We had no choice but to [illegible] While this tunnel looked to have roughly the same dimensions as the first when we entered, it seemed to shrink the farther we went. Four feet instead of five at the sides, with the ceiling a little closer to our heads. The acoustics of the reduced space amplified the sound of our breathing and footsteps. The initial illusion was of too many footsteps, but the longer it went on, the more I suspected the additional noise might not stem from echoes.

I grabbed at Josh and Elsie, holding my flashlight to my face and a finger to my lips. We all came to a stop. The footsteps did not. It's possible that my perception was off, but it sounded like at least two pairs, and not the heavy footfalls that would come from a man of Weeks' size and stature. Instinctively, we started trying to locate the source of the footsteps, but the flashlights revealed nothing. Then the footsteps halted.

We waited in silence for them to begin again, but after a minute or two, it became clear they wouldn't. Almost as soon as we started moving again, all three flashlights went out and the footsteps returned. Now it sounded as though there were at least four or five different people to account for all the noise—too small to be adults, too big to be animals. What's worse is I started feeling tugs at different places on my clothes, sensing the rush of air as the owners of those footsteps moved past me.

These were children.

Likely these were children that had died in this house.

ISBN 978-1-63789-785-0

For information address Crossroad Press at 141 Brayden Dr., Hertford, NC 27944
A Macabre Ink Production - Macabre Ink is an imprint of Crossroad Press.
www.crossroadpress.com

First edition

For Rachel,
Enjoy your trip to Slattery Falls.
Don't go in the basement.

SLATTERY FALLS

SLATTERY FALLS, BOOK ONE

BRENNAN LAFARO

04.07.23

MACABRE INK

For Dallas and Dustin,
My reasons for wanting to leave this world a better place than I found it.

PART ONE

A Glass Can Only Spill What it Contains

CHAPTER ONE

When you're about to investigate one of the most notoriously haunted houses on the East Coast, there are certain expectations. One revolves around thunder and lightning filling the midnight sky—the dark and stormy night trope. Yet there we were, traveling to the Weeks House in the middle of a cool, quiet August day. No sound. No fury.

I may have been misleading when I used the word 'investigate' before. That implies a sense of formality, a bit of professionalism, and truth be told, our crew was pretty far from that. We jumped through a few more hoops than usual, even had to start a ghost-hunting business, like you'd see on TV. All to get permission to enter that humble abode.

The name we registered, you ask? "Here Ghost Nothing". I still can't believe that wasn't taken. We made promises about monetized YouTube videos, and a book in the works that wouldn't be complete without a trip to Massachusetts' foremost location for all things paranormal. There's also a signed piece of paper somewhere saying the Slattery Falls Historical Society wouldn't be liable for any harm that befalls us to balance out the page count of that book I'm never going to write. Unless you count the document you now hold in your hands.

If you're thinking, *oh my, that is quite an elaborate ruse to gain access to a piece of property,* you're right. First prize. But we've always done what's necessary, whatever the cost.

Shit. I'm getting ahead of myself.

Some people get back to nature on the weekends. Others stay home and toast to forgetting the miserable work week they just suffered through and prepare to endure the next five days. Josh and I broke into haunted houses. It all began with a mutual affinity for avoiding the typical on-campus lifestyle and the eight-dollar twelve-pack. We met at the University of Connecticut in Storrs. He studied in the program for Animal Science, and I majored in Psychology.

One fateful Friday night, my roommate dragged me to an off-campus party. Showing up fashionably late guaranteed that almost everybody was pretty well wasted and not worth holding a conversation with. The lone exception looked like the human embodiment of Eeyore. The depressed donkey, right? Josh was tall and lanky with long, brown, curly hair that puffed out from under a backward Mets hat. His darting eyes and deer-in-the-headlights gaze broadcast to everyone in the vicinity that he wasn't sure how one should act in polite society.

After a series of abandoned conversations, I made my way over to the interesting-looking loner who had spent the better part of the last hour nursing a can of Coors.

"Travis. Morland," I introduced myself.

The reaction I received made me think of a camouflaged insect, so used to going unnoticed that it doesn't know what to do when it finds itself the center of attention. He had been blending in with that wall so well until I had the audacity to ruin the illusion.

"Josh," he said, watching his shoes carefully. "Josh Costa."

"Joshua Costa. You kind of look like you don't want to be here," I said, grinning.

"Josh," he said. "Not Joshua. Everyone just calls me Josh." His eyes continued moving every which way, desperately avoiding a meeting with mine. "I live here, so really it's all these people I don't want in my living room." At this, he came dangerously close to cracking a smile, and a hint of color returned to his cheeks.

"My roommate, Chris." He inclined his half-full beer can toward an animated extrovert wearing a skin-tight pink polo shirt. Chris waved his arms around with such vigor as he spoke, he appeared about to take flight. "He wanted to have a few people over and two became four became this." Josh gestured around the room to showcase an occupancy that must have violated some fire code or another. "I thought about going out, but that seemed like giving up. Admitting defeat, if you will."

"You're making a stand, then. That's quite noble."

"I'm a regular General Custer," said Josh with a nervous shrug. His gaze wandered the room again.

We'd said nothing of importance to each other, and yet something inexplicable kept me rooted there. I liked him immediately.

CHAPTER TWO

The wall between us stayed up for a while, but when it dropped the words flooded out of Josh. At first with caution and then later with reckless abandon. He was a lot. Josh and I shot the shit about anything and everything. It turned out we had almost nothing in common, but he didn't have many friends at UConn, and I had few good ones. What we lacked in mutual interest, he made up for in unbridled enthusiasm. One of the many interests we did not share was the paranormal. Supernatural fiction, true accounts, you name it and I was clueless about it. My expertise began with *Ghostbusters* and ended with *Ghostbusters II.* When future conversations would dive down such rabbit holes, Josh cited cases, locations, and details off the top of his head. You could blame me for being impressed with this ability, for being drawn in and intrigued, for all the shit we got into over the next ten years. You could make a case to hold me accountable for all the breaking and entering, too. My bad.

The first time we ever broke into a haunted house was during the fall of our junior year. We'd known each other long enough to build some trust, and Josh invited me to come stay at his family's house in Coventry over the long Columbus Day weekend. Josh's mom and dad were good people, if a little removed. They appeared every bit the rare late forties couple whose marriage still works. An uncommon occurrence in a world that treats divorce as no different than trading in a used car. Josh acted distant toward them, but I'd gotten used to seeing that out of him, and thought nothing of it.

The Costa household was pretty spacious considering it was just the three of them, and his parents left us mostly to ourselves. We did little that first night, a few beers each, the tour of the town, and some insight from Josh on what it was like to grow up there.

Out of the blue on Saturday, Josh asked if I had ever heard of

Nathan Hale, or the Hale House. I'd noticed signs when entering town declaring Coventry the home of Nathan Hale, but beyond a glimmer of recognition from high school U.S. history, nothing rang a bell.

"Nathan Hale was a spy during the Revolutionary War," he told me, speeding up as he approached the exciting parts. You could always tell how jazzed Josh was about a topic by his tempo. "One of the good ones, actually. On our side, is what I mean. Long story short, he gathered intelligence from the British and they eventually caught and executed him for it."

"Executed?"

"Yeah, hanged. In Manhattan at the age of twenty-one."

"Jesus," I said and opened another Sam Adams, my way of saluting another hero of early America.

"Jesus is right. Hale was the guy who said 'I only regret that I have but one life to lose for my country'. Supposedly, anyway. By the time those words got back to anybody who mattered, they had passed through so many sets of lips that it was like trusting the last person in a game of telephone."

"Purple monkey dishwasher."

Josh ignored my witty Simpsons reference and continued on.

"No one believes he single-handedly impacted the outcome of the war or anything, but the colonies regarded him as a bit of a folk hero, and Connecticut named him the official hero of the state at one point."

"I didn't know that was a thing. I don't even know if Mass has one."

"Samuel Whittemore."

"Now how the shit do you know that?"

"As you can imagine, the hero worship gets multiplied many times over in town, and the Hale House has museum status. It's even open to the public. The funny thing is, he never even lived in that house. His family bought it a few months after his execution."

"You're kidding. So what appeal is there to visiting the house that Hale never even saw, never mind grew up in?"

"It's haunted," he said.

"Oh. That'll do it."

"And we're going tomorrow."

CHAPTER THREE

Josh spent the rest of the night filling me in on all things Hale. I relaxed some when he told me the house was open to the public for tours and such through the end of the month. Even though Nathan Hale never lived there, his family went to great lengths to fill the house with his stuff. Anything for a buck, right?

I was less relieved when Josh told me we would be going in without a guide. Not to mention our private tour being scheduled for several hours after the museum closed. I might have mentioned something about breaking and entering earlier.

Apparently this house was relatively tame, at least as far as haunted houses go. Reported ghost sightings were limited to appearances from Hale's family, but not Hale himself. I sat through a lengthy lecture about how this lends credence to the story because attention seekers looking for a tale to sell more tickets would claim to see the ghost of the house's namesake.

Museum employees and guests rarely spotted ghosts on the grounds and more often heard footsteps on unoccupied floors or coming from outside, rattling sounds from the basement, and the occasional disembodied voice. Josh told me the hauntings didn't seem malevolent, and the museum had no difficulties keeping staff on. You can learn a lot about a haunting from turnover, apparently.

When I asked how we would get in, he said not to worry about it and moved on, which honestly made me worry even more. Usually when Josh gets going on one of his interests, changing the subject becomes a real problem and planning for a spooky outing was no exception. I never pushed him though. Over the last decade, I learned to trust Josh more than almost anyone else, and by the time we broke into Hale House, he already had my confidence.

CHAPTER FOUR

As far as preparation goes, there's not much to tell. We traveled light then, and the routine never changed much. Josh was a creature of habit and I deferred to his infinite wisdom. No cameras, recorders, EVP knick-knacks, infrared doohickeys. He held the opinion that such things were bullshit. His words, not mine, and I take it to heart when he curses, because it's a rare occurrence.

Josh packed flashlights, extra batteries, granola bars, water, and what I would later find out was a lock pick set, all packed away in a black messenger bag adorned with a Misfits patch. We waited until a little after midnight, then headed out. I hadn't thought to pack my criminal clothes for a weekend getaway to Coventry, so I borrowed a black hoodie and dark jeans and mentally prepared myself to see this bad idea through.

We parked the car on a dirt inlet off Skinner Hill Road in the Nathan Hale State Forest and went the rest of the way on foot. It wasn't long before we saw the house. The darkness lent a crimson hue to the normal brick-red coloring of the exterior. Not a great omen if you subscribe to such things.

Once we exited the woods, it couldn't have been over two hundred feet to the door. Even though the outside lighting was dim and there wasn't a soul in sight, the open ground seemed to stretch forever. When we reached the main entrance, Josh knelt and removed a slim case from the messenger bag. I stood watch while he set to work on the door, swinging my gaze from side to side, assuming an unaccounted-for night watchman would happen by at any moment.

I whispered, "There has got to be a great story about why you know how to pick a lock and own a set of tools to do it with. You'll have to tell it to me after we make bail."

"They'll never know we were here," said Josh. The volume of his voice boasted a lot more confidence than I felt. This clearly wasn't the first door he had opened without consent. "And… We're in." The door swung open, accompanied by the sound of hinges desperately crying for some WD-40. It occurs to me now that there should have been some kind of alarm, but I guess this was the type of museum that doesn't worry too much about theft.

We clicked on our flashlights and entered a large room full of antique furniture. Even with the traffic that passed through this house on a daily basis, the musty aroma of age overwhelmed the place. I eased the door shut behind us while Josh crossed to the center of the room and sat on a couch that likely had two hundred years on us, slowly and with a sense of something like reverence.

"We need to get our bearings before we go wandering around," he said, finally seeing fit to match my soft tone.

I nodded, made my way over to the couch, and tried to mimic the same careful way I'd seen him sit. His assertion that nobody would know we were there would not hold up if I decimated an antique sofa.

"First," he said, "we do not split up for any reason, inside or outside. There's no reason for it and no possible positive outcome. Second, we should establish and clear the main floor before we do anything else. Anecdotally speaking, the second floor and basement are where we're most likely to see or hear activity, so we want to treat this floor, this room even, as a base of operations. Kind of like a safe zone. Third, safe word. No jokes, Travis. I know you're picking between three or four right now, and I understand the connotations, but it's the best description of what we need. I propose we go with *husky*, the school mascot. If either of us needs to use it, we get out as fast and efficiently as possible, no questions asked, and take care to stay together. There are no reports of malicious hauntings here, but if we do this, we do it right. Oh, and this probably goes without saying, but don't take anything. Thoughts, concerns, or questions?"

"No, it all sounds… nope. Got it. Although I do resent you painting me as a thief who tells perverted jokes."

"If the shoe fits," he said with a smirk.

I was, admittedly, a bit in awe of him at the moment. Josh always showed himself to be a good friend, but a mouse of a man. I'd never seen him grab a situation by the balls and twist before. It wouldn't be the last time.

"Okay, good," he said, clasping his hands together. The soft smacking sound echoed through the deserted room "Then we're ready."

CHAPTER FIVE

Even with the house's isolation, we agreed it would be best to stick to flashlights and leave the overheads off. We made our way around the main room we'd entered, poring over the details, and looking for anything unusual or out of place. At least, that was the plan. I caught myself searching for any sign of movement and making good, if excessive, use of my peripheral vision. When it felt like we had explored every inch of the room, Josh returned to his spot on the couch. With a steady voice, he said, "If there are any spirits here, please make your presence known."

We sat in silence, listening for anything that resembled an answer.

I let a moment pass, then asked, "Does that usually work?"

"What makes you think I've done this before?"

"Literally everything."

"It's always worth a try. Come on, next room."

We repeated this ritual in every room on the main floor, as well as a few outdoor areas where Josh said employees and tourists had glanced figures in the windows. I don't remember any other occasions where my senses were so heightened for such a long time. Not before the Hale House, anyway. After we left, I remember feeling exhausted, and the two of us slept until early afternoon the next day. It was a serious rush, though. I understood why Josh enjoyed doing this. Despite the adrenaline, we had been gloriously unsuccessful so far despite searching for over an hour.

After the seventh or eighth location, Josh eyed the staircase. "Alright, we're going upstairs."

CHAPTER SIX

I don't want to bore you. I want to tell you about all the cool shit that happened upstairs, but nothing did. Not really. The house was a giant square, so I worried the upstairs might take as long to comb through as the downstairs. By the time we explored the second room, we hadn't seen or heard anything of note, other than a throw pillow reading "We'll scare the Hale out of you!".

We were just about finished when a metallic clanking sounded from below. A resounding toll like someone had dropped a heavy chain on a hardwood floor, and it reverberated throughout the house. Not that I had much doubt—it was deafening in the silence—but one look at Josh told me he'd heard it too, and the gears in his head were already turning.

"We make our way downstairs, but we do it slowly," he said.

I followed him toward the stairs.

Clank.

Again, but this one rang further away. Was it leading us somewhere? My ears were at attention, awaiting the next occurrence. My other senses remained on high alert as well. The shadows that had flown under my radar earlier now crept across the floor. I attempted to step around them because, at that moment, I convinced myself something lived in that darkness. Situational superstition at its finest, but my lizard brain knew no earthly good could come from getting too near. Whatever dwelled there had watched us from the minute we first set foot on the property, and now the time for waiting was up. Right there, my skepticism died, and what began as something to do on a three-day weekend became serious business.

A substantial part of me wanted to hightail it out of there and not look back, but I shut it down. Something was trying to get our attention, and this might be a once in a lifetime opportunity.

Clank.

A third time. We heard it as we reached the bottom of the stairs. The sound grew closer, coming from the basement. I remembered Josh saying something about rattling down there. The story contained bits with Hale's brother and a navy ship. Forgive me if I'm a little fuzzy on the details.

The moon's light, which had graced this room only twenty minutes earlier, made a hasty retreat and the creeping, crawling shadows returned. A portrait of a broad-shouldered man, balding, but sporting an enormous bright-red beard shone through the darkness, and I wondered how I could have missed it before. As we crossed the room to the basement door, I could've sworn the man in the portrait's penetrating sea-green eyes followed me.

Three more clanks sounded, one immediately after another, as though a chain were being dragged down a set of stairs. Josh reached out to grab me, and I think we both knew something was luring us to the basement. And it was working. Only a few steps from the door, he signaled we should sit.

I half expected he might give me the safe word, and I felt a momentary disappointment that surprised the hell out of me. Instead, he spoke just above a whisper and said, "This is why we planned. We don't lose our heads just because there's activity. We're going to take on the basement just like all the other rooms, but slower. More cautiously. We're going to sit here for another minute, collect ourselves, then make our way to that door, and you'll follow my lead."

Josh delivered the speech in a way that left me wondering whether he was talking to me or just himself. I didn't pick up on it then, but later I would think about him not giving me an out. I've spent a lot of time considering the motives, or maybe lack of motives, he had. Even ten years later, I still can't come to a solid conclusion. Josh Costa always did move in mysterious ways.

We stood and crossed the last fifteen feet to the basement door. As we closed the gap, the moon reappeared and the outstretched arms of the shadows rescinded. I barely picked up on this, though. My eyes were locked on the door. It was a dull blue or gray, paint peeling, and the colors indistinguishable in the limited light. Kind of strange in a museum regularly open to the public, like a single small corner of the house fallen into disrepair. Josh tapped the knob three times with the flat of his hand, as you might do when looking for a safe exit during a fire. Satisfied, he looked in my direction, took a deep breath, and opened the door.

CHAPTER SEVEN

Whatever I expected on the other side of the door—some grisly, decaying nightmare creature or maybe the ghost of Nathan Hale with an elongated neck—didn't come to fruition. The door swung open toward us, and the narrow staircase descended into a murky darkness. Even straining my eyes, I couldn't see the bottom.

"After you," I said.

Josh eased down the creaking set of stairs, shining the flashlight toward the basement, but also side to side, never keeping it in one area for more than a couple of seconds. Given the shabby condition of the door, we weren't confident about the upkeep of what lay behind it, and took each step with care.

"Do you smell that?" he said.

I inhaled deeply and caught a faint scent of cold, salt air. I'm not sure I'd ever thought of a smell as *cold* before, but there was no other way to describe it. Going down the stairs, the scent became stronger and stronger, and I had to remind myself that we were not actually descending into the hold of a ship. When we reached the bottom, we paused and got an idea of the layout. No windows of any kind appeared to be letting outside light in, and the open door at the top of the stairs wasn't as generous with its luminescence as one might expect.

Josh held up a hand to signal I should stay where I was and then maneuvered around me so that we were standing back to back. A bead of sweat dripped down my forehead. This was a position of defense.

"If there are any spirits here, please make your presence known," Josh called out.

No response.

"Don't all speak up at once," I said.

"Shut up."

As soon as I said it, the room grew darker. I could concede the movement in the upstairs shadows as adrenaline combined with an overactive imagination. I doubt I'll be able to convince anyone that imagination wasn't a factor in the basement. The darkness became absolute. Even our flashlights no longer cast light. They simply became pinpricks in the inky blackness.

"No husky yet," he murmured, as if reading my thoughts.

Josh reached out with his free hand, grabbed the sleeve of my sweatshirt, and inched away from the stairs. Despite their ineffectiveness, we kept the flashlights on.

A thunderous clank came from the base of the stairs, where we had stood only a moment ago. It had the clear timbre of metal crashing down on wood despite the basement's concrete foundation. When the reverberation settled, a sound like a foot dragging across the floor emanated from the same location.

A step. A shuffle.

A step. A shuffle.

Coming closer.

A step. A shuffle.

"I'm calling it," I whispered, "We've got to go. There's fucking somebody down here."

The door at the top of the stairs slammed shut.

Our flashlights returned from the dead, revealing a figure hunched over, facing the corner of the room. The burst of light lasted for less than a second, but that image etched itself into my mind, perfectly detailed. Something about its stance struck me as inherently male, though I couldn't see the face. Long, dark, dirty hair would have obscured the features, even if it had been looking toward us. It wore a trench coat, tattered along the bottom, which hardly concealed a pair of bare, filthy feet.

We continued moving to the stairs, eyes locked on the pitch-black spot we'd seen the specter in. The flashlights lit up again for a split second. Just long enough to divulge that the previously inhabited corner stood empty now.

It's funny. I recall every second in the basement of the Hale House so clearly, but the exodus is a blur. I remember getting to the stairs, scrambling up on hands and knees. I don't know who got to the top first, but the door didn't open right away. Maybe whatever was in the house was keeping us in. Maybe the door just didn't fit correctly in the frame. Hell, maybe we even momentarily lacked the capacity to push in the right direction. After multiple frantic attempts, it opened and we sprinted through the entrance room and outside, putting some distance between ourselves and the house.

One last thing I remember about getting out of there. I felt watched, even after we got outside. A chill, like icy fingers ran up my spine and kept me from looking back. The sensation made me move like the devil was chasing me.

CHAPTER EIGHT

"What the fuck was that? You saw that, right? Jesus!"

We burst out of the woods and headed toward the car, moving at a brisk pace that somehow didn't feel brisk enough.

Josh followed me without answering, listening patiently to the same questions asked over and over with slightly altered phrasing and different placements of the 'fucks' contained within. He didn't say a word until we got to the car. I expected him to be angry or loud, even if that was outside the box. When I didn't get those reactions, I figured he might act scared or upset. I did not anticipate frustration, especially geared in my direction.

"Travis," he said, a sigh, then a pause before he continued. "A glass can only spill what it contains."

"What the fuck is that supposed to mean?"

"Look, I know you're worked up, but can you stop cursing so much? It's exhausting."

"Sorry," I said, feeling a bit scolded and trying to figure out what to add next. "I..."

Nothing came to mind, and the silence lingered a moment. Finally, Josh answered for me.

"You didn't come because you felt pressured, or you thought I'd be mad if you said no. That's not you. You certainly didn't come because you felt the need to wander around bored in the dark. I think you agreed to come because you wanted what just happened, to happen. A glass can only spill what it contains. We can't help what's innately inside of us—our darkest desires."

I tried to interrupt, but he waved his hand, letting me know not to bother.

"Yeah, I know it's kind of a ridiculous assertion, but as Sherlock Holmes always says, 'once you eliminate the impossible, whatever remains, no matter how improbable, must be the truth.'"

"I'm supposed to be the psych major."

"Well, you're probably safe there. That's more in line with philosophy or English in its nature. Don't change the subject, though. There's a part of you that wanted to have an experience with the supernatural, to see a ghost. And Travis?"

"Yeah?"

"We saw a fucking ghost."

The frustration left Josh's face and the half-smile that occasionally cut through the glibness made an appearance. He added, "You're supposed to use fuck, and its derivatives to show emphasis. That seemed an appropriate place."

"Yeah. I don't disagree."

CHAPTER NINE

We had a few drinks back at Josh's place to unwind and ended up falling asleep near four or five in the morning. The sunshine and noise of the house collaborated to pull us out of bed in the early afternoon, and after a small lunch, we packed our belongings and got on the road back to Storrs.

We didn't talk about what happened at the Hale House. Not at Josh's house, not on the ride back to campus, not even in the coming weeks. Speaking it aloud would somehow diminish the personal nature of the experience, and I wanted nothing more than to hold it close and tight. Throughout the course of our third school year, I ran the events over repeatedly in my head, trying to process what we'd been through. It wasn't until spring semester that I finally brought it up.

"I think we should do it again."

"I'm not a fan of the pronoun game. I'm going to need context."

I couldn't tell whether that was Josh being sarcastic or just the blunt way he phrased most of his output on display. It's a personality quirk that takes some getting used to.

That night, we had a few people over to my room to partake in adult beverages and watch *1408*. I haven't seen that movie in years, maybe even since we watched it that night, but I always loved the idea of a haunting being isolated to a single room. Plus Samuel L. Jackson. The movie ended and everyone stumbled into the night to study for exams, or at least sit in front of books and make up excuses for not studying. As was customary, Josh stayed behind to have one more drink and talk. In a short amount of time, he'd done an impressive job of getting me caught up on all things paranormal. I still had trouble holding a conversation without my eyes going crooked, but I could follow most of what he said now.

"I think we should do *it* again," I repeated, emphasizing the pronoun mainly because I knew it would annoy him. "Like in October, with the Hale House."

"You want to go back to the Hale House?"

"Yes! No, I… I don't know. Maybe there, maybe a different place? I mean, I know you've done this before and probably in a few different places. So you're the expert. What do you think?"

Josh laughed. "I think I'm surprised. Look, I've actually been inside a couple houses with purported activity since October."

"Jesus. Alone or…?" Of course it had been alone. He didn't have anyone else to go with.

"Well, yeah. I didn't think you'd want to go after what happened last time."

"But you could've checked. We haven't talked about this in months. Months and months."

"Why didn't you bring it up?" Josh cocked his head slightly to the side.

"I don't know. I guess I thought we'd get there, and this thing came up and that fucking class, and I don't know, man."

Josh sat silently for a moment, just long enough to make sure I had nothing else to add.

"We kind of sound like a bickering couple," he added softly.

"Yeah, no shit. I just… I consider you a really good friend. All the people who walked out the door twenty minutes ago? Casual acquaintances. Bailing on each other is not something friends do."

Josh sat silently, staring at a point past my right shoulder. "I don't have a lot of friends. I'm sure that doesn't surprise you. I don't know how to act around people, and I never have. When I was young, maybe six, I learned how to copy what the people around me were doing—to look at people when I talked to them, to laugh even when I didn't find something funny, to talk about something another person was interested in when I didn't care about it. The list goes on. It's exhausting, though. It's like wearing a mask all the time.

"When I look someone in the eye, it's like… there's just too much happening. It's so much easier to listen to what they're saying if I can look at something stationary and just let my ears focus. That probably doesn't make any sense."

As much as it sounded like a place to jump in, I suspected he had more to say, so I let him go on.

"The thing is, that no matter how hard you try, you can't keep the mask on all the time and it wears you down. Eventually, when you spend a lot of time with a person, they get to see the real you. It's not socially acceptable if the real you is more interested in conducting research on ghost sightings that have occurred within twenty-five miles than, I don't know, playing a pick-up game of basketball or discussing what top the girl at the table behind you is wearing. Potential friends tend to drift away. I hit a point around my sophomore year of high school where I gave up, so to speak.

"It came down to acting in a way that made me comfortable and pushing people away, *or* covering myself up and then pushing them away eventually, anyway. High school is not the best time for self-discovery though. I got deemed a *freak* and a *retard* and the few people who associated with me, stopped.

"When I was sixteen, I tried to kill myself. It doesn't matter how, but I was told it was a 'cry for help', and I spent four months as a patient at a hospital in Rhode Island. I learned a lot of great coping techniques honestly, tried some medications. Some worked well, some didn't. When the doctors felt like I was in a good place, they discharged me, but I didn't go back to school. I finished my last two years of formal education as a homeschooler."

"What was that like? The homeschool thing?" I asked, sensing we had hit a point in the conversation where it was safe to join.

"It was great, actually. Everything I did was self-directed, and I could tailor it to the type of things I wanted to learn and the way I wanted to learn them. I ended up in an okay place, but I also lost the ability to trust new people. Even when I first met you, I just assumed you were making fun of me or you were just temporary. Honestly," and he smiled here, "I have a hard time not telling the truth. In a lot of instances it's out before I can stop it, and most people bail on me because they don't enjoy hearing it. You seem to thrive on it. You're a glutton for punishment, Travis."

"You're not wrong. I don't really know what to say. It pisses me off that there are people in the world who need everyone to act just like them. I'm sorry you had to go through all that. But I'm your friend, man, and I won't bail on you."

Josh simply nodded. "I appreciate that."

"So the next fucking time you're planning a haunted weekend excursion, you damn well better include me."

"Okay," Josh said. "I've got a few places in mind that I was hoping to visit over the summer. If you're up to go, so am I."

CHAPTER TEN

Josh handed over the names of a few places, none of which triggered any recognition on my part. He had more research to do on the history of each location, but we agreed to keep in touch about it and plan a weekend at his house to organize and try our luck.

As it turned out, we didn't get together until after the July 4th holiday. We planned a day and time for my arrival. What we hadn't planned on was Elsie.

When I turned into the driveway at the Costa residence, Josh stood outside by the walkway, waiting. I always expected a hunched stature on his tall frame, but today his shoulders hung lower than usual. If you've ever seen the guilty look a dog gets, just waiting to be caught, you know what I mean. Knowing Josh as I did, I steeled myself to drag whatever was wrong out of him. After all, we had big plans and it wouldn't do to put ourselves in a tenuous situation with an elephant taking up the better part of the room.

"Who shit in your cereal?" I asked.

He squinted his eyes in a way that either meant perplexed or sick of my crap.

"What's going on?"

"Elsie," he said. "My cousin."

"Okay, what about her?"

"She's staying with us for the summer. Got here three days ago. My aunt and uncle are going through some stuff."

"Stuff? No, sorry. Not my business."

"No, it's fine." He kicked at a patch of dirt and continued. "Division of assets is the way I'd put it. My parents agreed to allow one of said assets to live in our guest room for the next two months."

"I guess I'm still not seeing the problem."

"Elsie's a good person. She's a couple years younger than us. The problem is, she does not respect boundaries. On the first night she was here, I was downstairs watching a Mets-Phillies game. The Mets finished losing, and I headed upstairs and found Elsie in my room, sitting with my Misfits bag."

"Oh shit," I said. My heart crawled up my throat.

Josh's pace sped up. Sometimes nerves did that in place of excitement. "I said she's a good person, and I stick by that, but she also grew up in a house where people recognize what a lock pick set looks like, and how to use it."

He stopped for a moment, letting out a small laugh that seemed for him alone.

"So," Josh continued, "I'm thinking she's going to threaten to tell my parents, maybe even get so extreme as to call the police. Your face is looking kind of pale, Travis, so I guess that's probably where you thought I was going as well, but no."

He shook his head, looked down at his shoes, and paused again. "Really, she just wanted to know what I was up to and if she could help, or tag along, or whatever. Mainly, I think she was just—"

"Bored," added voice C to our A and B conversation.

The girl that walked around the side of the house looked just enough like Josh that I could believe they were related. She couldn't have been more than a few inches over five feet, but was every bit as lean as him, although she carried herself in a completely different way. Elsie broadcast a confidence Josh couldn't have hoped to match on his best day. Oh, and the hot pink hair that she later informed me was fuchsia. That was another difference. I'm trying to think of a more accurate way to describe her approach than 'strut', but words then, as they do now, failed me.

"Bored, yes. Travis, this is Elsinore."

"Remember what happened last time you called me that?" she asked Josh through a smile as she took a step toward us. Josh crossed his arms in front of his jeans, trying and failing to be subtle.

"Elsie," she said. "Pleasure to meet you. Josh has told me essentially nothing about you." She stopped a few feet away and put her hands in her jean pockets. "Oh, except that you two are ghost hunters, of course." She said this in a tone that conveyed not a bit of mockery, but I felt it anyway.

"It's nice to meet you too," I said, colder than was strictly necessary.

Josh and I had kept our activities and interests quiet, not so much because of the legalities, but the judgment. Reflecting on this now, the legal gray area was probably the better reason. I doubt we would have had a wealth of well-wishers at UConn if they knew we spent our summers planning to break into haunted houses, as opposed to the more socially acceptable model of getting blackout drunk until the calendar flips to September or, you know, getting a job. It was easy to see why Josh felt so alienated for refusing the status quo. It made no sense.

Long story short, we weren't interested in advertising and it surprised me and pissed me off a bit that Josh had let someone else in so easily and quickly, even if that someone was family. This belonged to us.

"Look," said Elsie, "I don't know you, but I'll tell you what I told my cousin if you can wipe that shitty look off your face for a minute?"

She seemed content waiting for me to oblige, taking her hands out of her pockets in order to cross her arms in front of her.

"Okay, I'm all ears," I said, trying to soften my tone. I assumed I had done just good enough, because the look of panic on Josh's face slipped away. Clearly, he had formulated an introduction and explanation, and Elsie had sent those plans through a wood chipper by jumping in too soon. Improvisation was never Josh Costa's strong suit.

"I need this," Elsie continued. "Maybe not this exactly, but something like this. You guys went straight from high school to college. Probably never questioned whether you would, just had to decide where and for what."

Anger tinged Elsie's voice, but I suspected I was no longer the cause or the target.

"I didn't really have the option. I graduated from high school in New Haven on a Tuesday and I started working in a shitty coffee shop on a Wednesday. I've been there for about two years now, and it's not even that bad a job. I mean, the customers can be annoying, but that's the service industry."

"Elsie, you're digressing," said Josh.

She shot him a look fit to melt the ice caps.

"It's just so dull," she continued. "And I've known way too many people that lose themselves in a dead-end job. Both my parents, for starters. You get so wrapped up in working open to close, you come home and crash, you get up the next day and you do it again. You start to lose the friends you had from school, you're too tired to start a new hobby, and nine bucks an hour doesn't fund them, anyway. Fuck, you're right, Josh, now I'm rambling."

I realized now that the confidence Elsie had been projecting up to this point was a pose, and it was slipping.

"No, you're fine. It's fine," I murmured and nodded for her to go on. I knew eventually I'd have to do something about these Costas laying their life stories at my doorstep, but this wasn't a good time to make a stand.

"I heard Josh tell you my parents have some shit going on. They pretty much have for as long as I can remember. My mom has left a few times, disappeared after an argument and showed up a few days later like nothing happened. My dad seems to have a semiannual appointment to do the same. And it's always the same shit. Things go back to normal and nobody talks about it. We reset the clock. This one is different, though. It's too calm. It's like the eye of the fucking hurricane. And we've never gotten to the point where we're moving stuff out of the house before."

Elsie slipped into a softer tone, not much more audible than a whisper.

"Coming here, even if it's just for the summer, is an opportunity to do something that isn't tied to brewing coffee, sleeping, or just wallowing in an atmosphere of perpetual bitterness. I want to be needed and I don't give much of a fuck what it's for."

"You know," I said, "you're really supposed to reserve fuck, and its derivatives for emphasis." As soon as I said it, Josh's eyes went wide, and he made a face like a fish gulping for air, but Elsie started laughing. Only a little at first, but then more and more until we couldn't help but join her.

"I'll bet," she fought through laughter, "that he told you that." She motioned to Josh. This was the moment where our trio came together. If she had stormed off like she probably should have—I mean, it was a pretty shitty joke—then the rest of this story definitely goes in a different direction. We didn't know it, mostly because we'd only tried this once, but Elsie would become an instrumental part of every late-night trip we would take from then on. She thought the existence of ghosts was utter bullshit, but that was just a minor obstacle.

"Is he any good with that lock pick set?" she asked me.

"Yeah, actually. I was surprised."

"Who do you think taught him how to use it?"

CHAPTER ELEVEN

Josh already had the next venue ready to go. The trip would be farther, but still in Connecticut. Our target was a place called the Benson House in Waterbury. Isn't it weird how houses of dubious repute always seem to have titles? I can't think of a time where we announced we would break into 16 Maple Drive.

The Benson House had no historical significance. It was mostly just known within the community. Elsie may not have believed in spooks, but she had been invaluable at helping Josh dig up old articles and stories about the place, even going to the library to find a couple articles stored on microfiche when we got to the point where search engines couldn't cough up anything new to us.

In 1956, the house was owned by, you guessed it, the Benson family. Thirty-six-year-old Michael, thirty-three-year-old Samantha, and their four-year-old son, Todd. One night in April of '56, Mr. and Mrs. Benson put their son to bed upstairs and returned to the main floor to read. According to multiple articles, this would have been around 7:30 p.m. Maybe twenty minutes later, Todd wanders down the stairs to get a drink of water. Mom gets him a glass, sends him back to his room, tucks him into bed, and kisses him goodnight for the last time.

The parents decide to turn in a little before ten, and while dad is brushing his teeth, Mom goes down the hall to do one last check of the kid's room, as moms tend to do. It doesn't take her long to realize he's not in his bed.

No panic at first. Like any young kid, he sometimes gets out of bed and falls asleep in a strange place. She flips the light on and checks under the bed, in the closet, next to the toy shelf, and nothing. Panic is rearing its ugly head now, and Samantha pulls her husband out of the bathroom. They tear apart the top floor to no avail. Next, Michael goes up into the attic while Samantha checks all the windows. They're locked from the inside.

Both parents are convinced he must be on the second floor somewhere. The chairs in the living room faced the stairs and no one could have gone up or down without Michael and Samantha noticing. They would later tell police that Michael got up several times between 7:30 and 10:00 to fix drinks and once to use the bathroom. Samantha also left once, but at no point was the living room vacant.

Once convinced that Todd was not on the second floor or in the attic, Michael phoned the police and Samantha frantically searched the main floor and basement. While Samantha waited for the police to arrive, Michael scoured the neighborhood.

When the police finally arrived, they performed a rudimentary search of the house and yard, and set up a perimeter in the neighborhood. They found nothing of note.

There were some trampled flowers underneath Todd's window, but nothing to suggest placement of a ladder or anything that might have granted access to the second floor. That night the police cordoned off the neighborhood and combed the small patch of woods nearby, but found nothing. They discovered no sign of Todd Benson inside or outside of the house.

Over the coming weeks, they questioned the parents countless times. We found twenty-three instances, but it was likely more. The officers interviewed all the neighbors first, then the detectives followed suit, but as time crawled on, no new information came to light. None of the neighbors saw or heard anything suspicious, and most had been taking part in the same activity as Samantha and Michael Benson—sitting in a quiet living room while the children went to sleep. Elsie felt it necessary to add that the Bensons had no alibis except for each other.

It was a close-knit neighborhood, and everyone who spoke to the police confirmed Todd was his parents' pride and joy. They never would have done anything to hurt him and were beyond reproach. However, with no new leads, suspicion fell on the parents. The only problem being there was no evidence to suggest that anything had happened other than what they claimed. After the initial search of the house, detectives conducted a more invasive search, which also bore no fruit.

Weeks passed, filled with additional interviews—Michael's co-workers, extended family, acquaintances, former acquaintances. Each straw grasped at more desperately than the last. Nothing new turned up. Waterbury police hit a point where they no longer suspected Samantha and Michael. Unfortunately, even though the judgment of the police subsided, that from the larger community never did.

I'm glossing over the weeks becoming months, the missing posters, the televised pleas for information from Samantha and Michael Benson, the false tips, and the dead ends. You can probably guess that nothing new ever came to light, and in 1966, the Bensons began the process to have Todd declared legally dead.

Neither parent would see that process through to completion. On January 3rd, 1967, Michael Benson hanged himself in Todd's old bedroom. The parents had left the room untouched. Given the circumstances, police did not suspect foul play. Following the death of her husband, Samantha moved in with an aunt and lived in seclusion until she died of pneumonia on July 17th, 1969.

With no clear next of kin, the house passed to Sylvia Jones, the aunt Samantha had lived with briefly. Ms. Jones hired a renovation team and then put the house on the market. Between 1970 and our research almost forty years later, the house was occupied five times, not counting the two buyers that intended to spruce it up then flip it. One family stayed for about three and a half years, but none of the others were there much longer than a year.

We dug up some secondhand accounts of things the people in and around the house experienced. The exciting thing about such old accounts is if this is what we could find, how much did we miss, or how much activity never even got recorded?

The most common report, shared by four out of the five families, was hearing a child crying softly. Anyone who investigated the noise never found a source. No matter which way they chased it down, it always sounded one room away. There was never any contact, no words, just a soft sobbing that resembled that of a young child, say age four.

One family that lived in the house during the early 1990s reported seeing a figure in the shadows, only in the room that belonged to Todd. Family members spotted the figure on multiple occasions, but whenever the viewer moved closer, the shadows would return to the form of whatever had been making them. The source mentioned most people wrote this experience off as literally jumping at shadows and letting the history of the house stake a claim on the owner's headspace, but this was precisely the shit we were looking for.

Two families reported seeing spectral figures that vaguely match descriptions of Samantha, Michael, or Todd. There was never any sense of danger associated with these sightings, more a sense of isolation, of loneliness. No reports exist of these figures being seen together. Sad, but fitting since all three family members, presumably, died alone.

Most of what we found were one-off occurrences. Floating lights glimpsed from outside, a figure in the window when the house should have been unoccupied, and the occasional, usually unintelligible, disembodied voice. In one instance, a neighbor came over to investigate a strange noise, and reported being told to "get out" despite not being inside the house. We agreed informally to disregard this one because it didn't really fit with the benign nature of most of what went on.

The last family moved out in 1997, leaving behind no record of what led them to spend eight months in the house and then vacate without trying to sell it. As far as we could tell, the house sat empty after that, possibly with the occasional squatter. We were not able to find any records of a transfer of ownership, so unless Elsie missed something, the family that abandoned the house still owned it.

Having this knowledge proved to be a happy accident. We made it commonplace in the years following to always know how likely it would be for the property owners to show up in the middle of the investigation. This last tidbit told us the likelihood in this case was 'not very'.

A few minutes online found us a public parking lot about a half mile from the house, which sat on Locust Street. The lot backed up to a patch of trees that would allow us to arrive in the backyard, away from prying eyes and passing cars.

We had everything we needed, so we packed up and headed out in search of the next glorious adventure.

CHAPTER TWELVE

I had arrived at Josh's to start planning on a Thursday afternoon. By Saturday night, we were on the road for Waterbury. Just under an hour's drive. We pulled into the lot on Division Street around ten and went for pizza before heading toward the Benson House. Thankfully, Elsie and I anticipated this possibility and convinced Josh not to dress like a cat burglar.

Despite our attire, I can't help thinking we must have looked like we were up to something. All three of us were outwardly nervous, even Josh who had done this more often, and rarely wore his heart on his sleeve. Around 11:30, the restaurant started closing up, and we decided we had lingered long enough. We tipped an agreed-upon and forgettable amount, then headed back toward the car where we grabbed dark-colored sweatshirts and a black knit cap for Elsie. It screamed robber, especially in July, but the alternative was attempting to be stealthy while donning fuchsia hair.

By midnight, nobody was around to see us duck into the woods. We walked in pitch blackness until we were far enough from the road to risk flashlights, which Josh took from his Misfits bag and distributed. The farther into the woods we got, the more my imagination kicked into high gear. It wasn't hard to envision police combing these woods over fifty years earlier, looking for Todd Benson. This place felt like it had a pulse. I guess I'll never know whether my knowledge of the events that took place there impacted my train of thought, but the woods felt alive, like something ancient and inhuman studied our every move. I never mentioned it later to Josh or Elsie—we had bigger things on our minds by then—but I recall taking every step with care, afraid to put a foot down in the wrong place in case it stirred up whatever made the hair on the back of my neck crawl.

A palpable sense of relief washed over me as soon as we emerged into the backyard of the Benson House, and I fought the urge to run from the woods' entrance.

The backyard was small, probably seventy feet from the trees to the back door. An above-ground pool sat empty and devoid of purpose, a hole punched through the side. Maybe by neighborhood kids, maybe the family who abandoned the house. A last-minute effort to make sure there were no more *accidents* on the property. Near the pool was a swing set that had seen better days. If this were a movie, the swings would have moved on their own, filling the air with some hearty creaks. However, it was a stagnant, humid July night, and those swings didn't have any stir in them.

We moved slowly and carefully to the back door, where Josh knelt and rummaged in the bag for his lock pick set. Elsie stepped around him and tried the knob, which turned easily, and the door swung inward.

CHAPTER THIRTEEN

The yard slanted up from the back, almost swallowing the house, so the door at ground level led into the basement. As we stepped inside, I thought about the basement of the Hale House, and I'm sure Josh did too. I reminded myself that almost all reports of activity in this house had been benign, ran it through my head like a mantra, and crossed the threshold. Anyone or anything that lived here didn't seem to interact with outsiders, but functioned more like a tape on a loop instead.

Since the backyard sat blocked off from the street, we went in with flashlights already on and stopped just a step inside the door. In theory, our research had prepared us for the house to look like no one had lived here in fifteen years, but the years of dust, stirred into the air by our arrival, created an ethereal scene. Boxes filled the room, stacked floor to ceiling, pervading the space. It made me even more curious about why we couldn't find a reason the last family left so abruptly and why they abandoned all their earthly belongings.

The heaps of boxes stretched throughout the basement and navigating through them was a bit like wandering through a labyrinth. If I'm being an optimist here, I did like that there wasn't much room for anything to hide in the shadows. I really did fucking hate basements. We took a few extra twists and turns, and managed to get to the stairs leading up to the first floor. At the base of the steps, Josh began his customary routine of calling out to any present spirits. I half expected Elsie to laugh at how seriously he took it. I even surprised myself by getting pre-emptively mad about it. To her credit, she remained stoic. That's how it needed to be. This was the ritual—the rite, almost—for each room, and she was part of it now.

Josh's questions and commands drew no response. Not so much

as a creak to suggest the old, empty house settling. Almost too quiet, like something holding its breath, ready to pounce.

We walked up the stairs and gazed through the open door and into the living room. Samantha and Michael had sat right here while God only knew what happened to Todd. The open floor plan, with the living room next to the kitchen and dining room, lent credence to the notion that Todd, or anyone else, could not have possibly come down the stairs unnoticed. Near the landing of the stairs were two armchairs. Not the same ones that would have been there in 1956, but possibly in the same location.

We settled in the approximate middle of the room, opting for a spot on the floor rather than the ancient and filthy furniture. I nearly jumped out of my skin when lights appeared on the wall and raced toward the kitchen. It took less than a second to get my head out of my ass and realize they came from the passing headlights of a car driving down Locust Street.

No one said anything, but I could tell it scared the shit out of Elsie too, and Josh made a concentrated effort not to let his face slip into a smirk.

"If anyone is here with us, please make your presence known," said Josh.

A moment passed.

"Michael Benson? Samantha Benson? Todd?" Elsie added. Unexpected, but it felt okay. "We're not here to cause you any more pain, and if we can help you, we will. If we can share what happened here with anyone, with the world…" Her voice quivered. Not with fear, but emotion. Raw.

Silence.

I put a hand on her shoulder and nodded. This part of the routine came with lowered expectations, and I mentioned as much when Josh brought up the same ground rules he'd gone over with me during our first trip. This time he did it on the car ride to Waterbury instead of inside a pitch-black house. A bit more logical, if you ask me. She knew what to expect once we got inside, at least from our side of things. Elsie had taken everything in silently, tossed back a few solid follow-up questions I hadn't thought to ask, and then started looking up local pizza places on her phone. A few days ago, she'd told us she needed something in her life, but I think we were both surprised at how invested she'd become in such a short time.

"It's like I told you," I said. "It's a good way to start these things off, but you—"

"Shut up," she shot back. A moment passed, the three of us listening for the house to give up any sign of life. "Do you hear that?"

We sat stock still, straining our ears. It was faint, but she was on to something. A muffled sobbing sound. Intermittent, the cry crept through the still air of the house every few seconds, followed by a heavy silence.

"It's coming from upstairs," she whispered.

We both looked to Josh for guidance. The goal remained the same—clear the 'safe' part of the house, which we hadn't done yet, then move on to the more active regions. The unspoken question: Do we fuck up our routine, or do we stick to the plan and risk missing out? We sat in silence for a moment while Josh thought it out. Routine was law in his mind.

"Okay, let's go," he said, "but I'm not comfortable with this and I'd like it on the record."

"Noted," said Elsie, getting to her feet.

Speaking later, he would tell us he had never deviated from his routine before. On his solo treks, he always went in order, even if it meant letting something pass him by. His reasoning? Sometimes you found activity and sometimes you didn't. Time would not have a strict bearing on results. A mature thought if ever I heard one. Elsie and I didn't ask why he made an exception this time, but we both knew. Even though it was hard for him, he sacrificed for us.

CHAPTER FOURTEEN

Elsie led us in the direction of the sobbing, and although the main floor had been relatively clean compared to the basement, more clutter greeted us on the house's second level. Boxes touched the ceiling, filling all available space on the landing at the top of the stairs. The cardboard appeared weathered and faded, as though packed away significantly longer than the decade since the last occupants abandoned the house. The stairs opened to the head of a hallway, two rooms on either side—Todd's room and a bathroom on the left, a guest room and master bedroom on the right.

All the doors were closed and there was something unnerving about it. The long deserted hallway harbored a sense of claustrophobia. We directed our lights down the passage looking for anything out of the ordinary—a stray shadow, a figure, but nothing presented itself. Through unanimous, yet silent agreement, we stood still as statues waiting for the sobbing to resume.

I didn't want to be the first to make a move or a sound. Just when I didn't think I could last one more second without giving into the tension, the cry returned—a requiem whose timbre flooded the top floor, not with its dynamic force, but its melismatic resonance.

I don't have children yet, so I'm not an authority to speak on this, but it wasn't a lament of pain, hunger, illness, or anything immediately rectifiable. This wail didn't tell of a child separated from their parents, desperate for an attempt at reconciliation. Resigned and hopeless might not be the right words, but they're the closest I can find.

"What do you want to do?" I whispered. "Todd's room should be the first one on the left, but it doesn't sound like it's coming from there. Doesn't sound like it's coming from any of the other doors either, though. More like it's... everywhere."

"Unless it wants to be found, I'm not sure it's going to get any more clear than this. I think we try each room, one by one. Elsie?"

She nodded and crept toward the first door on the left, put her hand on the knob, and then looked back at us. Josh nodded and as Elsie made to turn the handle, another cry came from the end of the hall.

She paused and looked at us again. "Bathroom."

A few steps took us to the end of the hall, this time without a sound, and Elsie opened the bathroom door. It couldn't have been over eight feet deep and five feet wide. I tried to throw the light switch, thinking there were no windows to give us away, but the electricity had been off for some time. It didn't take long to search everywhere, including behind the shower curtain. Let me tell you, pulling that back nearly sparked an arrhythmia, and the honor was all mine. Thankfully, the result didn't end up like the bathroom scene in *The Shining*.

With nothing of note in the bathroom, we opted to try Todd's room again. Josh closed the door behind us. It felt like the thing to do, and something didn't sit right about the idea of being on that floor with all those doors open, like watchful eyes.

This time, Elsie opened the door to Todd's room before anything could cause a distraction. A man stood in the middle of the room, taller than either Josh or me. Broad shoulders gave his silhouette the build of a lumberjack, but his features were obscured. Right off the bat, I considered this might be due to the darkness of the room, but I can see that moment in my memory still. The man's face blurred like a smudged oil painting in shades of grays and black, as though he were not quite there, which very quickly he wasn't. The figure appeared just long enough for us to register his presence, then vanished without pomp and circumstance. The interaction was so brief that I could have believed I imagined it if Elsie hadn't screamed. She quickly shut it down before it could reach bloodcurdling decibels, more of a startle than a shriek of abject terror.

"Josh, did you…"

"Yes."

We stood frozen in the doorway, no one wanting to go in, no one wanting to shut the door and leave. God knows how long we would have stayed in the doorway if we hadn't heard the sob again. More clearly this time, but also not in the room. The acoustics made it difficult to pinpoint where it came from, almost like hearing it underwater. Since we had already entered Todd's room, it felt like we should have a quick look around. Subconsciously, we avoided the area where the large man had appeared only moments ago, while also keeping an eye out for his potential return.

"Todd?" said Elsie. "Are you in here?" For a skeptic, she was coming around pretty quickly. Twenty minutes in and just as engaged as Josh and me. Despite the gravity of the moment, I recall smiling just then.

In short order, I had checked under the bed, in the closet, and in any other nook or cranny I could find. I noticed Josh sitting on the bed, eyes closed. As if he could feel my gaze, he said, "Not looking for a monster. Not much sense in checking under the bed."

"What are you up to then?"

"Listening."

Elsie and I found a place to sit and joined him. We hadn't been at it long when we heard the cry again. Still on the same level, but coming from multiple directions. It felt like a wild goose chase. Before we could react, Josh held up a hand to stop us. We waited. A minute or two would go by, then we'd hear it again. The first few times it sounded the same—that sense of being submerged underwater, then it cleared up. The volume didn't change, but a direction took shape and it was... unhelpful.

"That's coming from outside," Elsie said.

"Agreed," said Josh. "I think we should give the other rooms a cursory once over and then head out. Thoughts?"

By agreement, we all stood up and headed for the door. This room felt empty now. It held a certain presence, a vibe, after we saw the figure in there, but that had dissipated over the last ten minutes.

We set out to check each room. First, the bathroom again.

Empty.

Next, the master bedroom. A little more cautious this time, all of us likely expecting the reemergence of the dark figure.

Empty. A palpable sense of relief spread.

Finally, the guest bedroom.

Also empty.

We heard the cries twice while clearing the floor, and they still seemed to come from outside. The sense of being alone that had developed in Todd's room now spread throughout the entire floor. Like something had shown up to welcome us, but then decided it had better things to do. We closed each door after us and started back toward the main floor. Another fleeting glance around some rooms we had missed the first time, and then down toward the basement. However impossible, it looked as though even more boxes had appeared, and since there was no real order to the chaos, navigating was difficult.

"Guys, look at that," Elsie said. She motioned to the wall on our right, separated from us by a sea of abandoned belongings. "Was that there before?"

Scrawled in two-foot-high letters was the word *WEEKS*.

"I couldn't swear to it," said Josh, "but I don't think so. It doesn't fit with the decor, and it's not exactly subtle. One of us would have noticed it."

I moved a few boxes to the side to get closer while Josh and Elsie held the path and gave me light. I hoped to hell that the writing wasn't blood or shit or some other horror movie trope, so I was relieved to find out that it wasn't. Well, sort of relieved.

"It's… scratched into the wall."

"Scratched? Like a cat?"

"Not unless it's a big-ass cat. More like a knife, but the cuts are too wide."

I ran my finger down the indent of the letter W, then *WHACK*! A hatchet sliced into the wall, not six inches from my hand.

"Go!" shouted Josh, ducking low and putting an arm around Elsie.

I ran back to the path and the basement door we had come in through, but froze as soon as the scene outside became clear. The weather hadn't changed since we'd come in less than an hour ago, hot and stagnant, not a draft to be had. Except now, the swings were moving. Not just a gentle sway in the breeze, but steady with the force of carrying a large child. You could feel the accompanying creak vibrate throughout your entire body.

We had to go past the swings to get to the woods.

We hugged the pool as much as possible and slowly made our

way to the tree line, refusing to let fear make us run away. Not an easy feat considering that something in the house manifested to throw a hatchet at my head. At the edge of the woods, we heard the cry again, coming from behind us. I cast my gaze back toward the Benson House. In the bay window on the ground floor stood a dark figure. Correction, stood *the* dark figure. We were farther away than our first glimpse, but it was him. A shadow come to life, just like in Todd's bedroom. The distance and darkness obscured his features, but two pale bluish-green eyes glowed in the night, watching us cover the last patch of open yard and following our every move long after we lost sight of them. A hideous bellow of laughter reached us at the edge of the yard, coming not just from the green-eyed figure, but from all around us.

We backed into the woods, traversing our way back to the car, flashlights ablaze and the laughter trailing close behind. We didn't really give a fuck if anyone saw us at that point.

CHAPTER FIFTEEN

Our voices took a back seat to our thoughts as we traveled through the woods, nothing but the sound of our feet hitting the ground and our labored breathing. I'm almost positive the silence lasted until we were back on I-84. The atmosphere had been significantly less creepy than at the Hale House, but even at the most nerve-wracking point of that trip, I'd never felt in danger. All reports led us to believe that anything living at the Benson House was not sentient, but more like a projector playing a movie on repeat. A residual haunting. The first sighting of the dark figure fit that neatly, but we should have realized something was up when the crying started. It manipulated us, and a residual haunting doesn't have the consciousness to do that.

"Elsie, you spent the most time with the research. Could that have been Michael Benson?" Josh asked.

"No way," she said. "That guy was well over six feet and broad. All the pictures I came across of Michael, he wasn't a big guy. Skinny and under six feet."

"Sure as hell wasn't Samantha or Todd," I said. "So who was it?"

"I don't know. That house seemed like such a safe choice, and maybe that guy was just fucking with us, having some fun. Shit, guy. That was not a guy. We saw him disappear." She shook her head as if to clear it. "I could write a lot of what happened off to a playful spirit messing around, and then freaking us out with the swing set action, but I don't know. It felt... bad."

"It felt bad," agreed Josh. "Elsie, you've only been on one of these trips. Travis, only two. Most of the experience lies outside your main five senses. It's emotional. You learn to trust your gut. I've interacted with ghosts before, rolling a ball, something simple like that, never anything so physical as this. You can sense that in an active haunting, there's an innocence, a sense of exploration. This one exuded a feeling of cruelty. I've been in twenty-seven different places now, and I've never felt anything like that."

"The fact that it wrote on the wall with a fucking axe or something definitely doesn't help its case," I said. "Oh yeah, then threw it at my goddamn head!"

"Hatchet," Josh corrected. "No, I suppose not." His eyes held a distant, troubled look. "Weeks. That could mean anything. Is it telling us it's been there for weeks? That can't be right. Do we have weeks? And what happens when that absurdly arbitrary time period is up?"

The sound of the radio playing softly filled the car for the rest of the drive, each of us no doubt having an internal conversation similar to the one we'd just heard from Josh. I don't think the spirit trying to communicate with us could have been more cryptic. Might as well have scrawled the word *THE* on the wall and told us to figure it out. We were all feeling scared and confused, and it was probably a good thing no one had anywhere to be the next day.

I flexed my left hand, opening and closing the fingers, glad to have all five.

CHAPTER SIXTEEN

I stayed a few more days in Coventry, spending a lot of time trying to dig deeper into the Benson House, to see if we could associate the word *Weeks* with the house in any way. Elsie all but moved into the library while Josh and I sat in front of laptops. There was talk of going back to Waterbury to see if any records might be attainable in person, but it seemed like a lot of work for a likely dead end. Ultimately, the additional information we cobbled together was pretty slim and none of it related to the word on the wall.

When I went home I kept at it, albeit in a pretty half-hearted manner. Elsie and Josh did too. We kept in touch, but eventually the research fizzled out. Despite the common occurrence of the word—*Weeks*—there seemed nothing to unearth.

I couldn't get the word out of my head though. *Weeks. Weeks. Weeks. What did it mean?*

I would try to sleep at night and there it would be—in bold, neon lights, just waiting to be deciphered. Weeks.

Another visit later in August confirmed it hadn't left the forefront of anyone else's mind either. Because of the extreme lack of progress we'd made figuring out what happened that night, we decided to investigate a new location instead. Josh had a few places to choose from, so we selected an abandoned building at a business park in Bristol, Connecticut, and then dove into the research with our typical fervor.

Look, I wrote out a detailed rundown of the Hale House because I think it's important you know how Josh and I got started. I wrote about the Benson House because I think you need to know what kicked off the beginning of the end and has occupied our minds all this time. We went to the building in Bristol together that August, then went through our senior year of college and took four more trips—an abandoned house in Springfield, Massachusetts, another in Danbury, Connecticut, an out-of-commission hospital right down the road in Storrs, and another house in West Hartford, Connecticut.

Out of the collective five trips, only two were duds. Whether it be sounds, sightings, feelings, or what have you, we came out of the other three with a story. It wasn't the same, though. Nothing else communicated in such a straightforward manner. The house in Waterbury felt like going fishing in a koi pond and hauling in a white whale. We never talked about what would happen after college, going our separate ways mostly, but I think we knew our ghost hunting days were at an end.

One unexpected side effect of our extracurricular activities was that Elsie and I got over our differences. We both came at each other wielding a child-like standoffish mentality. Pulling from that oh-so-useful psych degree, I'd say we were both mistrustful of each other for the same reason—protecting Josh. Once we realized the other person had his best interests at heart, we let down our guards.

In December of our senior year, when we were in Coventry planning for our third trip after Waterbury, we realized having Josh in common might not be the extent of our feelings. Elsie and I were digging up material for our next trip while Josh stepped out to get food. We were laughing about who knows what, and she leaned in and kissed me, quick on the lips, then backed away almost like she was planning to say she'd tripped. It wasn't one of those profound moments because I think we'd seen it coming for a few months now. I kissed her back, and this time she didn't jump away.

We kept it on the down low for a few weeks, but I think Josh always knew. He often kept his face impassive, but when you developed the brotherhood we had, reading him became second nature. When Elsie and I decided we wanted to give it a real go, we told him. In typical fashion, he simply nodded and said okay. What some people might view as indifference, Elsie and I understood to be love and trust from a person who didn't easily give up either one.

Her fuchsia hair initially got my attention, but she was bright and tenacious, and I think that's what made it so easy to fall in love with her. We've been together for almost ten years now, married for three. I'm not sure any of us planned on the house in West Hartford being our last trip together, at least for quite a while, but it ended without circumstance, and we never discussed another. Josh applied for, and received, an internship at a local emergency veterinary hospital and stayed with his parents for a couple of years until he found an apartment.

Elsie and I moved to Southbridge, Massachusetts, and rented an apartment together. She worked in retail and I landed a gig as a case manager with Harrington Hospital. We were content, if a little boring, and we kept in touch with Josh. After all, he was family. When he visited we never talked about the days of wandering through abandoned houses in the dead of night. Not until recently, when the force that found us in the Benson House decided it wasn't done with us. Not yet.

PART TWO

Torches Together

CHAPTER SEVENTEEN

It doesn't take as much as you might think to flip your entire life upside down. At the ripe old age of thirty-two, Elsie and I settled into a nice little starter home. It needed some work, but it was ours. All it took to cause that upheaval was one word, and you already know what it is.

Elsie and I had never really forgotten about the Benson House. It still came up in conversation every few months, but we no longer allowed it to occupy all our headspace. We believed we'd never know what any of it meant, and had come to terms with it.

Josh called on a Friday night. We had settled in to watch a movie and go to bed at a reasonable hour. Elsie stopped dying her hair years before, but that was never the only thing that drew me to her. With her natural mousy brown hair, she looked more beautiful than ever. I recall looking forward to the bed part of that night, but we never quite got there, at least not in the fashion I hoped for.

My phone rang around 9:15. We heard from Josh regularly, but usually only during business hours. I picked up only to find him mid-sentence, talking a mile a minute.

"… think I figured it out."

"Hello to you too, sir. Figured what out?"

"Weeks."

A chill swept over me, and I felt the blood drain from my face. Elsie must have noticed because she sat up quickly and mouthed, *what is it?* I put the call on speakerphone.

"I, uh, Josh. You're on speakerphone. Elsie. Elsie's here." She looked at me like I was having a stroke. A mixture of confusion and concern. "Could, uh, could you say that again?"

"I know what Weeks is," he said. No arrogance or satisfaction in his tone. Just a statement of fact. My stomach dropped and that chill ran a second lap around my body.

"Well, don't keep us in suspense, Joshy. Do tell," said Elsie. Despite the playfulness of her words, her tone matched the way I felt.

"It's a house. In western Massachusetts, not very far from any of us. It's also the person who built the house."

"How did you find that out?" I asked.

"I've been looking for a long time. I haven't been on any more outings since the last time with you guys, but I still spend at least a few hours a week reading up on local attractions. It's how we started doing it in the first place. Remember, Travis?"

"Yeah, I guess I'm just glad you're not going it alone."

"So am I," Elsie agreed.

"The really strange part is not that I found it," continued Josh, "but that it took me so long. It's a pretty well-known house locally, for activity and the like. It's the type of place I should have discovered before I even met you, but here we are. I stumbled across it about twenty minutes ago for the first time, on a message board."

"I legitimately thought those were a relic from middle school."

"For the most part, they are. Obviously the name got my attention, so I followed up and there's so much out there. If this is related, and I'm almost sure it is, it's like it was being hidden from us. Especially odd considering the steps the Benson House took to get us to pay attention."

"I actually can't believe you called us before you had a chance to dive down the research rabbit hole," said Elsie.

"Well, it wasn't my intention," said Josh, "but I came across something that made me rethink going this alone. Hold on, I'm going to send you a picture."

A photo came through on Elsie's phone. An old black-and-white picture of a man and a woman, dressed in their Sunday best, and looking deadly serious.

"This is really old," I said. "Like very early 1900s old."

"1870s, actually. Do you recognize the man?"

"I don't think so."

"That's not surprising. It's been a long time, but there was a portrait of him at the Hale House. On the wall in the main room where we started out."

"Oh shit, you're right. Who is he?"

"Robert Weeks, the guy who built the Weeks House."

"Okay, what was his portrait doing in the Hale House? He didn't even live in the same time period as Hale."

"That I don't know yet," said Josh. "Like I said, I just discovered this place existed. I've got a lot of questions and a lot to figure out. I was hoping you guys might help me out on this one."

"Josh, man, I don't know." I paused, catching Elsie's eyes. "I mean, you know I'd love to, but we can't just drop everything to look into another haunted house."

"Travis, you know it's not just another haunted house. There's a connection here. I know there is. What if I come to you, just for the weekend? We see what we can dig up and go from there."

I could tell I wasn't getting around this, as much as I didn't want to dig any of that up. Elsie continued staring at the photograph, eyes wide and glistening. If she had an opinion, it wasn't forthcoming. "I guess so."

"Fantastic," said Josh. "I can be there at eight tomorrow morning." And with that, he hung up.

"Eight? It's a Saturday," but he was already off the line. I laid my head in my hands and let out an excessive sigh. Elsie hadn't said a word in the last three or four minutes of our phone call. I picked up my head. She looked more terrified than I ever remembered seeing her before, her eyes big as saucers and her lower lip trembling.

"Hon, what's wrong?" I asked. She still had her phone open with the picture Josh had sent.

"It's him," she said. "That's the man from the Benson House. The dark figure. I'm sure it is."

I took her phone and looked again. I'll be damned if she wasn't dead on. Obviously, the Robert Weeks in the picture was more than a shadow, but the build was exactly right. Even his stature in the picture matched the specter we'd seen, as though the man from the portrait had stepped out into real life. The penetrating eyes, though black-and-white, weren't difficult to imagine in an emerald-green hue.

"Let's go to bed," I said, shutting off the television. No one slept particularly well that night.

CHAPTER EIGHTEEN

As promised, Josh arrived at 8 a.m. sharp. Knowing his affinity for punctuality, Elsie and I were up and dressed, and I had made coffee. When I opened the door, he headed straight for the kitchen table to set up shop. First, he pulled a laptop out of his bag, the same Misfits messenger bag he'd carried around with him in college. At least I assume it was the same one. The only thing more odd than a man in his thirties carrying around that bag would be a man the same age going shopping for a new one.

"Make yourself at home," I said, trying to find a place for my coffee mug. "Elsie will be out in a few. Can I get you anything?"

"Already ate, thanks," said Josh, without looking up. "I, uh, didn't get much of a chance to sleep last night, so I left early."

"Wonder why that could be," I said, not expecting an answer. I let out a sigh. "We kind of had the same issue, although I'm thinking maybe for different reasons. You started looking into that house without us, didn't you? Just couldn't wait."

He still didn't look up, but allowed a trace of a smile to creep onto his face. "If it makes you feel better, I didn't get very far. A few biographical details on Robert Weeks, and some information about the town. There's quite a bit more to dig into, that's where I need Elsie, but…"

"Gee, thanks."

"I've never coddled your ego, Travis, and I'm not about to start now. She's always been better at the research portion. What I was saying is it seems like Weeks, and by extension the house, is pretty tied into the town it's in."

"Which is…?"

"Slattery Falls."

"Don't know it, but that doesn't mean much. Western Mass has a ton of podunk little towns."

"Yeah, it's not huge. It's right near Conway, Deerfield, and Hobson. You could actually follow Route 91 up from Hartford and get pretty close."

"Conway and Deerfield I know. What else did you find?"

Before he answered, Josh's eyes darted around the room. "Nothing much, really." I knew he had more to tell me, and I also knew that he was a better liar. He had something on his mind and wanted me to drag it out of him. I crossed my arms, letting the silence hang.

"Nothing much definitive," he amended. "There's a lot of speculation around both the house and the town—more message board stuff. I told you that was where I found out about it in the first place. I'm just curious to see what else we can come up with before we compare notes."

"Fair. There's something I've got to ask you before Elsie comes in." I waited until I was sure I had his complete attention. In other words, no more clacking keys. Josh didn't look up, but I knew he was listening. "What are we going to do with all this information?"

He chuckled, and then immediately stopped when he noticed that wasn't the reaction I wanted. "I mean, I thought we'd go, you know, like we used to. We'd check it out, see what there is to see. Maybe it needs something from us."

I shook my head. "We started the investigation thing for fun, this doesn't seem fun. It seems dangerous. This fucking thing crossed state lines to mess with us, terrified us, terrified Elsie, man. You didn't see her face last night when she looked at that picture. Fun wasn't the first word that crossed my mind. Now, after ten years, it's back in our lives. Why? Why now? You said it yourself, the Weeks House is something you should have come across years ago, and now you just happen to stumble across it. You think that's a mistake?"

"I had thought of that," he said, under his breath.

"And what? Didn't care? Wanted to go after this place like Captain fucking Ahab?"

"I don't know, Travis. It's not like that. I need to know, though. Step one is to learn more. I don't know anyone in the world who is a better fit to help me than the two of you. Can we start there and take it a step at a time?"

I stared him down, taking a deep breath as his eyes slipped back to his laptop.

"Yeah, I guess," I said, feeling myself calm a little. It was easy to forget in the heat of the moment that Josh didn't have a manipulative, malevolent bone in his body. "Yes. I just need to know that you have Elsie's best interest at heart. She's your cousin, and Josh, she's my world. We're not dragging her into a position where she could get hurt. Please agree with that."

"Of course."

We ended up changing the subject to baseball while we waited. The Mets were getting ready to miss the playoffs again, and as a lifelong Massachusetts resident, I was strapped in for the roller coaster ride that is a Red Sox season. We were knee deep talking about starting pitchers—Sale versus deGrom—when Elsie walked in, no inkling of the tension present only a few minutes ago.

"Morning, boys. We ready to get started?"

CHAPTER NINETEEN

Hours passed, feeling like minutes. We immersed ourselves in as much information as we could get our greedy hands on. Around noon, Elsie and Josh deemed me non-essential personnel and sent me out to get lunch. Occasionally, one of us would stop to bounce something we had found off the others, but mainly we worked in silence. Falling back into old routines happened a little too easily. We knew later in the day we would shut down the computers and compare notes, then use that to discern what else we needed to be looking for. It was all very methodical and scientific-ish.

Elsie set that chain in motion somewhere around 7 p.m. With a dramatic groan, she closed her laptop and sat back, arms crossed in front of her chest, looking back and forth between Josh and me.

"Everybody in a decent stopping place?"

We nodded, and she returned the gesture. "Let's make something to eat, pour some drinks, and see what we've got."

Elsie and I made chicken and rice, nothing fancy, while Josh ran to the liquor store to pick up some beer, also nothing fancy. We planned on getting something in our stomachs before we got to business, but everyone was visibly excited, and the conversation refused to wait until after dinner.

"So, recap of what we knew going in," said Josh between bites. "The house was built in Slattery Falls, Massachusetts, in 1868, mostly in 1868 anyway. It looks like construction spilled into the next year and there were additions put on following that. Robert Weeks immigrated to Slattery Falls from Bristol, England in 1869."

"So wait. Doesn't that mean he didn't build the house? That it was at least started before he came?" I asked.

"Yes, and no."

"I've got that one," said Elsie. "Slattery Falls is a pretty small town, which is probably one reason none of us knew the name when it first popped up. One day in 1868, construction sprung up. None of the workers would answer questions put to them by the townspeople, just kept to their job. They never came into town for food or drinks either, just brought everything they needed with them and packed up at the end of the day to leave. Well, supposedly. I found it noted in several places that no town residents ever saw them go, and that worried the people of Slattery Falls. The construction workers were hard at work one minute and gone the next.

"One day in early 1869, the residents noticed a towering man with a big red beard present at the site. At first glance, they thought the job might finally have a foreman. Reports said even though the workers still wouldn't interact with anyone, this man would come into town occasionally, buying items at random, and putting a very cold disposition on display. A length of rope here, a set of empty jars there, never a lot. Just knick-knacks." Elsie paused for a moment to catch our eyes. "This is speculation, but reading that part, the way they phrased it, almost reminded me of a shoplifter buying a pack of gum to avoid appearing guilty. The whole thing kind of has an urban legend vibe to it, especially the part about the workers."

"So did the town just, like, not trust Weeks? Have it out for him?" I asked.

"He was never very personable, but he did frequent pretty much every shop in the town. All those little items added up, and since they saw him as a wealthy man, there was little to no chance they were going to shun him." Elsie pushed her chair away from the table. "Give me a second. Let me grab my notes. I want to read you something."

She walked to the other room to get the red spiral-bound notebook she had written in all day, then returned to the kitchen. Not a sound in the interim.

"This is from the diary of Emily Stone, dated July 20th, 1869. *That man Weeks is a frightening one. I find myself putting it off to his size and the fact that he never smiles, but he has a way about him that I do not entirely trust. The shopkeepers, however, seem perfectly acquiescent to taking his money. When Mr. Weeks converses, his words are friendly enough, but they do not match the tone. They do not match the man. Everyone here walks on eggshells when he is around, but they have plenty to say when he is not.*"

"It's not super damning," I said. "Just makes him sound like a bit of an asshole. I noticed he was from Bristol, but I couldn't find anything about his life before he came to Massachusetts. Any luck on your ends?"

"None," said Josh. Elsie nodded in agreement. "You would think that someone of wealth would leave a record on how they attained it, but there's nothing. Like he simply appeared on the outskirts of England one day."

Something about including the word *appear* didn't sit well with me. We discussed nothing egregious, but it still felt as though something unnatural hung in the air.

"It's around 1874 that it gets rough," said Josh.

"The missing children of Slattery Falls," I said.

"Exactly. For about five years, Robert Weeks frequented the town. He didn't make any friends, but no enemies either. Like Elsie said, and I had the same notion, it just seems like a man trying to quash any suspicions that might lie on his doorstep by incorporating himself as just another citizen of Slattery Falls, although one with a much less modest home. The oddest part, and I also found this in Emily Stone's diary, was that even when the house appeared finished to the outside observer, the workers never went away. The people of Slattery Falls didn't see them as often, and assumed they must be renovating inside the house, but the workers would gather outside regularly, and not just a few, but just as many as the first day ground broke."

"Again weird," said Elsie. "Not necessarily sinister though."

Josh nodded. "It was the summer of 1874 when the first child went missing. Six-year-old Benjamin Hempel. He went off to play down by the creek with his older sister, Elizabeth, in the middle of the afternoon. She came back, he didn't. Now, the obvious answer is he fell in the creek and drowned."

"No," I said, "I read about that one. I found pictures of the creek and descriptions and whatnot. I mean, I know they say you can drown in an inch of water, but even if there was some freak accident there's no way they wouldn't have found the kid."

"Benjamin," added Elsie.

"Right. Benjamin. They said his sister had no recollection of what could have possibly happened, like she lost time. She blamed herself for not paying enough attention and losing him."

"And she killed herself," finished Elsie, looking down at her lap. "The next year, she couldn't live with it anymore, and she killed herself."

I shot Josh a look, and he quickly put in, "Elsie, we don't have to—"

"No, it's fine," she added quickly. "I mean, it was hard to read through obviously, but there were seven other cases just like that, even after Weeks was supposedly gone, there were still two more. And guys, I don't know if anyone else jumped to the same conclusion, but—"

"Todd Benson," I said.

"Yes. Everything we found about Todd Benson said there was no way someone could have taken him, but someone did, and who knows how many others. We just stumbled on that case, but it's been almost a hundred and fifty years. If this all pans out, it could be hundreds by now."

A moment went by while we took it all in. It was Josh who broke the silence.

"Okay, so children went missing, and the people in town became suspicious of Weeks. Outsider syndrome. No matter how many years one spends in the community and how well they acclimate, there's always a sense they don't belong. If something happens, that's where suspicion will fall. After the third child goes missing, that's when the side-eye glances and mumbling turn into more direct accusations. Weeks doesn't take kindly to this and abruptly ceases his visits to town. You would assume that the missing children would stop, or at the very least pause, but that doesn't happen. Children continue to go missing at the rate of one every two to three months. Elsie, you said you read about nine cases total, right? Details or just names?"

"Both." She pulled her notes closer, not because she needed to, but to steel herself before reading from them. "I mentioned Benjamin Hempel was the first, age six. After that, Theresa Warner, age five, Jessica Hampstead, six, David Wright, eight, Eugene Davieau, five, James Hembree, seven, and Lucy Gibbs, three. I couldn't find a ton of details on any one particular case, but honestly I think that's because there aren't that many. Recorded accounts, that is. It seems like they all kind of mirror the Benjamin Hempel story. The children were away from the parents, sometimes for less than a minute. You can imagine after a few children went missing, the kids weren't spending much time off on their own anymore. They were away from their parents, then they were gone."

"This is probably a shit question," I said, "but did they ever find any of them?"

She shook her head. Her mouth formed the shapes of the words, but only their ghosts came out.

"Not alive," Josh finished for her.

CHAPTER TWENTY

The reign of terror lasted almost two years, parents afraid to let children out of their sight, knowing that even their best efforts wouldn't ensure safety. The whole situation left local law enforcement baffled. They deputized several highly regarded community members and secretly assigned them to keep watch on the Weeks House to monitor comings and goings. Months of this turned up nothing. Robert Weeks had ceased leaving his house, and although people saw the workers outside sometimes, with a cigarette or chatting in groups, they never left either. On two separate afternoons where a child went missing, the house was under surveillance, and the deputies saw no one depart the premises.

Despite the evidence, or lack thereof, the people in town refused to acquit Weeks in their minds. According to Emily Stone's diary—a source we were becoming intimately familiar with—on October 10th of 1876, the frustration and anger present in Slattery Falls, Massachusetts, physically manifested, and a mob of almost two hundred people marched on the house, torches and all. The mass hysteria had boiled over to where it even involved the town's lawmen, sheriff included. Nobody hid their faces. They had a fucking monster in their midst and damned if they were going to wait for proof, or for one more of their children to go missing.

They stood at the gate and demanded that Weeks come out. When he realized the group wasn't going away, he did, appearing at the second-floor window. Several of the workers were present in the front yard, but made themselves scarce when the angry mob began throwing stones. I could paraphrase the rest, but I think it's probably best to go word-for-word here.

In an entry from later that night, Stone writes, *Robert Weeks appeared at the window of his house on the hill, overlooking the town. He stood bold as brass, unrepentant and unashamed, declaring his innocence with no more emotion than a man might use to inform a passerby of the color of the sky. As though stating a fact. The people of Slattery Falls had already rendered their verdict, however, and it was not a favorable one for Mr. Weeks.*

We set to breaking down the gate. True, we had no tools to do so, but we had manpower in droves. The gates began to give, and I looked up to see Mr. Weeks raise his hands as though pushing against an invisible wall. The gates seemed to draw renewed strength from this gesture, whether it be magick, I cannot say, but it took some heart out of the people who had seen it. In short order, the mass of human beings became too much for the gates, and for the man, to hold back. They came down with a clamorous roar and the townspeople rushed for the front door. It proved no such obstacle and came down without circumstance. About twenty men on the front line stormed the second floor to retrieve Weeks, including Wright and Hampstead, who had lost children to this beast.

The man, if man he was, I certainly have my doubts, was dragged down a flight of stairs and onto the front lawn where he stood surrounded and had accusations hurled at him. Robert Weeks showed no anger, yet there was a fire, a fury present in those startling sea-green eyes. One I suspect will stay with me for some time. The townspeople seemed at an impasse, and no one quite knew what to do next. I believe we all expected that such a gathering would force the truth out, and yet the man remained stoic.

As the tension neared an unbearable point, a scream cut through the air. The folk who were not interrogating Robert Weeks had ransacked the house. The crowd parted around Shannon Brown, who held the lifeless body of Benjamin Hempel. Brown cried out that there were more, and not just the missing seven, but at least fifteen bodies, all children, in the house's basement.

At this discovery, Robert Weeks' demeanor changed, not to fear as I might have guessed or hoped, but to joviality. This marked the only time that the people of Slattery Falls had seen the man smile, and it came at the public revelation that he had murdered their children. He laughed, a sound that penetrated the stunned night air. The memory keeps me from finding sleep even as I write this. I fear that sound will haunt my dreams until my final day. In the end, there was no admission of guilt, no final words, only laughter. It was like there was a joke that only he had been privy to. Swiftly, the people had their justice as they hung Robert Weeks from the sturdy branch of an oak tree on his own property.

The people continued making their way through every inch of the house, bringing out the bodies of the children, many of whom were not from Slattery Falls. I suspect we have quite the workload ahead of us in finding out where and from whom he took these other children. They dragged workers out, about twelve of them. Those who resisted were deemed complicit and beaten to death. Those who came willingly were judged equally guilty and hung. The last person brought out was a harsh-looking woman. Her attire suggested she'd been pulled from her bed, and tears gathered at the corners of her eyes, but refused to fall. No one in town had ever seen her before. When interrogated, she refused to give out any information, except that Weeks was her husband. That admission alone earned her a rope on the branch right next to his. Though Stone's journal had no record of the woman's name—perhaps they never learned it—Josh would later discover that it was Tabitha.

When all was said and done, several people were missing. Not children this time, but men of the town, William Riley and Michael Tucker. They were among the folks who raided the house looking for any and all damning evidence, but no one saw them come back out. It is, of course, possible that they returned to their homes without notice amidst the chaos, yet doubt courses through my mind. Only tomorrow will tell.

Finally, Emily Stone leaves us with this bit of wisdom. *It was a night of blood and vengeance. As we returned to our homes, no one was truly satiated. The monsters are dead. Still, it appears the evil has not been extinguished, but merely changed its form. Perhaps this is why Robert Weeks went to his grave laughing.*

CHAPTER TWENTY-ONE

You're probably thinking Josh and Elsie dug up quite a bit and I must have been sitting around with my thumb up my ass. Alas, you would be mistaken. I spent the day focusing on paranormal experiences in and around the house. Weird shit started up almost as soon as Weeks died. Immediately after stringing the man up, the town residents plundered every inch of his house and chained the gates shut. Despite the house being abandoned, people still saw figures passing by windows. One said to have strikingly resembled Robert Weeks. Passersby heard sounds coming from the house and described them as the noise of construction—the clang of a hammer driving in a nail, the rasp of a saw slicing through wood. Clearly coming from inside, but inexplicably amplified because how else would you hear that from outside the gate?

And those two men Emily Stone mentioned? Riley and Tucker? Nobody ever saw them again. As far as anyone from Slattery Falls knew, they went in looking for the kids—down in the basement—and never came out. Then the same thing happened on several more occasions. When townspeople first saw specters at the windows and heard sounds, they believed someone was squatting in the house and sent people in to investigate. Sometimes they came back, sometimes they didn't. Obviously they didn't have a never-split-up-when-investigating-spooky-fucked-up-houses rule. We couldn't find an accurate count of the men that entered the house in the months and years following Weeks' death, but the number who never came out again was five. Not including the two lost the night of the hanging.

Then two more children went missing, Sam Buckner and Nathan Stone. Almost identical circumstances to the original seven. And yes, Nathan was the son of Emily Stone. We first read about his disappearance in the diary entry from the day after he disappeared. Reading it together stopped us in our tracks for a bit. It made this whole thing a little more… real. If you really want to read it, feel free to do some internet sleuthing of your own, but I don't have it in me to read it again, never mind writing it out.

Both kids went missing in the house's vicinity, but outside the gates. It served as the straw that broke Slattery Falls' back and finally prompted the community to do something about the house, because by 1879, even the skeptics believed Weeks was haunting or cursing the town.

Here's where it gets interesting. They elected a group of men to burn the house to the ground, but it didn't work. How do you fuck up burning a house to the ground, you might ask? Well, it sounds like they did everything right and the house just refused to burn. No matter what they used as an accelerant, no matter how many times they tried, the flame would ignite, then extinguish almost immediately. Eventually, the men had to concede. The house didn't take anybody that night, and if I had to guess why, it was probably so those men had to walk back to town with their heads hung low and admit defeat.

Not entirely sure what to do with the house that had decided it wasn't going anywhere, the town doubled down on keeping distance. The house's relative isolation near the woods on the north end of town made this not only possible, but relatively easy. They basically drew an imaginary town line and banished the Weeks House from within the borders. After this entry, we didn't find any record of disappearances, child or adult, for quite some time, so on the surface this worked. For a while anyway, because there were two issues there.

Number one, trying to make a problem go away by ignoring it absolutely never works under any circumstance. Number two, eventually the true stories that happen to one generation become the urban legends of the next. I suspect that's what happened, because there are reports of disappearances from 1880 to the present day, twenty-six in all. On a long enough timeline, it doesn't look like an epidemic, but it struck us as a higher number than a town with a population of about 10,000 should probably have. I suppose I did neglect researching what an acceptable amount of disappearances might look like.

CHAPTER TWENTY-TWO

By the time midnight rolled around, we had gone through everything. During past cram sessions, we had spread all our materials and discussions out over the course of a few days, but this one demanded a sense of urgency. As a result, we were pretty wiped out.

"We still need to find some more about activity in the house between 1880 and now," said Josh, rubbing at his forehead and eyes to keep sleep at bay.

"I'm not sure there's much else to find," I said. "For a while, it seems the town kept the place on lockdown, and even though later generations didn't believe the curse aspect, they seem to have had the good sense to stay the hell away from it, and not let anyone else in either. The town's dirty little secret."

"So how do we get in?" Elsie said.

I guess I should have been expecting that, but it still surprised me. "Whoa, why would we go inside?"

Blank stares from my cohorts told me I was alone in this line of thought.

I rambled on. "Not only does that place have a record of making people disappear, but it's been actively trying to get our attention for ten years. Nothing about that says *good idea*. Nothing!"

Elsie rolled her eyes. "Do you honestly expect anyone to believe you just spent a whole day learning everything you could about a cursed little town in Massachusetts, so that you could sweep it under a rug? You don't have that in your personality, honey." There was a trace amount of sarcasm in her voice, but she wasn't joking. "Josh, what do you think?"

"I abstain, courteously."

"That's bullshit and you know it," Elsie said.

"Okay." Josh paused, seeming to search for the right words. A quick dart of the eyes in my direction before he spoke told me what those words would be. "I think we should do it."

"Of course you do," I said. "Because you're obsessed."

Josh shrugged. "I am a bit, but that's not why. You need to remember we've been looking into this for less than twenty-four hours, and so far, we've named sixteen people who have disappeared under mysterious circumstances, all presumably related to that house. Seven adults, nine children. Sixteen total. And ten children if you want to count Todd Benson, and I, personally, do. Elsie?"

"Yes. Me too."

"So," continued Josh, "my theory is that if we had a considerable amount of time and resources, we would likely find more tentative connections. Do you know how far Waterbury is from Slattery Falls? About ninety miles. With that in mind, Weeks could affect most of New England. At minimum."

"That's speculation, though. You went to school for science, animal science granted, but how are you suddenly going to throw the need for proof, for evidence, right out the window?" I asked. "That's not like you at all. We don't even definitively know that we can link all the people in Slattery Falls who went missing to Weeks."

"What's your gut feeling?"

"That doesn't matter."

"It does though." Elsie this time. She dropped her gaze before going on. "It sounds like Josh is in, and even if he wasn't, I'm going. Fuck it, I'll go alone if I have to, Travis. I think you know we have to, and you're just scared, that's fine. I'm petrified. Josh?"

"Scared shitless, and yeah, I'm going too."

"Christ." I pulled at my hair and paced the room. "You fucking two. You know goddamn well I'm not going to let you go alone. And yes, I'm scared. Know what of? We don't have a fucking plan. We know how to break into a house with minimal security and walk around with flashlights. What we don't know, is the first thing about stopping an evil entity that's been around for over a century. Thoughts, anyone?"

Neither one had an answer to this. "We'll figure it out, and we won't go until we have a plan," said Elsie.

"That could be months," said Josh. "It could be never."

"Then I guess we better get to work," said Elsie.

CHAPTER TWENTY-THREE

Having done everything possible over the weekend, we took Josh out to lunch on Sunday, then sent him on his way, disappointed. Ten years and I'd never seen him that despondent. Josh was the type of person who planned breakfast five days in advance. He rarely rushed into anything with uncertainty. Everything about the Weeks story burrowed under his skin, showcasing a side of him I'd never really been aware of before. We agreed to keep in touch if anything new came to light.

Josh agreed in order to get regular updates. Elsie and I agreed because it scared us to think he might go up there by himself.

Days and weeks passed with few developments. Running web searches on how to vanquish ghosts gets you results that deal in fiction or crackpots, not much in the realm of useful tips. It seemed like maybe we needed an expert on the occult, but where the hell does one find that? Yellow pages? Elsie and I kept this at the front of our minds, but we also spent some time trying to dig up other reported expeditions into the house—either freelance or professional, we weren't picky—and came up short.

The town of Slattery Falls still kept a firm grip on the property. Surveillance cameras galore and alarms on the fences. We found plenty of people who had tried to break in and failed. None who had succeeded and wrote about it, posting to the darkest corners of the internet.

This left us with two unique problems. Number one, we'd have to figure out a way in and it would be outside of the way we usually did things. That didn't bode well. Problem two, we liked to know the details regarding paranormal occurrences before going in. You know, hotspots of activity, rooms to watch out for, figures that might pop up, sounds to listen for, things like that. With no reports available, we were going in blind. Elsie pulled floor plans for the house, but that was about it.

It had been three weeks since we started trying to plan when Josh called us again, a little after nine. The guy still had no phone etiquette. When the phone rang at that hour, my stomach dropped. I put him on speaker and he sounded over-the-top excited.

"I've got it! I figured it out. I know what to do."

"Spill it," said Elsie.

"Okay, I was able to find a doctor who dabbles in this stuff. His name is Jericho. I can't go into details right now, but he gave me a ritual that will get rid of Weeks. The only catch is we need to be in the house, since that's the source of power. We also need some items, but I've got that covered."

"That sounds too easy," I said, more to Elsie than the phone.

"I thought so too," said Josh. "But he's done this before. He told me the whole story. Guys, we can do this! So, when do we go?"

"What are the items? How long do you need to get them?" asked Elsie.

"Already done," he answered.

"Holy shit! Okay," said Elsie. "Um…" Her eyes met mine, expectantly.

I looked for any excuse to put it off, to doubt my friend, but his enthusiasm was catching, and before I could slow the momentum, it had claws in Elsie. Nothing I could say or do would turn the ride around at that point.

"Okay," I said. "This weekend. Come up on Saturday, not so damn early this time. Anything you need from us?"

"No, I've got this, but, uh, as much as I appreciate that you're on board, maybe we should put it off until the following weekend. We still have to figure out how we're going to get in."

"Shit, I don't suppose you came up with something for that too, did you?"

"Actually, *I* might have something," said Elsie.

It was a great idea, although I admit to being a little disheartened that she had been rolling this over in her mind and hadn't run it by me. She told me later she wanted to figure some more stuff out before she laid a half-assed plan on my doorstep. The excitement of Josh having figured out how to deal with the house and the lingering spirit of Robert Weeks caused her to blurt it out.

That made sense. As much as I hated to admit it, I felt eager, too. Throughout our friendship, the man on the other end of the phone had never steered me wrong, but fuck, I wish I hadn't listened to him just that once.

CHAPTER TWENTY-FOUR

Like the best-laid plans, Elsie's was simple if it worked, infinitely more complicated if it didn't. You might recall the mention of a ghost-hunting business—Here Ghost Nothing. That idea belonged to Elsie, and was she ever proud of her brainchild. She made up shirts, pamphlets, the whole nine yards, then set to work finding out who in Slattery Falls one might contact to gain access to the Weeks House.

Turns out a Mr. Jeremiah Tedeschi, the head and presumably only member of the Slattery Falls Historical Society, held that distinguished responsibility. We got Mr. Tedeschi on the phone, admittedly under a false pretense, then ever so gently steered the conversation toward our main objective. At the beginning of the conversation, he showed reluctance to even admit the house was on the town's land, and we knew this might be a bit more work than originally expected.

We based a substantial part of the plan on this guy taking our word for a lot of things and not conducting any further research. Josh had set a website up, and while Tedeschi's voice said he would check into it, his tone suggested he would rather not deal with the computer machine. The pièce de résistance came when he referred to our "documentaries" as being on "The YouTube"—a pretty solid sign the background check would be shallow. The hardest portion to sell Tedeschi on was a book deal dependent on this trip to the Weeks House, twenty-five percent of the advance to go to the Slattery Falls Historical Society. What's twenty-five percent of zero? Okay, it was mean, but when you think about it, it's kind of their own fault for making it impossible to just break in. The logic is there, I promise.

Mr. Tedeschi hemmed and hawed, but it was all a show. He was good to go based on that advance money, but his reluctance created an interesting predicament. When we were setting a time to meet, we pitched late at night. That's when we did our investigating. He was quick to counter, saying he would be in bed by nine, and unable to let us in or lock up after us, so no, that simply wouldn't work. The conversation volleyed back and forth on that point, but I think it struck Elsie and me at the same time. Did we need to go at night? We always had, but that's only because it proved to be the best time to commit breaking and entering. An exploration by daylight would definitely be… different. We pushed for the night thing anyway, even tried saying it might affect the size of the advance, but despite agreeing to let us in, I believe we had pushed good old Mr. Tedeschi to the end of his limits. That's how we came to agree to a noon ghost hunt, perfect after a spot of lunch. We made our reservations, so to speak, worked out a timetable, said our goodbyes, and hoped to high hell that Jeremiah Tedeschi wouldn't realize how stupid the thing he had committed to really was.

"It's almost two weeks out," said Josh, "so let's figure out what needs to get done between now and then."

"I think the top of the list is the daytime thing," I said. "I'm a little pissed at myself for not anticipating that the old guy who's letting us in wouldn't want to lock up at three in the morning. Is there any reason to think this will change our approach?"

"It shouldn't. Nighttime is synonymous with ghost stories because it's scarier, but there have been plenty of sightings during the day. All the Civil War sites south of us have activity day and night. No, it shouldn't be a problem," said Josh.

Elsie piped in. "The other thing to remember is we're not necessarily looking for activity this time. We're going to get in, perform Josh's ritual, and get out. Although, I wouldn't mind sticking around long enough to make sure it worked. I'd hate to think all this work was just to piss off a ghost who already seems to have it out for us." She looked at Josh. "Any reason to think the ritual needs to be performed at night?"

"I'll look into it, but I think it should be alright."

"Ready to tell us what's involved yet?" I asked. "You're not going to sacrifice a pig, are you?"

"Nothing like that. Actually, I think I feel better keeping it close to the chest until it's time, and I'll ask you two to trust me. I will tell you that you don't have to play a role in it, it seems easy enough."

"Alright, I trust you, man. Els?"

"C'mon, you have to ask?"

With little to do, the next two weeks were interminable. We'd get Josh on the phone every few days, but there wasn't much planning left to do. We tried finding out more about the house and the town, but it appeared we had dug that well dry. Just when it felt like waiting another minute would push one of us off the deep end, the day finally arrived. Since Elsie and I lived closer to the Weeks House, Josh crashed on our couch the night before, and at 10:30 the next morning, the three of us set out for Slattery Falls.

CHAPTER TWENTY-FIVE

An eerie calm settled over the ride to Slattery Falls. We were about to perform an occult ritual to banish an evil... what? Spirit? Entity? Who the fuck knew, and two weeks of needling Josh confirmed to Elsie and I that he would not tell us what it involved until the moment came. Since there was nothing else to discuss, we rode in silence. Elsie drove, I rode shotgun, and Josh with his Misfits messenger bag on his lap sat in the back. Whenever I'd look in the mirror, he appeared lost in thought. Serene, but a world away.

The sun beat down as we took the highway exit and passed by a rustic, weather-beaten sign welcoming us to Slattery Falls. We turned down the town's main road, and only access point, then continued to a fork at the end. Our first view of the destination came over the tops of the trees. Not a mansion, but the Weeks House was a story taller than any of the other buildings in town. Being on a hill overlooking the town made the size differential a bit more glaring than it actually was. I'll just come out and say it. The place looked evil.

I know, I know. I saw what I expected to see and imprinted the history associated onto the face of the actual thing itself. But damn, you weren't there. The layout of the house was a style popular at the time called Gothic Revival, and honestly, it's exactly what you think of when you picture old haunted houses.

I guess I expected the place to look condemned. As far as we could tell, the historical society wasn't taking care of this place. Nobody was. Yet here it stood, appearing much the same as I imagine it must have in the late 1800s. Gray siding with black shutters gave the house a dark-as-night exterior, even in the middle of a summer day. The gates loomed high enough to keep amateur trespassers at bay, with spikes at the top in case they were wily enough to try climbing. They hid the cameras well, but you could spot them if you knew where to look.

Standing by the front gate was a man who could only be Jeremiah Tedeschi. Tall and thin, he lacked any hair on top of his head, and dressed as though he was on his way to teach an English course at university. We pulled up right at the agreed-upon time, and he still greeted us with crossed arms, a tapping foot, and a frown that stretched from nose to chin.

"Time to look professional, my people," I said. "Shirts on."

This ruse played better coming from a trio of semi-reputable looking adults than it would have from a bunch of college kids. Intuition told me Tedeschi wouldn't open the gate if Elsie turned up with her hair still pink.

"Hello, you must be Mr. Tedeschi. I am Travis Morland, proprietor of Here Ghost Nothing Productions, and soon to be Publishing." I shot him a wink. "This is my wife Elsie, our lead research analyst, and Joshua Costa, lead investigative specialist." Josh shot me a side-eye glance. I don't think I had called him by his full name since the first time we met. Evidently it hadn't grown on him. Tedeschi held out his hand to shake, and I put a pamphlet in it.

"Yes," he said. "Of course. It's, err… a pleasure to meet the three of you. I have high expectations, you know. I get several inquiries a year from people like yourselves who would like nothing more than to step into this house and sully the good name of Slattery Falls. I daresay you'll treat the house, as well as the town, with respect regarding your findings?" It was a statement, but without the proper gumption behind it, turned into a question.

"Oh, Mr. Tedeschi, have no worries on that front." Elsie adopted my carnival-worker-selling-to-a-rube tone flawlessly, and I don't even think she realized it.

"Very well. Do you have equipment to unpack?"

"No sir, everything we need is in that bag right there." I gestured to Josh. "Technology is a wonderful thing, everything so much more compact and advanced than it was twenty years ago. Am I right?"

"I would imagine you are." He looked as though he regretted skipping his noon tea to help us rapscallions out.

"Quick question, uh, for my notes. For the book. For my notes for the book." *Smooth.* "My understanding is that no one has occupied this house for well over a hundred years, and that the historical society doesn't do any upkeep on it. Shouldn't it look a lot more dilapidated?"

"Yes, that is quite strange, isn't it? Well, I can't speak to how the interior of the house has held up. I've never been in there. However, yes, the exterior has certainly retained its… quality."

So basically, he did not know, and the house scared the fuck out of him, too.

"You've never been inside?" Elsie's tone no longer upheld the facade.

"I have not," said Tedeschi, with an unmistakable air of finality. "Well, if that will be all, I will return at five o'clock sharp to lock the gates. If you finish earlier, please wait for me. It would not do to leave access to this house… available to the general public. Oh, and one more thing."

He reached into his tweed jacket pocket and removed an envelope.

"These are standard liability waivers in the event that one of you is injured during your visit to the property. I will require all three of you to sign one before I can permit you to enter."

"Just boilerplate, huh?" I said. "No problem." I took the paper, pretended to read it for a cursory amount of time, then signed it and handed it back. Josh and Elsie did the same.

Tedeschi tucked the folded papers into his jacket pocket and patted them. "Well, that's everything in order, then. The front gates are open, as you can see. Please close them behind you. This key will unlock the deadbolt on the front door," he said, holding it out between thumb and index finger, the way one might hold a tissue containing the carapace of a nasty bug. "If there are any other locked doors within, the historical society does not have a key for them, and you are quite on your own." He handed the key over and smiled, not allowing it to touch his eyes. "I wish you good luck and I shall see you at five p.m. sharp."

We shook hands and then watched him get in his car and drive back to town. Standing in front of the open gate, the realization hit. This was what we'd been working toward, not just for a few weeks, but for years. Before we could register what a godawful fucking idea this was, we stepped through the gate and approached the house.

CHAPTER TWENTY-SIX

Having Josh open the door to what came next felt like the natural move, so I handed him the key. Although the exterior of the house wasn't extravagant, the door's size and intricacy screamed money. Power. You've seen this type of door before—a taller arch than any human being could possibly require. And while the average door is probably under seven feet tall, these were at least ten and loomed over the three of us. Ornate designs separated the glass panels in a way that couldn't have been cheap or easy to craft when they built the house. A massive brass lion door knocker adorned the right-hand side. It begged to be used, but ultimately felt a little too much like tempting fate.

Josh unlocked the deadbolt with no difficulty and pushed the door open to reveal a well-maintained living area, unnaturally so. The furniture could have arrived just before us. The truly eerie part was how clean everything had stayed. Shouldn't there have been dust, settled or floating through the air? At the very least, wouldn't the furnishings be faded from the sunlight streaming in the window?

The style of the late 1800s pervaded the house in decor and furniture choice, but setting that aside, it wouldn't have been surprising to find an occupant. None of us expected a welcoming environment, but that's exactly what we walked into. The living area inside the front door was relatively large, with a grand staircase to access the second floor straight ahead. Never one to break tradition, Josh found a spot in the middle of the room and settled on the floor. Criss-cross applesauce, as the kids say. Elsie and I joined him.

"It's been a while," he said, letting the words hang. "Anybody need a refresher on ground rules?" Despite our predicament, smiles found their way onto our faces. I looked over at Elsie, who let her gaze fall to her lap. Her hair covered her eyes and a big grin lit her face. God, she looked beautiful at that moment.

"Stick together, don't steal, 'husky' means we bail, and don't talk about fight club. Does that do it?" I asked.

"Close enough."

Elsie shot him a sideways glance. "Close enough? You getting lax in your old age?"

"What?" said Josh. "I trust you guys. Should I not?"

"Speaking of trust, we're inside now. You ready to let us in on your secrets, or do we have to guess what's going to happen?" I asked.

"Not quite yet." He pulled the messenger bag close, wrapping one arm around it. "The ritual needs to be performed in the basement. I don't like the idea of going straight there. We may not know much about the history of this house, but we do know that's where they found all the kids, thanks to Ms. Stone. Presumably, that's where whatever happened to them took place."

"So you want to explore the house, make sure Weeks knows we're here and give him plenty of time to get good and pissed off before we go to the place where all the bad shit happens?"

"Sounds great," said Elsie. "Josh, I don't know if you put any thought into this, but let's say we skip the part where we call out for spirits that want to talk to us."

"My thoughts exactly," said Josh, "and Travis, don't kid yourself. He knows we're here."

CHAPTER TWENTY-SEVEN

The living room opened out in several directions, leading to different parts of the house. On the right side, a smaller living room—not the kind for receiving guests, more like the type every grandma has, where she covers the furniture in plastic and no one is allowed to sit. I believe it's called a French room. The rear exit led to a hall that existed solely to accommodate a giant and moderately inconvenient set of stairs.

After a quick look around, we entered the library off the left-hand side. It was nearly the size of the living room and contained books stacked floor to ceiling. I suspect that if Tedeschi knew what was in there, he might have been less hesitant to set foot on the property. Wading through and selling the contents of this room could probably have kept the town of Slattery Falls afloat for the rest of its existence. That almost two centuries had passed, and no one had the courage to come in and explore this house, made the skin on the back of my neck crawl. That's how much the legend scared them. There could easily have been ten thousand books in this room, but we didn't have time to peruse, so we moved on.

On our way out the door, I thought back to Emily Stone's words. She said Robert Weeks used some kind of magick to keep the angry townspeople at bay, and it quashed my dreams of riches, as a cold sweat broke out on my forehead. *What kind of books might be in here?*

Across from the hall containing the grand staircase was a dining room—a large table and thirteen chairs filling the space. A bay window let in a modest amount of light, enough to reveal a small hallway at the rear. The passage appeared to be designed for servants, and sure enough, it took us back to the kitchen, complete with a pantry that made our kitchen look like a closet. It couldn't have taken us over twenty minutes to go through the main floor.

The welcoming atmosphere that we noticed upon our arrival had not dissipated at all. The lack of negative emotion and creepy feelings actually contributed to a disquiet that hung over us. The calm, peaceful mood made it feel like a goddamn trap.

We climbed the stairs cautiously, despite how the exploration had proceeded so far. Opening the door to a large closet filled with towels, bedsheets, and spare clothes, we found the inexplicable phenomenon of preservation from downstairs mimicked. Everything inside should have been musty, moth-eaten, and worn by time, but these items appeared as though someone folded and put them away that very morning. There were two guest bedrooms, one above the French room and the other above the dining room.

"There's no way these rooms could have housed all the workers reported to be doing construction on the house," said Josh.

The thought hadn't crossed my mind until Josh spoke it. "Are we assuming this place is too classy to have them sleeping on the floor of that library?"

"Probably not. Still, it's strange. Unless their quarters were in the basement. Seems the most likely possibility."

We passed into the master bedroom and found nothing of note, although it was harrowing to see the balcony on which Robert Weeks had reportedly stood, using some unknown force to hold the gates against the invading mob. Then we came to the last room on the top floor—a study, or an office with bookshelves a plenty, in case the library was insufficient.

We sat in the middle of the study, no one wanting to be the first to break the silence. I couldn't help feeling disappointed, and I had to imagine Elsie and Josh felt the same. I can still remember how the sun felt streaming in through the window and coming to rest on the back of my neck. Warm and comforting.

"If there's going to be anything to see, anything to happen, the basement is where it's going to be," said Josh.

"So we go right down, do whatever the ritual entails, and get the fuck out, right? It's been fine so far, but I can't help feeling like I'm being lulled into a false sense of security. Am I crazy?"

"No," said Elsie. "I've got that too. Call it paranoia, but it can't be this easy."

Josh nodded.

"Okay, Josh," I said. "If we're all in agreement that the potential for something waiting in the basement is very real, I think Elsie and I need to know what you're planning to do down there. We've given you the benefit of the doubt, but now it's two minutes to midnight."

Josh put his hand over his bag, keeping his eyes on the floor six inches in front of his feet, but said nothing.

"There isn't any ritual," Elsie whispered.

"Of course there is," I said. "It's the whole reason we came here. Josh, tell us what you're planning."

He didn't move, save for a gentle rocking. Otherwise, you could've mistaken him for a statue.

"Josh!" I said, angrier than intended.

He shook his head.

"You've got to be fucking *kidding* me," I said, trying to keep my voice down, but coming up short of successful. "You knew I wouldn't agree to come without a plan. You fucking knew it, so you made one up? And you knew I'd trust you. God dammit, man. That's low. And you dragged Elsie into it, your fucking cousin by the way. Did you even give a shit about putting your family in danger?"

Josh didn't move a muscle, wouldn't or couldn't answer.

I turned to Elsie. "How long did you know? Did he tell you?"

"First of all, you can cut the shit attitude right now." She held me in her stare and let me ruminate on just how terrifying she could be. When she spoke again, a sense of calm had returned. "He never told me. I suspected the first time he refused to let us in on what he planned to do, but I hoped I was wrong. I also hoped that he had a secondary plan for when we got here." And with that, she punched Josh in the arm. "Doesn't matter though. Travis, I know I betrayed your trust, but if you knew we would wing it, you would've put your foot down in the name of protecting your damsel in distress, and we would've come without you."

"Without me? If I refused to make this trip, you guys would have done it, anyway?"

"In a heartbeat. Because it's the right thing to do. You may be skeptical, but there's evidence that suggests children are still going missing because of this house and the guy behind it. If there's the slightest chance we can stop it, we have to do it, even at personal risk."

About three thousand replies ran through my head in a second, and not one of them was the right thing to say, so I chose silence.

"Travis, I love you. More than anything. That's why I agreed to spend the rest of my life with you, but this is something I have to do. *We* have to do. I'm going to love you no matter what you decide, but we stand a better chance with the three of us, and if this show has as much to do with protecting my dainty ass as I think it does, you're not going to do me any fucking good waiting in the car. Be pissed off at Josh, pissed off at me all you like, but later. For now, we trust each other. Can you manage that?"

Another three thousand potential replies, some close, but none of them just right. I nodded my head, not trusting my words.

"Good," said Elsie. "Get your asses up and let's go."

CHAPTER TWENTY-EIGHT

The burgeoning avalanche of nerves and anxiety as we made our way back downstairs became almost unbearable, knowing every step could spring the trap we knew must be set.

"Did you notice the entrance to the basement on the plans?" I asked.

"No, and I didn't notice anything when we looked around the first floor either," answered Josh. "We can make some educated guesses, though. It might even be outside. Some of these older houses have the cellar access outdoors."

"There was a door in that massive pantry. I'd bet it goes to the basement," said Elsie.

"You are just full of surprises today," I said.

"Not the best time to be passive-aggressive," she replied in a sing-song voice that seemed exceptionally out of place given the current setting.

Josh stopped, scrunching his shoulders up to his ears. "I kind of felt like we had this sorted upstairs. It's on me, I get it, but I can't overstate how important it is we leave any issues we have for later. We don't know what we're going to find down there, what's in store for us. I lost some of your trust, and I'm sorry, and if you want to yell and scream and hit me later, that's fine. Now, we've got to have each other's backs. Agreed?"

"Yeah, sorry. I've got this," I said.

From the bottom of the grand staircase, we retraced our steps through the kitchen and into the pantry. I'd given this room a cursory glance on our first trip around the house. This time, even looking for the door, I still almost missed it, but sure enough, Elsie was right. On the back right side of the room, seamlessly blending in with the shelves where they would've kept food, stood a door.

"Hey," I said. "This house hasn't been touched since the 1880s for the most part, right?"

They nodded.

"Clothes still in closets, beds still made up, a picture of the night the town came for Robert Weeks, but..."

"There's no food in the pantry," Elsie finished. "How did we not notice this before? It's a room full of bare shelves."

"It's strange, no doubt, but I think we should keep going," said Josh.

We headed toward the door, Josh in the lead. Opening the gateways to scary basements fell to him, and I sure as hell wasn't about to break from tradition now. He tapped on the knob three times, another custom, and then eased it open.

A brick wall. While they had left the rest of the house alone, some proactive townsperson took the time to seal off the basement.

"Shit, what now? We came all this way, and now we can't even finish this?"

Josh stared at the wall as though he could break it down with a gaze. He reached out and placed his hand on the wall, closed his eyes, and left it there for a moment. Another moment.

The first brick tumbled out of place, clattering down the stairs behind the wall. Piece by piece, the other bricks followed, revealing an endless, dark hollow. A chilly breeze blew out of it, reminding me of an exhale. The wind carried the scent of mildew and decay—the first inkling we'd received that not everything was sunshine and roses. Elsie grabbed Josh and me by our collars and yanked us back several feet.

"What the fuck was that?" she asked, eyes wide and directed toward Josh. "You just knocked down the wall, like a superpower thing."

He smirked. "Oh no, that would be much better. I didn't take that wall down. It granted us access. I keep telling you, it wants us here."

"It wants us here?" I repeated. "You said it *knows* we're here. That's different."

"How? Two sides of the same coin. It knows we're here and allowed us to explore its domain because..." The gleam in Josh's eye was a little frightening as he left the sentence hanging, like a lifelong smoker spotting their first cigarette of the day. Reading the curious expression on Elsie's face, I could tell she had seen it too.

"Because it wants us here," she said. "Josh, can we do this?"

"You said it. We have to try."

Elsie nodded.

Josh distributed flashlights from the messenger bag, and then led the way down the stairs. We treaded carefully so as not to trip over any discarded bricks, but there were none. Each stair creaked, sounding like a scream announcing our arrival to the unknown darkness below. A typical flight of stairs couldn't contain over ten or twelve steps, and yet we kept descending well past that number. I started counting once I realized we were going down too far. I got to twenty-seven, putting the number of stairs going to the basement around at least forty.

It was difficult to tell how far we were from the top. We had left the door open, but since the pantry was an interior room, no light shone down to aid us. Like in the Hale House, the flashlights were technically working, but didn't seem to give off as much light as one might expect. Finally, we hit what felt like a dirt floor. Not uncommon in a house this age. As we went down, the smell, which was powerful enough at the top of the stairs, only got stronger.

"They took the bodies out of here, right?" I asked, pulling my t-shirt over my nose.

"According to an unsubstantiated journal entry from a woman of no historical significance, yes," answered Josh.

The floor plans included a detailed map of the main and top floors, but no information about the basement. We assumed an open room the approximate size of the main floor, but the bottom of the stairs opened into a long, thin tunnel that stretched at least the length of the house. The walls were solid concrete about five feet apart, with no breaks, doorways, or rooms to speak of.

We did the only thing we could, pushed forward. There was no rush, not with over three hours before Tedeschi would return. Would he lock us in if we were still down here? No, of course not. Our car was out front. But still…

We turned every so often to track our surroundings, eventually losing sight of the stairs as they disappeared into darkness. And then there he was. I turned to check the stairs, and standing ten feet behind us was Robert Weeks, more fully formed than at the Benson House, evidently waiting to be noticed. His green eyes pierced the darkness far more effectively than our flashlights. Without losing sight of him, I slapped at Josh and Elsie to get their attention. Elsie let out a small scream, then quickly stifled it. As soon as he had our full attention, Weeks smiled, displaying the same grin that must have spread across his face when the people of Slattery Falls strung him up. He walked toward us and almost immediately dissolved into a cloud of dust.

We stood frozen, eyes locked on the spot where Weeks had stood, waiting on what felt like his inevitable return. I don't know how long we would have stayed there except a bout of laughter broke our trance, and it came from in front of us—the same horrible, grating laughter that sent us fleeing from the Benson House.

We spun around, but only concrete, dirt, and darkness surrounded us.

"He's still doing it," whispered Elsie. "Showing off that he can lead us wherever he wants."

"The alternative is turning around and leaving," said Josh. "I, for one, vote against that. Least of all because I'm not convinced he would allow us to leave."

Nothing else needed to be said. Josh was right, so we continued on. We moved slower than before and checked our backs at least twice as often. In the silent dark, waiting for the next thing to happen, it was hard to tell how far we walked, but it definitely felt like more than the length of the house. Finally, we saw a wall ahead. But this couldn't be the extent of the basement, right? A long skinny tunnel? There had to be more. When we got closer, it became apparent that what looked like a dead end branched off in two separate directions at ninety-degree angles.

We had a choice to make. The first of many.

CHAPTER TWENTY-NINE

"Well, left or right, lady and gentleman. What's our choice?" I said. "Or we could split up."

"Not on your life," said Josh. "Elsie, thoughts?"

We took a minute to study each direction, but there was nothing to glean. Each tunnel appeared identical and endless, like the one we currently stood in.

"I think it's a flip of the coin," said Elsie.

"Anybody opposed to left?" I asked. No objections. "Left, it is."

We headed down the left tunnel with as much caution as before. A small cry from Elsie stopped us in our tracks.

"The other path," she said. "It's gone." Sure enough, where the path to the right had stretched out seconds before, a concrete wall as solid and unyielding as the ones on every other side blocked the way as if it never existed. You may not believe me since I've made it no secret that I opposed the trip in the first place, but this was the first point I sincerely thought about dragging the two of them outside against their wills. I still wish I had. We had gone from a tinge of supernatural to the utterly impossible in the blink of an eye, and it only reinforced Elsie's notion that we were part of a game. Rats being led to the cheese. What would happen when we found it?

We had no choice but to go on, so that's what we did. While this tunnel looked to have roughly the same dimensions as the first when we entered, it seemed to shrink the farther we went. Four feet instead of five at the sides, with the ceiling a little closer to our heads. The acoustics of the reduced space amplified the sound of our breathing and footsteps. The initial illusion was of too many footsteps, but the longer it went on, the more I suspected the additional noise might not stem from echoes.

I grabbed at Josh and Elsie, holding my flashlight to my face and a finger to my lips. We all came to a stop. The footsteps did not. It's possible that my perception was off, but it sounded like at least two pairs, and not the heavy footfalls that would come from a man of Weeks' size and stature. Instinctively, we started trying to locate the source of the footsteps, but the flashlights revealed nothing. Then the footsteps halted.

We waited in silence for them to begin again, but after a minute or two, it became clear they wouldn't. Almost as soon as we started moving again, all three flashlights went out and the footsteps returned. Now it sounded as though there were at least four or five different people to account for all the noise—too small to be adults, too big to be animals. What's worse is I started feeling tugs at different places on my clothes, sensing the rush of air as the owners of those footsteps moved past me.

These were children.

Likely these were children that had died in this house.

As though in tune with that realization, the scurrying stopped, and our flashlights lit up again. A young boy, no more than six or seven, materialized in front of us, pale as the moon with dried blood caked at the corner of his mouth. His wide eyes and quivering lips showed a fear no child that young should have to contend with. That day held a lot of unforgettable events, but the look of that child is something I expect will come to me in dreams for the rest of my life.

"What's your name?" said Elsie, crouching down to meet the child's eye level, but keeping her distance. The waver in her voice suggested she was holding back tears. "What can we do to help you?"

In response, the boy shook his head, backing slowly beyond the reach of our flashlights.

Elsie and I watched the form disappear into shadow, helpless to do anything but stare. A moment passed as we waited for the child's return before Josh broke the heavy silence.

"Guys," he said, "what time would you guess it is?"

"Can't be past three, right?" I tore my gaze from the thick shadows and checked my watch. It read 12:43. "Fuck, that can't be right. We would've been upstairs then."

"Mine says 6:10," said Josh.

"I've got 10:07 on my phone," said Elsie.

Josh and I glanced at our phones. They were way off, too.

"I think we just have to count on our internal sense of time, and hope Tedeschi doesn't lock us in here. What else can we do? We've got five separate times, and I doubt any of them are right."

"My phone just rolled back to 8:29, so yeah, I don't trust it."

"Do you see that light up ahead?" asked Josh.

I had to squint. But yes, a glowing pinprick in the distance. "Yeah, let's go."

As we moved closer, it became clear the luminescence wasn't an illusion, but in fact appeared to be coming from a room off the main tunnel.

"It's… water," said Elsie as we approached the doorway. "Like an underground grotto or something. It looks like it's lit from beneath."

"I can't tell how deep it is," said Josh. He was right, too. It would have been useful to know the depth, what was on the other side, and if there were other ways across. Not to mention what the fuck a grotto was doing in this guy's basement.

"I don't want to just pass this by," I said. "What if it seals itself behind us like before?"

"Seems extremely likely," said Elsie. "Can you guys see anything farther down the tunnel? Josh!"

He had moved away from us, a little way down the tunnel. "We don't split up, dude."

"I'm staying within your sightline. There's something here." He took another step forward, fading into shadow. "It's stairs."

"Another way out?" I asked.

"They don't go up," said Josh.

CHAPTER THIRTY

"If I'm honest, I don't like either choice," I said. "I don't see a way across the pool that doesn't involve swimming, and going down a set of stairs when you're already in a basement strikes me as a bad idea. What do you guys think?"

Elsie thought for a moment. "Since we're being guided along, we want to choose the way that makes the least sense. Does that make sense?"

"Oddly enough, it does," I said. "So which way is the one we're not supposed to choose?"

"The water. What self-respecting nitwit would wade through water when they could stay dry?" asked Josh. He sat and rifled through his messenger bag, pulling out a couple of plastic grocery bags. "It's not perfect, but I think we can put some stuff in here to keep it from getting wet. Ideally, we would take off our shoes but, uh, we don't exactly know what's in there, do we?"

I hadn't even considered that aspect. We were making an unappealing choice between wet mystery and dry mystery, and opting for what we hoped was the lesser of two evils. "Good point. Think I'll leave the shoes on."

Josh went first. An ethereal glow emanated from beneath the water, but gave no help in establishing the depth. Josh waded in gingerly, taking a step at a time, the bag slung over his shoulder. He kept to the edge, claiming that if a variety of depth existed here, the middle would be the deepest part. Elsie and I followed, staying a few feet away so if something happened to one of us, the other two would have time to react. The water felt just above room temperature and had a dirty, almost viscous, feeling to it. Not exactly inviting.

As we suspected, the water level dipped down as we went, gradually climbing from ankle to waist to shoulder height. Josh pushed on, bag perched on top of his head. Thankfully, it didn't seem to get any deeper from there. I turned to check on Elsie and froze.

Blood.

She was covered from chest to the bottom of her chin in blood. The entire pool had turned crimson. How had none of us noticed this? And the accompanying smell? Like a slaughterhouse in the middle of summer, clawing at my nostrils. My stomach dropped nearly to my toes.

"ELSIE!" I screamed. It cut through the silence, and Josh nearly lost his balance. I rushed to close the five-foot gap between us, and when I got there... nothing. Not a trace of red on her. The water surrounding us returned to normal. I wrapped my arms around her, noting a look of sincere panic in her eyes.

"What? Travis, what's wrong?"

What could I tell her? This place was getting to me. "Nothing," I said. "It's, uh, nothing. I thought I saw something, but the light... must be playing tricks on me."

"You're scaring me," she said, eyes darting around the cavern. "You sure it's alright?"

"Yeah, let's just get out of here."

As we pushed on, I kept expecting the water to change to blood again, and the notion made me more vigilant. The light coming from beneath the water threw strange patterns and shadows across the wall, complete with spots of light ebbing and flowing, mimicking the interior of a lava lamp. Some shadows made their way to the surface of the water, sinking beneath and calling to mind a creature prowling beneath the calm exterior. I couldn't help thinking of the Hale House, feeling like the shadows were reaching out, coming to life. The total effect made the walls feel less like a solid slab of concrete, more like a forest at night. The walls had eyes. The illusion held the entirety of my attention when I bumped into Josh, who had come to an abrupt stop.

"What's up?" I said, no longer trying to disguise the panic in my voice. "Did you feel something?"

"Something like that," he answered. "There's a wall."

It didn't take long to figure out that the wall ran the entire length of the room. We had traversed the blood-water for nothing, and now had to retrace our steps and try our luck with the stairway to hell.

"There's got to be more here, a hidden passageway or something," said Josh. "Just give me a couple minutes." He started tracing the wall with open palms. I mirrored his movements, not entirely sure what I was looking for, but assuming I'd know it if I found it.

"Over here!" Elsie cried.

I trudged through the water, but failed to see what had caught Elsie's eye. "What are we looking at?"

"There's a hole in the wall, under the surface. Feel here," she said, pointing to a spot below the surface.

I swung my foot into the space she'd indicated and felt it go further than expected, the surprise almost causing me to topple over. "How does that help us?"

"We've come this far," said Josh. "We swim through it. The path continues on the other side." Whether for show or not, he sounded considerably more confident than I felt.

"I'll do it," said Elsie. "Scope it out."

"The hell you will," I said. "We don't know how long it is. You could drown. We don't even know if it comes out on the other side. It could be a dead end. Oh, and best-case scenario, you pop up on the other side of the wall, and we don't know what's there. It could be dangerous."

She stood, arms crossed, looking at me with a stare I knew well. The kind that said *you're not winning this.* "You finished?"

I stayed silent. There wasn't anything I could say to come out on top here. Even in the dim light, I could see Josh had a smirk on his face.

"I said I'll scope it out. Go in a little ways and come back out if it's a dead end. Thirty seconds, tops. If there's nothing, we'll go back and take the stairs. Assuming they're still there, that is. The alternate path has a tendency to disappear."

I held her face in my hands. "There's no way I can talk you out of this, is there?"

"Not a one." She smiled, pulled in a deep breath, and disappeared under the water. I thought the fear brought on by seeing Weeks, or the ghost children, wrecked me. It was nothing compared to the wait for Elsie to come back up. Every second felt like a lifetime. Twenty seconds went by.

Thirty.

"I'm going in after her," I said. I dove under the water and went to enter the underwater tunnel when Elsie appeared. We came back up together, greedily sucking the stagnant air from the cavern.

"Jesus Christ. Thank God you're okay," I said. "I was freaking out." I grabbed her face and kissed her.

"It's not far," she said. "It comes up into another room with only about ten feet of water, then it leads back up onto the floor like a boat ramp. You won't love what's on the other side, though."

"Oh shit, It's fucking stairs again, isn't it?" She answered with a small nod.

One at a time, with Elsie leading the way, we entered the underwater tunnel.

CHAPTER THIRTY-ONE

The area underneath the Weeks House—it got harder by the minute to call it a basement—didn't fit the size and shape of the structure above. This struck me as the reason the workers never left, even after the house seemed complete. It would've taken years to hollow out the area beneath the hill. Who knew how many rooms or caverns were down there? Even though the setup of the basement didn't make a ton of sense, the ability to change its nature had us baffled, as well as nervous. Almost every new location we stumbled upon came with a choice. Once we made our decision, the alternative disappeared. Even the way we had come from occasionally vanished, typically turning to solid rock or concrete.

The journey through the underwater tunnel gave us no issues, just as Elsie promised. When we came out the other side, a slight incline led us to another downward staircase, which appeared identical to the first one. Stone steps brought us farther into the heart of the hill, looking every bit as old as the house should have, perhaps even more ancient. Almost as if someone built the stairs long before they laid the first bit of foundation.

With no other choice apparent, we descended the stairs, not too slow but with a sense of caution held close.

The staircase brought us to what looked like a ballroom. The ceiling loomed as high as a cathedral overhead, and the interior spread out expansively in every direction. Light shone from the ceiling, though I couldn't identify the source. Tapestries hung from the walls, and a large wooden table surrounded by chairs took center stage in an otherwise empty room. Ten chairs on the sides plus one at the head of the table.

Josh examined the tapestry closest to us.

"Friendly reminder, we don't have all day before that guy locks us in here," I said.

"I'd rather not be the one bringing this up, but we've got no plan. It's possible that there might be some relevant information somewhere, and it's probably worth the extra few minutes to check it out."

"And whose fault…"

"Don't," said Elsie. "Later."

Point taken.

We moved around the room, studying each piece of fabric. About half were the same—a deer skull, a buck actually, complete with antlers; a crossed pair of swords passing behind it. I'm no sword expert, but they looked more like the type you might duel with rather than something heavier or medieval. A family crest, maybe?

The other six tapestries told a story in sequential order. The first displayed a ship sailing across an ocean, a man standing at the prow, gaze fixed on the horizon. The man was too small, the detail not quite fine enough, but I had no doubts who it represented. Number two showed a simplified, yet recognizable, version of the house's exterior. It sat at the top, the hill it rested upon taking up most of the negative space. At the bottom, Weeks leaned on a shovel. The third shared some similarities with the second. Again the house on top of the hill and Weeks at the base, only this time he held a flute to his lips. Off to the side, three children were pictured listening to the music. It made my blood boil and the hair on my arms stood up.

We crossed to the other side of the room to view the rest. The next one had removed Weeks from the bottom of the picture and replaced him with a gallows tree, two nooses dangling from a bare branch. One for Robert, and one for Tabitha. The first four were relatively straightforward, telling the same story we'd uncovered in not so many words. The last two made no sense, and that was the worst part—the attempt at prophecy. Number five repeated the same outline of the house on the hill, this time Weeks standing next to it, either taking up the foreground or every bit as big as the hill. No, definitely larger than before. In his right hand, he held the gallows tree, and it looked no bigger than a drumstick. A smile stitched onto his face. It didn't look happy; it looked… knowing.

The final hanging contained no trace of Weeks. The house on

the hill had returned, but this time the hill shared the features of a skull, caved in as though someone had taken a bat to it. I leaned in to study it further, then the interruption came.

"I'm so glad you could join me." A booming voice, with a British accent. No, not quite British, but similar. We'd heard the man laugh, but never speak. Still, no doubt lingered about who the voice belonged to.

We remained quiet, attempting to communicate with eye contact as we narrowed the distance between us. A passing silence filled the room, followed by all eleven chairs shooting back at once, inviting us to sit. The sound of wood scraping stone reverberated, piercing through the peace in the large room.

Weeks continued. "Rest yourselves and have a seat. You are my guests, after all." Definitely not British, but sounding more and more like an accent one might hear on *Game of Thrones* or some other fantasy influenced by medieval England.

"I'll stand, thanks," I said, mentally reprimanding myself for thanking the malevolent spirit we came to stop. The fear of being in the same room as Weeks caused my adrenaline to surge.

When he spoke again, the initial tone of welcome was absent.

"Why are you here?"

Leave it to Elsie to decide that powerful spirit or not, she's had it with your bullshit. "What do you mean, why are we here? You were pretty demanding of our attention last time we saw you, and you've obviously been getting your jollies by leading us around your fucking maze like a rat to a piece of cheese."

A soft chuckle, but one that brought to mind the image of boulders rolling. "I like her. It's a shame I'll have to kill her and leave her to rot down here."

"Hate to break it to you, but we're not children you can control like some pied piper," I said, gesturing to the third tapestry.

Another chuckle. This time it sounded more like a thunderstorm rumbling underground and shook the entire room. "I've already done just that. You're here, aren't you?"

He paused to let the last part sink in. The room ceased shaking after the last laugh, but still pulsed as though in time with a heartbeat.

"You've come to kill me, but you're not the first and you won't be the last." His voice softened, but still resonated throughout the room.

Of all the things I expected to encounter here, a supervillain monologue wasn't one of them.

The voice continued. "You're right. I've been watching you for a long time now. Perhaps longer than you realize."

"What's so special about us?" said Elsie.

"I'm not sure. That's what intrigues me. The first time you saw me was a few short years ago. I watched you flee from a house in Connecticut, but I've been with you much longer than that."

Before our eyes, he materialized, more substantial in form, like when we first entered the basement. He towered over us, easily a few inches over seven feet now, and turned his gaze toward me. I froze when those icy, sea-green eyes met mine.

"I knew," he said, "that you and the girl would end up betrothed before either of you even knew the other existed. Once that bond formed, the three of you would make up a power source the likes of which I've not seen in centuries. You see, children are the purest fuel cells, but they don't last as long as they once did, and I must go hunting every few years to… replenish myself."

Even with a corporeal body, his voice still surrounded us and shook the room.

"You eat children," I said.

"Nothing so crude as that," Weeks snapped back. "I utilize their essence. Meanwhile, I allow them an opportunity to become a part of greatness, a part of history. My gift to them,"

Josh stepped forward, meeting Weeks eye to eye, if not exactly face to face, with stoniness. "What do you mean by centuries? Like since you moved to Slattery Falls?"

"I would imagine you could not find much about my time in England, and before that?"

Our silence answered the question for him.

"Of course not," he chuckled again, no merriment present. "Truth be known, the story from Bristol is much like the story here. I got greedy, took too many children from too small an area, and they burned me at the stake. Before that, Scotland. Beheading. Before that, dear me, I can't remember, but the path originally began in Norway." *Norwegian, that's the accent.* "Eventually, one simply needs to move on and try again."

"And your wife, Tabitha?" spat Josh. "Do the villagers kill her every time as well?"

A pained look crossed his face, and I worried for a moment that Josh had fucked up royally.

"Tabitha, I met in England, and brought here with me." His eyes seethed with fire. The room even felt warmer. "Slattery Falls made a terrible mistake acting so rashly and dispatching her with me. I have gone out of my way ever since to see that their future generations pay for it. I pick up stock and find a new place every so often, but this time, I see no reason to leave. Not without her."

He waited for us to reply. Probably not a good idea to antagonize him.

"So now what?" said Josh. "You've got us here. You're going to… what? Utilize our essence and live here for another couple hundred years?"

Weeks took a step forward, meeting our gazes one at a time. "Yes," he answered after a moment. "And it's going to be most unpleasant for you, I'm afraid."

CHAPTER THIRTY-TWO

You've heard the phrase "all hell broke loose", I'm sure of it. Maybe you've even used it, and let me assure you, you did so in a hyperbolic fashion. I don't want to brag, but I've seen all hell break loose, and you haven't.

After informing us of his intentions, Robert Weeks didn't move at first, arms crossed and closer to eight than seven feet tall now. As he waited for us to make the first move, the mysterious light pouring down from the ceiling took on hues of red and orange, flames licking down all around us. The temperature jumped from uncomfortable to scalding and the ground shook. The sound of concrete grinding and splintering drowned out everything else.

I turned toward the stairs we had come down, only to find another doorway transformed into a solid wall. Shucks and son of a bitch, wouldn't you know it? We kept to the far side of the room, trying to keep away from Weeks. He stood watching us scramble about the room with a half-smile on his face until we discovered a doorway and ducked in. I say ducked in, because the door, and the tunnel it brought us through, couldn't have been over five feet tall.

Trying to escape a vengeful spirit is hard enough, never mind when you're sweating bullets and have to run hunched over like an absolute dipshit. The tunnel narrowed as it went, eventually coming to a rounded end with nothing but a hole in the floor. A rope hung down, tethered to the wall by a mounted hook. Another obvious trap, but what other option did we have?

"I'll go first," I said, adrenaline finally lending the inspiration to stop letting everybody else take all the risks.

"We're being bottlenecked," said Elsie. "I don't love the idea of you going first."

"And if you cut in line, will that make it less of a trap?" I smiled, gave her a peck on the lips, and lowered myself down. A lifetime of choosing a trip to the drive-through over the gym caught up with me all at once. I hadn't even been able to climb the rope to the ceiling in high school gym class. What hope was there for me now?

I continued down, arms burning, losing my grip and sliding a foot or two down the rope occasionally. I could see Elsie rappelling above me, having a far easier time. After what felt like a thousand feet, my feet hit solid ground. I stepped away from the rope to let the others down and attempted to get my bearings. This new room was dark—like cave-in-the-center-of-the-earth dark. The light trickling down from the hole above barely made a dent in the tangible blackness.

After the sudden onset of heat in the last room, a welcome draft made it feel huge. Keyword is *feel,* since I couldn't see more than a foot in front of my face, and I had stowed my flashlight in Josh's bag at the grotto. I saw an Elsie-shaped person hit the ground followed by a Josh-shaped one, complete with messenger bag. As Josh adjusted to the Stygian gloom, he fished around for our flashlights, then froze as an alternative source of light emerged.

The light came from two pinpricks. Two sea-green pinpricks. Eyes. Fuck me.

As the eyes came closer, we retreated, scraping up against a wall behind us. I expected Weeks to step into the little bit of luminescence cast by the hole in the ceiling. Instead, an unspeakable monstrosity filled that gap.

The closest comparison I can make is to a buck, but with no skin or musculature the description doesn't do it justice. Calling it a skeleton wouldn't be accurate either. That implies it was skinny, or somehow frail, but the buck appeared broad and fierce, tattered pieces of rotting skin hung from bones, the smell of dirt and decay arriving right before the rest of the beast. This thing had died a very long time ago.

It lumbered toward us, then came to a stop and let out an inhuman combination of a groan and a roar. When the unearthly sound ceased, it charged. I dove to the left, and the beast collided with the wall, sounding like a Flintstones car crash.

I think this was the closest we ever came to breaking our "never split up" rule. We hauled ass in the direction the buck had come from, hoping the creature had knocked itself unconscious. At least I think that's what happened, since I couldn't fucking see anyone else. I went at a flat-out sprint, surrounded by the sounds of footsteps and heavy breathing. Blood pounded in my ears. Hoofbeats joined the din. A crash and a scream told me it had overtaken Elsie. I changed direction, hoping against hope that I was heading the right way, when I slammed into a wall of bone. I didn't know if I could hurt this thing, but I'd sure as hell try.

The pain registered immediately, and the beast's mass gave no quarter. I tried reaching, scratching at anything I could get my hands on. My fingers latched onto what felt like an eye socket, and I knew I had its undivided attention. I heard Elsie scoot out from underneath as my fingers mashed through wet gristle, extinguishing one bright sea-green eye.

The buck swung its head wildly, trying to dislodge my hand. As much as I wanted to get away, I was hurting it and wanted to press that advantage. I applied as much pressure as possible, then felt a searing pain overwhelm my left thigh.

An antler? What else could it be?

Elsie got to her feet beside me, panic in her voice. "Travis, what is it?"

"GO FOR THE EYES!" I shouted.

I heard a sickening wet crunch that must've been its other eye, and the second green light blinked out. The beast let out a wounded cry and pulled away, running back toward where we had descended from the floor above. There was no outlet that way, but I was sure it would find or create one.

This fucking place and its "anything goes" policy. I felt a momentary twinge of sadness for the thing that had just tried to gore us. Why did that fucker have to send an animal after us?

"Are you okay? What happened?" said Elsie.

Oh yeah. I'd been stabbed. "I think so. It hurts like hell and I can't see how bad it is, but it doesn't feel life-threatening. Can you feel if an injury is life-threatening?"

Against all odds and common sense, she laughed, and I couldn't help thinking of the first time I'd met her. How that strange sense of humor drew me in from the start, even if it took me a while to realize it. I felt her reach out and cradle my head against her chest.

"I guess I'm not trained in mortal injuries. Can you walk on it?"

"Yeah, pretty sure." I grunted and grumbled, getting to my feet. "Hey, where's Josh?"

"Here," he called back right away.

"Could have used some help there, man," I said, immediately feeling Elsie's gaze cut into the back of my head. "Shit, sorry. No, don't worry about it."

"I froze," he said. "I've never seen anything like that. I'm the one who's supposed to know what to do here, and I just left you and Elsie to get torn apart."

"Josh, man. You can't beat yourself up. I don't think anyone has ever seen anything like that and gotten out of this fuck-faced basement to tell about it."

"Did you just call a basement fuck-faced?"

"Well, you know what? It is a fuck face. I can put some weight on this thing. Elsie's fine, right? I feel like I was probably supposed to check on that."

"Yes, fine, thank you. My knight in shining armor."

"So we've got to keep going. Otherwise we just sit here and wait for him to, like, rip our souls out? I don't know."

"Yeah," said Josh. "That's a pretty fair point. Any guesses what's ahead?"

"Dark. And lots of it."

CHAPTER THIRTY-THREE

My leg wasn't horrible. I could walk on it, but it was definitely worse than I let on. It actually worked to my advantage because we walked pretty slowly. The house had done little in the way of earning our trust and any excuse to avoid charging ahead would do. Then that fucking voice again.

"My children, have you resigned yourself to walk in the dark forever?"

"Just looking for the exit sign," I called. Look, quick aside here. You might think I've added in some snark at this point to make myself look more courageous, but I was scared, completely and utterly shitless. No shit, whatsoever. I was also fed up and frustrated. I thought, if this fucker is going to kill us anyway, I might as well have some fun in my last few minutes with the people I love.

"You won't find an exit, not unless I want you to. These caverns go on infinitely. You could walk for days, weeks until your legs collapse beneath you and dehydration sets in. You may as well give in now."

"Kindly fuck off, and let us walk in peace," said Josh, surprising even me with the flippant way he said it. Then the ground shook. The tunnel flooded with a dim hellish light, and the surrounding walls roared.

Weeks appeared directly before us, even larger than before, well over eight feet tall. The green in his eyes glowed like those of the buck.

"I have centuries, an eternity to wait you out, bastard scum, but it's been long enough. So I'm going to take you one at a time. I'll pull your limbs off your bodies, and I'll suck the meat off your bones. Then maybe crack them open and drink the marrow. Don't want to miss any of that essence." The impatience in his words and the light show, however unimpressive, spoke to his fury, but the calm with which he described his plans for us contained a chilling air.

"The others," he continued, "will watch." He held a hand up and I felt my feet sink as if I'd stepped into a warm mud puddle. As soon as the liquid reached my ankles, it hardened again. Elsie was in the same predicament on my right, trying desperately to pull herself free, but to no avail. Josh's legs remained free. A look of panic flashed across his face so quickly that I might have missed it if I'd blinked. Then my friend was back. He reached into the Misfits bag and yanked out a small book just as Weeks grabbed him around the middle. The bag dropped from Josh's shoulder and fell to the ground with a sense of finality.

"As a rule, I take no pleasure in this," said Weeks, "but you three are particularly troublesome. I don't think I've ever had to work for a meal like this before. All this struggle, and for what? You could never have hoped to escape this place with your lives. You've been destined to end up here, like this, your entire existence. I'll be able to stay here and continue my crusade against this cursed town, or maybe pick up and go somewhere new. I quite like America, perhaps the West Coast this time."

While Weeks spoke, Josh flipped through the book he'd plucked from the bag. Frustration and anxiety turned to hope in his eyes as he settled on a page. He whispered while reading from the page. Had the son of a bitch found a ritual, after all? A frenzy ran through his voice, as if he had a mile of words to speak and only a meter in which to do it. I couldn't make out much of what he said, but it didn't sound like English. Then Weeks paused.

"What are you doing? What is that?" He tried to snatch the book from Josh's hand. As soon as it met his skin, a loud sizzling sound erupted and the air filled with the acrid reek of burned flesh. Weeks snatched his blackened fingers away from the book and let out a roar. The same wounded but dangerous sound that had come from the buck earlier. Something told me he would not be running the other way this time.

With no warning, Weeks grabbed Josh's arm, the one that held the book, and wrenched it from his body with a sound like tearing a drumstick from a roasted chicken. He casually tossed it to the side. Elsie and I both screamed, frantically tearing at our feet, our concrete restraints every bit as solid as before. Josh bellowed. He clenched his teeth and closed his eyes, continuing to speak in the unknown language. Whatever he had in mind, I hoped he could do it fast.

Weeks still had Josh by the torso with his left arm. He wound his right fist back to deliver a crushing blow, and time slowed to a standstill. The chant ceased. I could only hope because it was finished. A sense of calm washed over Josh in that split second, and a half-smile crept onto the right side of his face. It would be a few more minutes before we knew what had happened, but in that moment, Josh knew he had won. He never got to see the aftermath. He didn't need to. This was why he'd come, and he knew it all along.

I couldn't help thinking that I'd never get to hound him about that.

Weeks' massive fist connected with the side of Josh's head, resulting in a sickening *thwack*. A crack resonated through the underground cavern. Whether it came from his skull or his neck, we never found out. Josh's body went limp just before Weeks unceremoniously tossed him to the floor.

"I don't know what kind of game you little shits think you're trying to pull, but he got off easy. You two, not so much." His unflappable exterior had finally cracked.

"Robert?" A voice came from behind him, heavy with reverberation. It sounded like a woman.

The anger drained from his eyes, his shoulders slumped. He didn't even turn.

"Tabitha."

An apparition, bathed in white light, materialized behind him. I recognized her instantly from the original picture Josh had found. She wore a floor-length evening gown, her skin unblemished, and her eyes kind. Was this the ace up Josh's sleeve?

She approached Weeks and stopped a few feet behind him, waiting for him to turn. As he did, tears rolled down his cheeks.

"You're done here," she whispered. A sound so soft it didn't seem capable of reaching our ears, yet it did.

"Years of study, I've learned how to cheat death. It's my right to be here." Some of the confidence that had drained away at the initial sound of her voice returned. "I have missed you… fiercely, over the years, but I have no desire to join you in death. Not yet."

"What great deed are you performing here, Robert?"

He waited for her to go on.

"When we first met, I will admit I was drawn to your power. The ways one could change the world with the ability to live a hundred lifetimes, but what exactly have you done with that power, that time? Darling, you have become so obsessed with living to see the next day that you make no plans for it, and even worse, you do not care what you have to do to see it. I spent my last day on this earth being dragged out of my home, shown proof that my wedded husband murdered children, and then was hanged. I cannot speak for you, Robert, but the people of Slattery Falls did not hang me high enough to snap my neck. It was an awful way to go.

"You, more than anyone, know that the dead have time to plan. I suppose I could have haunted you. Made you pay for my unfair death with sleepless nights and a lack of peace, but I pitied you. I pitied you and I loved you. The man I married had so much potential, and the man I have watched since I died is just cruel. Robert, do you know why I am here?"

"I was murdering children long before I loved you, Tabbie. I didn't stop for an instant either." There was no venom in his declaration, just a statement of fact. "It's the only way I could survive."

"Then perhaps surviving is not worth the cost. I ask again, Robert, do you know why I am here?"

"I guess they sent you here to kill me. I'll tell you, love, what I told them." Tears flowed freely now, collecting in his beard. He gestured at Elsie and me, callously ignoring Josh's body. "You won't succeed."

"You cannot kill what is already dead. You have been killed many times and it never seems to stick. I came back to take you with me, to help you cross over."

"And how do I know what kind of judgment awaits me on the other side?"

"You do not, but you can trust me like I once trusted you, and you can trust that I love you, and I believe that somewhere inside you is a good man. Your faith will be better placed than mine was."

I couldn't believe my eyes. His tone, his body language, his stature. How could this be the same man that had terrorized us? He stood, defeated.

"And what if I refuse to come?" said Weeks with resignation in his voice.

"Oh, darling," and here Tabitha looked at me, looked at Elsie, looked at Josh before continuing. "You've been around for centuries and centuries. When it comes to a woman's request, do you really believe you have a choice?"

She leaned in and kissed him. Weeks stood stock-still at first, then gave in and wrapped his massive arms around her. The white light that had been issuing from her all along developed a green tinge. It became more and more intense until it culminated in an emerald flash. When the brightness cleared, they were gone.

With Weeks having left this plane of existence, the concrete holding our feet in place released us. We ran to Josh, hoping life remained in him, but I think we both knew. He was gone as soon as Weeks' fist connected with his head. He'd saved us, though. Without his last-ditch effort to summon Tabitha, Weeks would have murdered us in a gruesome fashion.

Holding his limp head in my arms, I lost a few minutes, but that paled in comparison to having my best friend stolen by a monster. I remember screaming, cursing. I remember Elsie there, but the whole world was a vacuum in that moment. Any pain that she projected, any comfort she tried to give was lost.

I don't know how long I remained in that state. I don't know how much longer I would've stayed in that state, except the earth started shaking.

CHAPTER THIRTY-FOUR

When Weeks disappeared, his power did too. The instant effect being that our feet were no longer bound in concrete. The more lasting problem was that we were in a house, a basement anyway, whose size and scope defied physics. Natural law didn't care for that. Unfortunately, it also didn't care that we were still inside.

"We have to leave him," said Elsie. She grabbed me by the arm before I had time to argue. Smart, because I would have, and we had no time for that. I grabbed the book he had read from and stuffed it into my back pocket.

We ran in the direction Tabitha had come from. The red light Weeks had conjured remained in place, allowing us to see cracks forming all along the walls and ceiling, racing alongside our path. We ran harder. A large crevice formed in the wall to our left, so we took it on a whim and emerged in the dining hall. The tapestries had all fallen to the floor, the chairs strewn about the room, and we kept moving. Where the stairs had been earlier, there was now an entrance to a tunnel with several small rooms off it.

Inside every room, and there must have been more than a dozen, stood a… creature—all of them gaunt with long, dark, dirty hair. The workers, perhaps? Rather than defiance, the creatures appeared lost in panic, unable to leave their quarters and doomed to be buried under the hill. Recognition dawned right before we passed the last room. I'd seen one of these workers before, in the basement of the Hale House. Weeks told the truth. He had been keeping tabs on Josh and me there.

Josh.

No time to dwell. We followed the tunnel as it got thinner and thinner, the light dimming, until the floor vanished, dropping us into a pool of water.

The grotto! We were back in the grotto, next to the wall with the underwater tunnel. We swam for the opposite end, no longer caring what might be underneath our feet, and pulled ourselves up onto the shore. We stopped for the first time, listening and taking in the surroundings.

Above us, we heard the house creaking and groaning. Ready to collapse on itself. We chose the path to the left, feeling the ground change from concrete to dirt under our feet. A light appeared directly ahead and became our target. When we arrived, it was barely large enough to crawl through. Elsie went first, and I followed, leading with my head as the rest of me followed. I realized two things quickly. One, I was outside, and two, I was on the side of a steep hill. The latter, I realized as I rolled down, eventually coming to a rough stop at the bottom next to Elsie.

We sat together and watched as the Weeks House gave up the ghost, so to speak. The hill, no doubt hollowed out and supported by some otherworldly force, collapsed under the weight of the house above, transforming into a crater that consumed the house. Shattering wood and breaking glass harmonized in a symphony of destruction. Cathartic music to our ears after everything we'd been through. I don't think I'll ever see anything like that again. God, I sure hope I don't.

Elsie and I sat for a long time, hand in hand, eyes locked on the wreckage. The decision to leave, knowing Josh remained under there somewhere, hurt. Still does. A morbid part of me thinks that he might have been okay with being left there. Being present at his own wake would have been the last thing Josh wanted. All those people gawking at him, pretending they knew him, knew who he really was. Thinking of his sacrifice broke my heart, but I managed a smile at that moment.

"We have to go," I said to Elsie, taking her by the wrist.

"Yeah, Tedeschi might have us arrested," she laughed. "Although, I don't know. Maybe this town will just be glad to have this place off their hands. Can you imagine? No more living in fear of a house?"

"I can imagine very well. Come on."

CHAPTER THIRTY-FIVE

We made it home without incident, but the car ride felt, well, empty. We tried music, half-hearted conversation, even silence, and nothing worked, so we gave in to the heaviness. It didn't help that when we got home, Josh's car was still in our driveway. We would have to figure that out the next day. We settled in as best as we could, had a drink to take the edge off, and just tried to keep thoughts about what came next at bay.

Then I remembered Josh's book, still in the car. I told Elsie I'd be right back and went to get it so we could flip through it together. The plain black notebook contained a lot of entries about Robert Weeks and Slattery Falls, some of which we had covered together. The remainder of the notebook comprised notes taken between the first time we met about this and today. There were three pages mixed into these newer notes that only contained symbols or runes, no words. I assumed these were the pages Josh read from in his final moments. Nothing of great importance in there, not anymore, but I liked the idea of having a memento. After the symbols, the rest of the book was blank. Except for the last page.

Here it read:

Elsie and Travis,

I wrote this in a place you won't find it unless I'm not there to stop you. I guess what I'm saying is that if you're reading this, you made it back from the Weeks House, and I didn't. Given what I've discovered in the last week, that's definitely a possibility. I looked tirelessly into the possibility of a ritual to banish a ghost, and it's pretty much all nonsense. I fabricated a ritual because I didn't think I'd be able to get you guys to go otherwise. I'm sorry about that. Sorry for exploiting your faith in me. You deserve to know the two things that made me do that. First, I had a Hail Mary up my sleeve. Second, we're a great team, always have been, and I knew we'd figure it out.

You can probably see from the beginning of this book that I kept doing research after we had completed our initial round. Tabitha Weeks caught and held my interest. It's mostly because of how little there was about her. Slattery Falls' history painted her as some kind of witch complicit in everything Weeks was up to, but unlike him, there were records of her birth and life in Bristol. She was the well-to-do daughter of a shop owner, and she met and fell in love with Weeks. I even found a record of their marriage in Bristol. I just had to know where to look. The marriage took place a month before Weeks first showed up in Slattery Falls. I took a gamble. But I suspected she had been a pawn in the whole ordeal, drawn in by his prowess. I hoped that with the way things ended up, if I could contact her, she might be on our side. Maybe looking to get some revenge.

Oddly enough, as difficult as finding a spell to banish a ghost was, finding a summoning spell was easy, although the pronunciation proved difficult. I guess I should be thankful I don't have to deal with the aftermath of doing internet searches for all those weird things. The one thing I kept finding was that it took a lot of energy, a lot of life force. It was not something I wanted to try alone in my apartment as a test run. I'd have to play to my strengths, study the theory and trust it to work in practice. Again, if you're reading this, I'll assume it did.

I can't thank you enough for being in my life. I've always felt like an outsider in every aspect of my life, but you guys are family. You make me feel like I belong.

With Love,
Josh

CHAPTER THIRTY-SIX

That Sunday will go down as the second-worst day of my life. It took a lot of hard work, but we somehow pulled it off with little to no suspicion. We notified authorities that Josh, and here we really played up the family angle, had been spending the weekend with us. We took a day trip to the Blue Hills for a hike, settled in for some lunch, and Josh went off to piss behind some bushes. Then he never came back. The police initiated a search. Elsie and I took part, knowing full well we would find nothing. The worst part was seeing Mr. and Mrs. Costa there, knowing they'd never get closure on their son, and not being able to tell them anything. They were good parents, loving parents. Their son had just been different, and the connections between them and Josh didn't fire on all cylinders. They never really understood him.

The search turned up nothing, and they declared Josh missing. Posters went up, and all that jazz. How fucked up that all this started with people going missing and here we are again?

Elsie and I miss him every day. We're oddly comforted by the fact that he knew he would probably die in that basement. Less so by the fact that he had to hide it from us. He did it so we could get out, so that a few more parents could get up in the morning and find their children still asleep in their beds, never having to know the fear and heartbreak that comes with inexplicably losing your child.

Josh was the fact-based person, yet he accepted the intangible, far better than I ever could. Nearly 600,000 children go missing in the United States every year. Many of those kids return home alive and well, but not all. It's fucked up. First, I had trouble wrapping my head around the notion that a ghost could be responsible for any of them. Now that we know it's true, I can't accept with absolute certainty that we actually stopped it. Sure, we saw a big greenish white light and then the monster was gone, but don't monsters sometimes come back? I'm paraphrasing here, but didn't Emily Stone say evil never really gets extinguished? It just changes its form. Is there any way to know definitively that we made the lives of some kids a little bit safer?

Elsie believes it with all her heart. I can tell. Josh believed it too, and part of me thinks I owe it to my friend, my brother, to be less of a skeptic. Besides, Elsie and I are expecting our first child in a few months. If it's a boy, I think we've got the name all set. I want to believe so badly that we made the world safer for our child. I want to believe that.

To be continued in:

Decimated Dreams

Slattery Falls, Book Two

ACKNOWLEDGMENTS

As I write these acknowledgments, I'm looking at a sticker on my laptop that says, "Write Epic Shit," a gift from Aron, my wife of thirteen years and the love of my life. Great encouragement, yes, but also a constant reminder of her unyielding support. When I told her I wanted to try this writing thing, she didn't laugh or tell me I was already too busy, though I was. She selflessly gave me the time to pursue it and is a key reason you hold this book in your hands.

Thank you to David Niall Wilson and David Dodd at Crossroad Press for bringing this baby back to life and giving the complete story a home. Thanks to Ken McKinley at Silver Shamrock Publishing for being the first to believe in this book. Credit also goes to Patrick McDonough, my brother in horror, an early supporter of this story, and the loudest voice telling me to keep going.

Donnie Goodman knocked this new cover design out of the park and I couldn't be more proud to have it grace the front of this book.

Janine Pipe, Michael Tichy, and Kayla Meehan proved essential beta readers, steering the story home, and providing essential insight on what worked and what didn't.

None of this would have been possible without an incredible bevy of horror readers, writers, and enthusiasts. To name a few, and unfortunately forget many, thank you to the people who cheerlead at every corner and make the genre a better place—Ronald Kelly, Tyler Jones, Hailey Piper, Erica Robyn, Kenneth W. Cain, Laurel Hightower, Eric Raglin, Briana Morgan, Ross Jeffery, Andrew Fowlow, Brian Keene, Shane Hawk, Todd Keisling, Kevin Whitten, Gabino Iglesias, Cina Pelayo, Jonathan Janz, Daron Kappauff, Nico Bell, and many more.

I never would have finished this without the support system we've built here.

About the Author

Brennan LaFaro is a horror writer living in southeastern Massachusetts with his wife, two sons, and his hounds. An avid lifelong reader, Brennan also co-hosts the Dead Headspace podcast. *Slattery Falls*, the first entry in a trilogy, is out now from Crossroad Press. Be on the lookout for *Noose*, coming soon from Dark Lit Press. You can read his short fiction in various anthologies and find him on Twitter at @brennanlafaro or at www.brennanlafaro.com.

CROSSROAD
PRESS

Made in the USA
Middletown, DE
05 January 2023

20776178R00076

A Spectacle Unto God

The Life and Death of Christopher Love (1618-1651)

by

Dr. Don Kistler

Soli Deo Gloria Publications
...for instruction in righteousness...

Soli Deo Gloria Publications
P.O. Box 451, Morgan, PA 15064
(412) 221-1901/ FAX 221-1902
www.SDGbooks.com

*

Printed in the United States of America.

*

1-877611-98-0

*

To Dr. John H. Gerstner
—the last Puritan

and

To my daughter Michelle
—the next one

Contents

List of Illustrations

Foreword

Don Kistler and Soli Deo Gloria Publications have greatly blessed Christendom by bringing to its attention the life, and especially the death, of this 17th century martyr. Much larger now, at the end of the 20th century, the Protestant church has fewer Christopher Loves and needs them more. Though he died at thirty-three years, his wisdom is for the ages, especially the impending "Third Christian Millennium."

There is another grand irony in the story of Christopher Love. He seems to have died for something he did not really believe in—the ecclesiastical overthrow of the evil government. You will see from his letters here published that he claimed not to have participated in the revolutionary return of the Stuart King, Charles II. He was insistent that no evidence had been presented to the contrary. So he was martyred for the zeal of the Cromwellian Independents, the laxity of the Stuart Cavaliers, and the non-revolutionary character of his fellow Presbyterians.

Kistler's account suggests what I think is the truth, Christopher Love made all the actors on the religious scene of his day more or less his enemies because he told the truth across the board. As I said above, we can use a few more Loves for the 21st century.

This introductory volume doesn't stress it as much as the *Works I* to follow, but Love was a *jue divino* (divine right) Presbyterian. 1640-1660 was the double decade of the church government struggle, par excellence. Episcopacy and Independency vied with Presbyterianism for the sole right to biblical existence. That is far from the current era of virtual indifference to such matters. With Samuel Rutherford in Scotland, Gisbert Voetius in Holland, and Christopher Love in England, this was the gold age for church order, not from top-down (Episcopacy) or bottom-up (Independency) but top-down and bottom-up (Presbyterianism).

That a stickler for regulations would be the devout pietist of the letters here included is instructive. High Calvinistic theology, meticulous discipline, and heart religion were providentially and sanctifyingly mixed together and out came Christopher Love. He had to die young.

John H. Gerstner
Ligonier, PA
July 1994

Preface

Some years ago, while reading Benjamin Brook's *Lives of the Puritans,* I read several of the letters Christopher and Mary Love wrote to one another while he was awaiting execution in the Tower of London. I was struck by their deep love for each other, and by how that love had been augmented by their love for God. I wept as I read their affectionate and tender farewells. As I began to obtain and read Christopher Love's sermons, I was even more impressed with the keen insights he had into God's Word and the fine logical structure of his thinking.

Christopher Love was, for me, the first person to acceptably answer the question I had heard asked so many times, "Why did God ordain sin?" His answer was that God ordained sin so that we would know Him in the fullness of His attributes. If God had never ordained sin we would only have known Him as a Creator, but because of sin we can know Him as a Redeemer. Others had said this before, I'm sure, but I had never come across it in my studies. Time and again, as I read Love, I saw thoughts and answers I had not seen before. The brilliance of his mind made me want to know him better.

The story of a man who lost his life for his convictions (while others of his colleagues were released) and a wife who was left with young children and no husband touched me on a emotional level to the same extent that his sermons touched me on an intellectual and theological level. I began to think that others might appreciate their story as much I as did.

I have spent several years collecting Love's writings, letters, and the transcripts of his trial. It has been as much a detective's work as an author's work. There is as much a human interest story here as there is a theological story. It is refreshing to see the human side of historical figures come to life. The Puritans have been caricatured for centuries as cold and unfeeling, but here are real people in a real-life drama with real-life emotions and responses. In this story, the characters feel sorrow, respect, longing, devotion, and anguish, but most of all they are resigned to the will of the God in whom they believed so deeply.

I would like to acknowledge the help of Mr. William H. Clennell of the Bodleian Library in Oxford. The good people at Dr. Williams' Library in London were most co-operative. It was there I found Mary Love's handwritten memoirs of her life with Christopher. The records at the city library of London next to the Guildhall, adjacent to St. Lawrence Jewry church, were helpful in determining marriage, baptism, and burial dates. Thanks to Rachel George of the library at the Reformed Presbyterian Theological Seminary in Pittsburgh for her co-operation in making some scarce works of Christopher Love's available. A hearty thanks goes to John Stone who first let me touch and handle his old Puritan books, then actually let me borrow and read them.

The format for the book is built around the letters to and from Christopher Love while he was in prison. The odd numbered chapters contain those very letters, penned nearly three hundred fifty years ago. The even numbered chapters are the story of his life and ministry, authored through my own research on Love.

It is my hope that this book will spark interest in one of the most fascinating figures with whom I have come in contact. I hope that Love the pastor will be as compelling as Love, the "tragic" figure.

May the reading of this book spark your interest in the godly legacy left by this one man who was willing to be "a spectacle unto God, to angels, and to men."

Don Kistler
Pittsburgh, PA
March 1995

Christophorus Loue

1

My Dear Heart

July 14, 1651

Before I write a word further, I beseech thee think not that it is thy wife but a friend now that writes to thee. I hope thou hast freely given up thy wife and children to God, who hath said in Jeremiah 49:11, "Leave thy fatherless children, I will preserve them alive, and let thy widow trust in me." Thy Maker will be my husband, and a Father to thy children. O that the Lord would keep thee from having one troubled thought for thy relations. I desire freely to give thee up into thy Father's hands, and not only look upon it as a crown of glory for thee to die for Christ, but as an honor to me that I should have a husband to leave for Christ.

I dare not speak to thee, nor have a thought within my own heart of my unspeakable loss, but wholly keep my eye fixed upon thy inexpressible and inconceivable gain. Thou leavest but a sinful, mortal wife to be everlastingly married to the Lord of glory. Thou leavest but children, brothers, and sisters to go to the Lord Jesus, thy eldest Brother. Thou leavest friends on earth to go to the enjoyment of saints and angels, and the spirits of just men made perfect in glory. Thou dost but leave earth for heaven and changest a prison for a palace. And if natural affections should begin to arise, I hope that spirit of grace that is within thee will quell them, knowing that all things here below are but dung and dross in comparison of those things that are above. I know thou keepest thine eye fixed on the hope of glory, which makes thy feet trample on the loss of earth.

My dear, I know God hath not only prepared glory for thee, and thee for it, but I am persuaded that He will sweeten the way for thee to come to the enjoyment of it. When thou art putting on thy clothes that morning, O think, "I am now putting on my wedding garments to go to be everlastingly married to my Redeemer."

When the messenger of death comes to thee, let him not seem dreadful to thee, but look on him as a messenger that brings thee tidings of eternal life. When thou goest up the scaffold, think (as thou saidst to me) that it is but thy fiery chariot to carry thee up to thy Father's house.

And when thou layest down thy precious head to receive thy Father's stroke, remember what thou saidst to me: Though thy head was severed from thy body, yet in a moment thy soul should be united to thy Head, the Lord Jesus, in heaven. And though it may seem something bitter, that by the hands of men we are parted a little sooner than otherwise we might have been, yet let us consider that it is the decree and will of our Father, and it will not be long ere we shall enjoy one another in heaven again.

Let us comfort one another with these sayings. Be comforted, my dear heart. It is but a little stroke and thou shalt be there where the weary shall be at rest and where the wicked shall cease from troubling. Remember that thou mayest eat thy dinner with bitter herbs, yet thou shalt have a sweet supper with Christ that night. My dear, by what I write unto thee, I do not hereby undertake to teach thee; for these comforts I have received from the Lord by thee. I will write no more, nor trouble thee any further, but commit thee into the arms of God with whom ere long thee and I shall be.

Farewell, my dear. I shall never see thy face more till we both behold the face of the Lord Jesus at that great day.

Mary Love

Cardiff in the 17th Century

2

Love's Beginnings

Cardiff in Wales is an ancient city, some one hundred seventy miles west of London. It was a fortified station for the Normans and, most likely, the Romans, largely due to its position between the rivers Taff and Rhymney, and also between the mountains and the sea. Cardiff means, in fact, "castle on the Taff." There are few remnants of her antiquity—the castle, the old church of St. John, and the noble pinnacled tower—but the ancient walls and gates have been swept away. When the Arthurian legend speaks of Sparrow-hawk, it is referring to Cardiff.

It was here that Christopher Love was born in 1618, the youngest child of his parents and the son of their old age, his mother being fifty when she gave birth to him. Christopher carried his father's name. According to John Quick, who knew Christopher and wrote of him after his death (his handwritten remembrances are in the Dr. Williams Library in London), his parents were "not so rich as to merit envy, nor so poor as to deserve contempt."

His parents gave him a good education, though they never intended him for the ministry. As a child, he was unusually fond of books and never neglected his learning. In fact, he devoted much of his time, both day and night, to his beloved studies.[1] This was in spite of the indulgence of his parents, who gave him great liberty for play and recreation. Love's family was not a church-going one; in fact, young Christopher was fifteen years old before he ever heard a sermon.

William Erbery was the new vicar of St. Mary's in Cardiff. He was a local, having been born in 1604 at Roath-Dagfield in Glamorganshire, Wales. He did his studying at Brasenose College in Oxford, then entered the ministerial office. Erbery leaned toward the schismatic[2], and was an independent with regard to church government. The Bishop of Landaff visited his diocese in 1634 and pronounced him to be dangerous. His refusal to submit in various ways led to his ultimate resignation under fire. But in 1632 his preaching drew a curious Christopher Love to hear him. It was novel, but little else.

Love went often to hear this preacher, but, in his own words, it was only to see a man in a pulpit. Yet in that first sermon, wrote his wife, "God met with him and gave him such a sight of his sins and his undone condition that he returned home with a hell in his conscience." Something had happened in this young boy's life and heart. By the time he reached his home, the change was so dramatic that it made his father wonder about him. In fact, his father concluded that young Christopher had been seized with a strange fit of melancholy, what we would call depression. Mr. Love's antidote was to suggest that Christopher find

---

[1] Benjamin Brook, *Lives of the Puritans,* 3 vols. (London: 1813), 3:115.

[2] John Wood, *Athenae Oxon,* 2 vols., 2:100-101.

some of his companions and play with them, but Christopher refused. All of a sudden, he could find no pleasure in their company. His father suggested he go to some gentleman's house and engage in his usual card games, but Christopher requested permission instead to go to church on the next lecture day. His father refused and blamed the present sadness on his recent trip to church to hear Mr. Erbery, Mary Love recalled.

To prevent Christopher from going to church, his father locked him up in a high chamber of the house to confine him till the service was over. But the determination and tenacity that was to characterize Love in later life was evident even then. His desire to hear the Word of God preached led him to escape by tying a cord to the window and sliding down the side of the house. He went to church, where it pleased God to deepen his earlier convictions so that the result was a sound conversion of his soul to God.

Christopher returned home to an exasperated father and an awkward condition. He could displease his earthly father on the one hand or his heavenly Father on the other. The former was the only choice. The thought of offending God was deplorable to this new convert. And his situation was only aggravated in that he had no friend with whom he could share his burdens or triumphs. Christopher unburdened his heart to Mr. Erbery, who was "of great edification and benefit to him."

However, several of Love's young companions in vice had, at the same time, been brought to a relationship with Almighty God. Now, they would often assemble together for the purpose of fasting and prayer.

When their parents were in bed, they would meet twice a week. The meetings were always late at night so as not to neglect their school work or displease their parents. His wife later wrote that "this young scholar in Christ's school endeavored with double diligence to regain those 15 years of his life past."

Love's father, however, seeing Christopher continue in this course, withdrew his affection and branded him a hopeless youth. The young boy who had once been known as a young gamester, and such a one who would regularly beat older men at both cards and dice, was now stigmatized as a young Puritan.[3] Mr. Erbery intervened with Love's father, but to no avail. At last, Erbery requested that Christopher be allowed to live at his own house. He would take care of him and see to his education. To this, Mr. Love consented.

Christopher grew greatly under the arrangement, but his father saw it as temporary. Mr. Love went to London and entered into an arrangement to have Christopher become an apprentice to a master, even paying the fee up front. Christopher, however, was very opposed to the arrangement. His heart was set on going to Oxford. His father consented, but did so with obvious displeasure. He refused his son any aid other than a horse on which to leave home. While at Oxford, Christopher's support was divided between his mother and his mentor, Mr. Erbery. Mary Love remembered, "His father gave him only a horse to ride upon, only his mother, being very dearly affectionate to him, gave him (unknown to his father) a bond to receive some money owed her by a lady who lived in the way to

3 Brook, 3:116.

Oxford."

Later in his life, Mr. Erbery came under much criticism for aberrant theological views. Whether valid or not, he was accused of teaching universal redemption, antinomianism, "and other dangerous errors." Wood, the Oxford historian, accused him of speaking blasphemies "against the glorious divinity and blood of Jesus Christ." He appears to have become heavily involved in mysticism. In one debate, Wood says, Erbery declared that ministers were beasts, dogs, monsters, asses, and false prophets; that they were the beast with seven heads and ten horns; that Babylon is the church in her ministers and that the great whore is the church in her worship. His wife joined the Quakers, whom Erbery greatly admired.

In spite of all this, Christopher Love later observed, "As for Mr. Erbery, though he is fallen into dangerous opinions, yet, he being my spiritual father, I do naturally care for him; and my heart cleaves to him more than to any man in the world. I speak to the praise of God, he was the instrument of my conversion nearly twenty years ago, and the means of my education at the university; for which kindness, the half of what I have in the world I could readily part with for his relief."[4]

Christopher Love's wish would be granted; he was going to Oxford.

---

[4] Christopher Love, *A Clear and Necessary Vindication of the Principles and Practices of Me, Christopher Love,* (London, 1651), 36.

The Tower at Oxford
(Across from the Bodleian Library)

3

Dear and Precious Friend

June 1, 1651

I cannot but congratulate your liberty, and the singular honor God hath laid upon you. The Captain of our salvation is wise and knows whom to call out for His champion. He hath pleased to call you to the forlorn hope; we are leading up the van. Our brethren in the black bill are like to bring up the body; and for our rear (blessed be God) we have armies of prayers and tears. Yea, through mercy, we may say, "Our righteousness goes before us, and the glory of the Lord shall be our reward," Isaiah 58:8. Well might we fear had we not a good God, a good cause, and a good conscience; but where our God justifies, who shall condemn? Certainly, that God who hath done us so much good by a prison (blessed be His name) can do us much more good by our trial. He bids us not fear them who, at worst, can but kill the body. And why should we be afraid of man that shall die and forget the Lord our Maker, yea, our Redeemer?

It is too much honor that God lays upon us, to suffer anything for His name and covenant's sake; that, hereby, we are so endeared in the hearts of His faithful people, and have been occasions to blow up the spirit of prayer that was almost extinct. Will not God incline His ear when He hath prepared the heart? Did He ever set His children to begging but He had a boon for them?

I need not stir up your Christian resolution, but rather desire to light my candle at your lamp. Yet, when lately I looked upon Revelation 2 and 3, I spied no less than seven rare cordials to persons in our condition. Revelation 2 verses 7, 10, 17, 27 and Revelation 3 verses 5, 12, and 21: (1) a tree of life; (2) freedom from hurt by the second death; (3) the hidden manna and white stone; (4) the morning star and wielding the rod of iron; (5) the white garments, the Book of Life, and owning us before His Father; (6) that we shall be pillars in His house, having His new name graven upon us; and (7) that we shall sit in His throne, and all this is made over to him that is overcoming. A Christian is sure to conquer if he dares but fight, and no soldier but he can glory when he puts on his harness.

The Lord arm you with such courage and wisdom that you may avoid the snares and be above the fury of your adversaries. God, angels, and men look upon you; and, while you are fighting, Christ is weaving your crown. He, by your example, so heartens His people and dampens the adversary, as they may rejoice and bless God who favor your righteous dealing, and all iniquity may stop her mouth. So prays your unworthy brother and companion in tribulation, and in the kingdom and patience of Jesus Christ. I beg your prayers and present my best affections to yourself and Mistress Love.

I'd rather die with grace than live with blame;
Far better die with Love than live with shame.

For my most honored friend, Mr. Love,

Roger Drake

New Inn Hall, Oxford
(As it appeared in the 17th century)

4

Love at Oxford

At one time, Oxford was little more than that which its name suggests, a ford for oxen to cross the rivers. It was not the major center of learning it is now. Students who wanted to do serious study would go to London or Paris. But in the 12th century a falling out occured between the kings of England and France, and English students in Paris were sent home. It was only then that Oxford began to expand as an educational center.

Oxford was not, at first, a university of colleges. The University of Oxford was born in the 12th century, a full century before the foundation of the first college. Many of the Oxford colleges were originally monasteries, some Dominican, some Augustinian, some Franciscan. There are now many colleges in the University; there are also a number of "halls." A hall was a smaller society. While the colleges had their quadrangles around which students walked while asking and answering questions of and from their mentors, the hall was more sequestered. It was a building all to itself in which a few young men lived and learned. In 1552, at New Inn Hall, there were forty-nine members; twenty years later, there were but twelve, and that included servants.

These little democratic societies, with their rules, their rivalries, their intense vitality, were for generations the academic homes of the majority of Oxford men.[1] These societies had rules—rules for religious observances, sermons, Bible reading, and grace at meals. There were rules about behavior: no dishonest games, no evil gossip, no bad language, no fighting, no dogs, and no solitary walks. After all, students were there to learn!

New Inn Hall was originally called Trilleck's Inn, named for John Trilleck, who died in 1360. Through a succession of gifts, the buildings were given to New College in 1391. During the times of Queens Mary and Elizabeth, as few as six students were there; but when Christopher Rogers, a leading Puritan in the University, was appointed Principal of New Inn Hall in 1622, the hall began to flourish. During his tenure, as many as forty students matriculated per year at New Inn Hall. Like Magdalen Hall, New Inn Hall became largely a Puritan center. In fact, it was known as a nest of Precisians and Puritans.

Christopher Love arrived at Oxford not knowing anyone or whom to choose for his tutor. One evening soon after his arrival, sitting by a fire in a local tavern, he overheard several young scholars railing against the Puritans and cursing them, particularly Christopher Rogers whom they called an "arch-puritan." They raised the point that no other Puritan besides him was head of any house in Oxford.

---

[1] Charles Edward Mallett, *A History of the University of Oxford,* 2 vols. (New York: Barnes and Noble, 1968), 2:286.

This peaked the interest of young Love, who resolved to see if these charges against Dr. Rogers were true, for, if they were, that was exactly the kind of tutor he was looking for. Christopher Love entered New Inn Hall under Dr. Rogers on July 29, 1635 at the age of seventeen.[2]

While there, he had little to live on, being careful to honor the sacrifices of his mother and spiritual father, Mr. Erbery, in sponsoring him at Oxford. He was a diligent student, devoting certain hours to academics and the rest to the study of Scripture. He allowed himself very little sleep and little or no time for recreation.[3] Love seemed to be very mindful of time misspent in his youth; the memories of his earlier years were a source of constant and bitter lamenting. His wife wrote that he did double diligence to make up for his fifteen misspent years. Additionally, according to Mary Love, "he knew that as grace was absolutely necessary to make a good Christian, so learning was of the same importance to make an able minister."

During this time, the British nation was troubled, and the sympathies of the citizens, like those of most of the middle-class people throughout the country, were with Parliament. The King had the loyalties of the nobility and greater gentry and, of course, the Church of England. The University was overwhelmingly loyal to the King. Puritan sympathies were to be found in a few colleges, but mainly in the halls.[4]

---

2 *Alumni Oxonieses*, 3 vols. (London, 1891), 3:940.

3 Brook, 3:117.

4 A.L. Rowse, *Oxford in the History of England,* (New York: G.P. Putnam's Sons, 1975), 93.

If a young man went to Oxford or Cambridge in the 17th century he was, most likely, desirous of entering the ministry. There were exceptions, of course, but the majority of hopeful divines knew full well that the best road to the pulpit ran this way. Most subjects taught at the universities would serve as a preparation for preaching. Joseph Glanville, in *An Essay on Preaching,* said that the young Divine will need "the knowledge of Philosophy, Languages, History, and a competent acquaintance with the most substantial writings of the ancient and modern divines." Though there had been a formal professorship of Divinity at Cambridge and Oxford since Henry VIII's time, there was no formal training in preaching as an art. But the young bachelor of divinity, because of the method of instruction, would have regular practice in public speaking.[5]

Oration was referred to as the composing of a theme. There was much practice in not only developing a subject but also in the selection of appropriate illustrations and figures of speech. Thus, every student was to keep a notebook called a "Common Place Book," in which he wrote down phrases from the authors he read. There was specific training to acquire dexterity in vocabulary and illustrations (something with which Puritan sermons are replete), and when a student studied for his Master of Arts degree, he trained in theology, philosophy, and medicine. Note the numerous references in Puritan sermons to "physic," or medicine. The future preacher realized

---

[5] Caroline Francis Richardson, *English Preachers and Preaching: 1640-1670*, (New York: The MacMillan Company, 1928), 3.

that if the sermon was the means instituted by God for the conversion of sinners, then his duty was to be an accomplished rhetorician. Negligence in the latter might be a cause of failure in the former, for God had not only ordained the end but the means as well. That worthy Divine, Joseph Caryl, endorsed a book by John Smith entitled, *The Mysterie of Rhetorique Unveil'd.* The author divided rhetoric into two parts:

1. Garnishing of speech, called Elocution.
2. Garnishing of the matter of utterance, called Pronunciation.

Caryl must have learned his lessons well, for he preached twenty-five years on the book of Job alone!

A typical grammar school boy in England would have come to the university having learned the orations of Cicero and Demosthenes, among others. He would have had training in Greek, Hebrew, and Latin, if not Arabic, and would have memorized many orations in their original languages. If a student had viewed a calling to the pulpit, he would have learned to keep phrase books. He would have studied ancient languages and practiced disputation and oration. He would have compiled books full of answers to stock arguments and elaborate figures of speech. And he would have learned to construct themes with a beginning and an end.

At the university, declamations (or debates) were a required exercise. Sometimes they were given to the tutor alone, other times in front of small or large groups. The students would often attend these gatherings simply to gain further knowledge about elocution, or the art of proper public speaking. Sir Simonds D'Ewes, in his *Autobiography,* stated that "my increase of knowledge (was not) small, which I obtained by the ear as well as by the eye, being present at the public commencements. . .at problems, sophisms, declamations."

When a young preacher took a church, he would realize that his university experience in speaking in public intelligently and effectively, in bearing himself when assaulted with arguments, was a most conspicuous advantage. Note the typical Puritan sermon with its numerous objections and answers thereto. The great instrument of high education was disputation, or debate, often repeated, and conducted with the most elaborate forms in the tournaments of the Schools. And, when a young man received his Bachelor of Arts, he was proficient at logic, the only course in which he spent as much time as in Bible and theology; for the Puritans felt deeply that if a man could not think clearly, he could not interpret God's Word clearly or correctly. So he knew his arguments and could defend them with logical precision. In fact, the Puritans would often be derisively referred to as "Precisionists." They could thank their classical education for that.

An undergraduate student at Oxford attended lectures twice a week in grammar. Twice a week he attended lectures on Aristotle, Cicero, Quintillian, or Hermogenes. He attended lectures in logic and moral philosophy, and every Monday, Wednesday, and Friday he observed disputations. After two years he engaged in some of these disputations himself.

The undergraduate would study logic for four terms and then dispute twice before being granted his degree. On Mondays, Tuesdays, Wednesdays, and Fridays at 9 a.m. he would attend the college lecture in rhetoric, and at 1 p.m. those same days he would attend the college lecture in Greek. Students were additionally required to "declaim" in Latin or Greek on alternate Saturdays.

Debating was a primary means of preparing a young student to be a divine. These disputations had originally developed centuries earlier as a means of resolving questions which could not be agreed upon even by the most learned authorities.

E.G.W. Bill, in his *Education at Christ Church Oxford, 1660-1800* (New York: Oxford Press, 1988) is very helpful for a better understanding in this matter of disputations:

> A question in grammar, logic, rhetoric, or philosophy was posed in the form of a question which could be argued by the canons of Aristotelian logic. The respondent first offered an answer to, or interpretation of, the question and advanced arguments in support of it. The opponent then stated contradictory propositions and attacked flaws in the respondent's reasoning. The determiner finally summed up the arguments, pointed out the fallacies in the reasoning of the participants, reconciled the differences, and pronounced a decision or determination. (P. 245)

By the latter part of the 17th century, however, these disputations were not so much a seeking of truth, but they had become a contest to win. They now were exercises to train the logical faculties. Obadiah Walker, in his *Of Education*, wrote that students were put:

> . . .upon a continual stretch of their wits to defend their cause and it makes them quick in

> replies, intentive upon their subject; where the opponent useth all means to drive his adversary from his hold; and the answerer defends himself with the force of truth, sometimes with the subtility of his wit; and sometimes he escapes in a midst of words, and the doubles of a distinction, whilst he seeks all holes and recesses to shelter his persecuted opinion and reputation.[6]

Bill also gives this insightful description of logic at Oxford. Though the time frame of which he writes is such that it is under Archbishop Laud, who restructured educational codes after Love's time at Oxford, we can still get a good idea of the nature of learning at Oxford during Love's tenure there.

> The study of logic was an important element in liberal education. At Christ Church, from the foundation until late in the eighteenth century, each of the four *Classes* had its own lecturer in dialectic or logic, whose duty was to moderate at disputations and to deliver lectures in logic. Neither the lecturer in rhetoric nor the lecturer in Greek was assigned to a particular *Classis:* only logic was deemed to require such extensive provision. Disputations were the most important logical exercises. . . .The main defence of logic was that it trained the mental faculties. Edward Bentham, who had been a tutor at Oriel before becoming Regius Professor of Divinity in 1763, wrote that it enabled a man to view a subject in all its branches, to judge which parts deserved to be considered more minutely, to consider the arguments of opponents, and to determine whether they proved their conclusions.

---

6 Quoted in Bill, p. 246.

> The deductive methods of logic, unlike the inductive methods of scientific inquiry, were especially suited for reasoning on matters of law, morals, and divinity, where the premises were provided by the unquestionable texts of statutes, classical authors, or the Scriptures. Logic was thus concerned with words and ideas rather than with the observation of nature or of fact.

The student at Oxford preparing for the ministry in the 17th century was well-versed in logic, in rhetoric, in public speaking, in illustrations from life and in clear, precise, analytical thinking, which most separates him from the college graduate today. Bill asserts that mathematics was studied by undergraduates mainly as an exercise in logic.

John Morgan, in his *Godly Learning: Puritan Attitudes towards Reason, Learning and Education, 1560-1640,* states that logic was chief among the academic weapons the Puritans sought to bend to their use, for it was logic that could drain the last drop of meaning from God's Word.[7]

There was a great deal of change taking place at Oxford and Cambridge in the study of logic, however. Aristotelian syllogisms were being displaced by Ramean divisions. Peter Ramus, a French Protestant who had been martyred in the previous century, had revolutionized the study of logic. Since the papists who had begun the universities had used the scholasticmen such as Aristotle, the Puritans felt that a true Christian would have deeper insights into God's Word than an

---

[7] John Morgan, *Godly Learning*, (Cambridge: Cambridge University Press, 1986), 105.

unbeliever or pagan. Ramean logic went beyond the syllogisms of Aristotelian logic ("All men are mortal; Socrates is a man; Socrates is mortal.") to the complex divisions and subdivisions of Ramean logic. To illustrate this, we can examine a sermon by Christopher Love on 1 Thessalonians 5:21 entitled,

A Divine Balance to Weigh all Doctrines by
"Prove all things; hold fast that which is good."

He first gives the context and then defines what is meant by prophesying. Next he states the doctrine: "Those that have attained unto the highest perfection of grace and knowledge that it is possible for men in this life to attain unto, are not to despise or neglect the ordinances of Jesus Christ." Then he gives two reasons for the doctrine:

1. Our sanctification is not perfect in this life.
2. Sin lies hidden in the secret corners of the heart.

Next he explains the words of the text: "We must hold fast the truths of the gospel in judgment, that we run not into error." Then he states a second doctrine: "It is the duty of all hearers of the Word to try and prove all doctrines which they hear." Then come four cautions about trying of doctrines:

1. We must not take liberty to try all teachers.
2. We must not be skeptics in religion.
3. We must not bring the Scriptures to our opinion, but our opinion to the Scriptures.
4. We must not be over confident of our opinions.

Following this he gives four reasons why we should try all doctrines:

1. Because erroneous teachers may carry a resemblance to them that preach the truth.
2. The Scripture foretells that there shall be many false teachers in the latter days.
3. False doctrines are published very craftily.
4. There is an aptness in our nature to be turned aside unto error.

Then come three general directions about trying of doctrines:

1. The Scripture is to be the standard by which we are to try all doctrines.
2. Clear principles of truth must rather be maintained than disputed.
3. We must not be confident in any opinion until we have tried it thoroughly.

There are nine rules for trying all doctrines we hear:

1. Whatsoever the Word of God doth expressly hold forth to be believed and received.
2. Whatsoever doctrine advanceth the grace of God in Christ.
3. Whatsoever doctrine doth advance the will of God.
4. Whatsoever doctrine doth advance all the attributes of God.
5. Whatsoever doctrine discovereth the sinfulness of vain thoughts.
6. Whatsoever doctrine advanceth all truth.

7. Whatsoever doctrine tends to settle a troubled conscience.
8. Whatsoever doctrine intends to the advancement of godliness.
9. Whatsoever doctrine will abide the trial.

All these doctrines are sound and to be embraced, Love says.

Last, he gives nine reasons to reject doctrines:

1. Whatsoever doctrine is not to be found in Scripture.
2. Whatsoever doctrine debases the grace of God in Christ.
3. Whatsoever doctrine makes the will of God for obedience and the grace of God for salvation to be contrary.
4. Whatsoever doctrine doth rob God of His glory in any of His attributes.
5. Whatsoever doctrine requireth only outward reformation.
6. Whatsoever doctrine is pleasing to the corrupt nature of man.
7. Whatsoever doctrine leaves a distressed conscience without any bottom to rest upon.
8. Whatsoever doctrine tends to licentiousness.
9. Whatsoever doctrine will not endure the trial.

All these doctrines are false and to be abhorred, Love concludes. And all of this in fifty-one pages! This is Ramean logic displayed in all of its tedious but meticulous dissecting of a passage.

The Puritans adopted Ramus' system of thinking and saw it as being from God Himself. Since God's mind was logical, then logic could help unravel the seeming mysteries of God's Word.

Undergraduates also studied ancient Greco-Roman literature as an instrument for training the mental faculties, but also in order to have a model for moral and social behavior. Says Bill on page 275, "By construing classical authors and by writing verses and themes, they learnt to think logically, to speak and write with fluency, clarity, brevity, and occasionally wit, and to acquire the virtues of moderation, prudence, fortitude, and the rest."

Additionally, the promising divine would study ethics, religion, and the original languages of Scripture. The belief was that ethics were based upon reason, and that was the main basis for studying the Greek and Latin moralists of classical and pagan antiquity.

Christopher Love did so well in his studies that his tutor, Christopher Rogers, invited him to move into his own home and live. Love graduated with a B.A. from New Inn Hall on May 2, 1639. He began pursuit of his M. A., another three year term (Bill asserts that "most of those who stayed on to obtain the M.A. did so to pass the time until they reached the canonical age for ordination of twenty-three"), but was expelled for not conforming to the mandates of the Church of England under Archbishop Laud. He was later re-admitted, however, and received his M.A. on March 26, 1645. He was the first to refuse to subscribe to Laud's new canons of 1640 (see chapter XVII, "Archbishop Laud and the Caroline Code", in volume two of Mallet's *A History of the University of Oxford*). Love said that "when I was a scholar in Oxon, and master of arts, I was the first scholar that I knew of, or ever heard of in Oxon, that did publicly refuse in the congregation house to subscribe unto those impositions, or canons, imposed by the archbishop touching the prelates and common prayer."[8]

Love had practiced his skills as a preacher for hours in the church known as St. Peter-in-the-Bayly, across the street from New Inn Hall. He was zealous to hear sermons and zealous to preach them. But the road to the pulpit would not be an easy one for him, as he was soon to discover.

---

8 *The Whole Trial of Mr. Love* (London, 1652), 36.

St. Peter's Church
(Where Love preached his student sermons)

5

Dear Friend

June 17, 1651

I cannot be unmindful of your person and condition, as being not only in the body but also in a special manner bound with you, Hebrews 13:3. And certainly, if habitual and active grace are such motives of Christian love, is not passive grace much more? To suffer for Christ is a grace as well as to believe in Him, Philippians 1:29. Christ and His people are never more lovely than upon the cross. May we not, under God, thank our prison that we are so gracious this day in the eyes of God's people, yea, and I am persuaded, in the eyes of some enemies? Doth not Christ, by this means, set a higher rate upon reformation, the ministry, and the government? How do the Northern people prize the sun who see it but once in three or six months, and do not our dunghill hearts ordinarily value blessings much more by their want than by their enjoyment?

In particular, sir, how you are endeared to God and man in this call, to be the proto-confessor or proto-martyr. The Lord enable you, by His grace, to bear the honor as well as the burden. I bless God for your cheerfulness and constancy, whose flames contribute much to the keeping of my poor spark alive.

But my errand is, if it may be, to prevent the latter; and, may it stand with God's will, I would not have you yet to be a martyr. Haply, you will say, I wish you worse than your adversaries do; if so, yet I am sure it is with a more honest heart.

Sir, I have only one thing to add, which I apprehend as a providence not to be slighted. Namely, that your day of trial is your day of jubilee, and your day of Pentecost is being precisely the fiftieth day from your apprehension; ordered so, I am confident, by special providence, not by the intention of the Adversary. The Lord make it a jubilee to you for liberty of spirit, and a day of Pentecost for effusion of the Spirit of grace, wisdom, and utterance. I shall say "amen" to the omen, and follow it with what poor interest I have in heaven, still choosing rather to die with Love than to rule with lust, which is the Magna Carta of these apostatizing times. My best affections to yourself and dearest consort. I beg your prayers and rest,

Yours,

Roger Drake

St. Gile's in the Field Church
(Where Christopher and Mary Love were married)

6

The Ministry of Love

Christopher Love was expelled from New Inn Hall in Oxford for non-conformity. In 1639, he received an invitation from Sheriff Warner to come to London to be his domestic chaplain. The Warner family grew to love him deeply, and he was instrumental in the conversion of several members of that family. He spent much time teaching and catechizing the children and servants. It was here also that he met his future wife Mary Stone, the sheriff's ward. Her father, Matthew Stone, had been a successful merchant in London. Christopher and Mary lived in the Warner house for six years before they married on April 9, 1645 at St. Gile's in the Field church in London.

It was also while he was chaplain to Sheriff Warner that Dr. William Twisse, one of the leading Puritans of his time, came to hear him preach. He was so impressed that he asked Christopher Love to come and live with him, offering him not only personal assistance, but the use of his library as well. Dr. Twisse died, however, before Love could move in.

Love was invited to become lecturer at St. Ann's, Aldersgate, but the Bishop of London was opposed to his appointment and for three years refused to allow it because Love had not been ordained. Love declined episcopal ordination and went to Scotland to seek ordination by the presbytery there, but met with great disappointment because the Scottish presbytery had decreed to ordain only those who would settle in Scotland and minister there. He had many large offers to stay in Scotland but refused them all, wishing to return to England.

Upon returning, about 1641, he preached at Newcastle by invitation of the mayor and aldermen of the city. In his sermon in the afternoon, he expressed his sentiments against the errors in the Book of Common Prayer and the superstitious ceremonies in the Church of England. For this, he was immediately taken to jail and imprisoned with thieves and murderers. He slept in his cell with only straw for a bed. While in jail, the people flocked to hear him but were refused admittance, so he preached to them through the prison grates. Later, his friends were allowed to come and clean his cell. He preached to all who came and was used mightily of the Lord. Christopher Love was a very popular preacher, which exasperated his enemies, and he had no sooner entered into his public ministry than he was silenced.

He was imprisoned for some time and was later taken to London on a writ of *Habeas Corpus,* was tried in the court of king's bench, and was acquitted.

About the time of the outbreak of the civil war there, he preached as a lecturer at Tenterden, Kent, on the lawfulness of a defensive war. In his own words, he said, "About the beginning of the wars, I was the first minister that I knew of in England who was accused of preaching treason and rebellion merely for maintaining in a sermon in Kent at Tenterden the lawfulness of a defensive war at the first breaking out and eruption of our troubles." Of this, too, he was acquitted and recovered damages.

Shortly thereafter he was made chaplain to Colonel John Venn's regiment, and, later, preacher to the garrison at Windsor Castle. The royalists nicknamed him "Venn's principal fireman at Windsor." His ministerial work was highly esteemed, however, even by those who disagreed with his views on ecclesiastical matters. The unnamed author of a brief sketch of Love's life, which prefaces a 19th century book of prophecies by him, wrote, "I am bold to say that no man was more generally beloved than he was, and, I believe, as great a seal was set unto his ministry as God doth usually set to the ministry of any of His servants."

A plague came upon the town and castle of Windsor, and many died; but Love continued to minister there, unafraid of death. He visited the homes of the sick and dying, exposing himself to infection and possible death, but through this period of danger the Lord protected him. Many died, but Love's life was spared. He was said to have made the Lord his refuge and the Most High his habitation, so that he was not afraid of the pestilence that walked in darkness, nor of the destruction that wasted at noonday.[1]

When the Presbyterians were established in government, Christopher Love finally received the ordination he had so strenuously sought. On January 23, 1644, at the instigation of Edmund Calamy, who was later to be responsible for getting so many of Love's works printed after his death, he was ordained in

[1] Brook, 3:120.

Aldermanbury church by elders Horton, Bellers, and Roberts, which was done by fasting and prayer and the laying on of hands.

As part of his examination prior to ordination, the question was put to him whether he thought he could suffer for the truths of Christ which he had professed if called upon to do so. He answered, "I tremble to think what I should do in such a case, especially when I consider how many have boasted what they could suffer for Christ; and yet, when they have come to it, they have denied Christ and his truths, rather than suffered for them. Therefore, I dare not boast what I shall do; but if this power be given me of God, then I shall not only be willing to be bound, but to die for the sake of the Lord Jesus." Mr. Ley, his examiner, commended Love's gifts and graces at the conclusion of his examination.

Christopher Love was lecturer at St. Ann's, Aldergate for a period of three years. A sermon printed December 24, 1647 lists him as such. St. Ann's is about two hundred yards from St. Lawrence Jewry, where Love would minister from 1650-1651. St. Ann's is also next to the site of St. John Zachary, where at least three of Love's children were baptized. St. John Zachary was destroyed by the fire of 1666 and was never rebuilt, though a plaque marks the site on Gresham street in London where the church once stood.

The records in the City of London library at the Guildhall show a Mary Love, daughter of Christopher and Mary Love, being christened on March 5, 1646. Their first child lived only a few days, and was buried on March 13 of that same year.

A second daughter, whom they also named Mary,

was christened on July 27, 1647. She too lived a short life and was buried on May 14, 1650. Christopher Love, their first son, was christened on December 15, 1648. In a letter to his wife from prison, Love mentions two of his children whom he believed to be in heaven. These would undoubtedly be his two daughters. Christopher Love wrote of another child whom he referred to as Mall, but I have been unable to find any birth, christening, or death records of this child. A fifth child, James, was christened on September 22, 1651, having been born just thirteen days after Christopher Love was executed. The child lived less than seven months, and was buried on April 26, 1652.

Love later ministered at St. Lawrence Jewry in the Guildhall section of London. The church had existed on its site since 1136, but that building was destroyed in the great fire of 1666 (Christopher Wren redesigned the new church—as he did so many of the London churches destroyed by the fire that destroyed four-fifths of London in four days—and it re-opened for worship in 1677). St. Lawrence, for whom the church was named, was treasurer of the Church of Rome in 258 A.D. When Emperor Valerian ordered Lawrence to produce the treasures belonging to the Church, he gathered together the sick, the lame, and the poor and said, "Here are the treasures of Christ's Church." For this remark he was martyred by slow roasting on a grid-iron. The word "jewry" refers to the church being built on the western edge of the Jewish trading area. Edward I expelled the Jews, but the suffix was retained to distinguish it from other dedications to this saint at a time when there were one hundred twenty-six churches within a square mile of this one.

Christopher Love's name is not listed on the plaques in the narthex listing all the vicars and rectors of that church, but Love was a Presbyterian not an Anglican. He is always referred to as *minister* of St. Lawrence Jewry rather than rector or vicar. The parish minutes show that on March 21, 1649, Christopher Love was chosen over a man named Coles to be the minister by a show of hands of the church leaders. The terms of call were for him to be paid £150 per annum in quarterly payments, and to have the use of the vicar's house and all the utensils in it. For this, he was to preach twice every Sunday and on fast days, and to administer the sacraments monthly. The sum of £20 was also approved for repairs to the vicar's house.

The congregation must have been pleased with their new minister, for in 1650 they augmented his salary with £51 from the parish members, and in 1651 with another £126.

Christopher Love was also chosen as a member of the Assembly of Divines at Westminster. In the proceedings of the Assembly, however, he was largely inactive. In Daniel Neal's list of Divines, he is marked as one who seldom appeared.[2] Most likely Dr. William Twisse's admiration for him had much to do with his selection.

As a pastor he was prolific. While little of his material was published in his lifetime, after his death his sermons were printed by those Puritan ministers who were friends and admirers. The following list of his sermons and writings is from Benjamin Brook's *Lives of*

---

[2] Miss Dorix A. Nix, *Journal of Presbyterian Historical Society of England*, Vol. XII, No. 4, May 1967, 139.

the Puritans (published by Soli Deo Gloria), 3:138, and from a printout supplied by the Bodleian Library at Oxford of pre-1920's manuscripts in their collection at the Duke Humfrey's Library:

- The Debauched Cavalier, or The English Midianite, 1642 (with George Lawrence).
- England's Distemper, having division and error as its cause: wanting peace and truth for its cure, set forth in a sermon, 1645.
- Short and Plain Animadversions on some Passages in Mr. Dell's Sermon before the House of Commons, 1646.
- Answer to an Unlicensed Pamphlet, 1647.
- The Main points of Church-Government and Discipline; handled by way of question and answer, 1649.
- A Vindication of England's Distemper, 1651.
- Love's Case, 1651.
- Love's Trial, 1651.
- Love's Advocate, 1651.
- A Full Narration of the late Dangerous Design against the State, 1651.
- His Speech and Prayer upon the scaffold on Tower Hill, 1651.
- The Truth, and Growth, and Different Degrees of Grace, 1652.
- A Sermon at the Funeral of Mrs. B., 1652.
- Heaven's Glory, Hell's Terror, 1653.
- The Soul's Cordial: in two treatises: 1653.
  1. Teaching how to be eased of the guilt of sin.
  2. Discovering advantages by Christ's ascension.
- A Treatise of Election and Effectual Calling, 1653.

- Scripture Rules to be Observed in Buying and Selling, 1653.
- A Christian's Duty and Safety in Evil Times, delivered in several sermons by Christopher Love, 1653. The sermons included herein are:
  1. Christ's Prayer the Saint's Support, John 17:15.
  2. A Divine Balance to Weigh all Doctrines by, 1 Thessalonians 5:21.
  3. A Christian's Great Inquiry, Acts 16:30-31.
  4. A Description of True Blessedness, Luke 11:28.
- The True Doctrine of Mortification and Sincerity, in Opposition to Hypocrisy, 1654.
- Combat between the Flesh and Spirit, 1654.
- The Sum or Substance of Practical Divinity, 1654.
- The Christian's Directory, 1654.
- The Dejected Soul's Cure, 1657.
- The Ministry of Angels to the Heirs of Salvation, 1657.
- The Omnipresence of God, 1657.
- The Sinner's Legacy to His Posterity, 1657.
- The Penitent Pardoned, 1657.
- A Discourse of Christ's Ascension and Coming to Judgment, 1657.
- The Natural Man's Case Stated, 1658.
- The History of the Holy Bible, by question and answer, 1783.

These, and other works not listed but received in photocopy from the Folger Shakespeare Library in Washington, D.C., are to be included in *The Works of Christopher Love* currently in production by Soli Deo Gloria.

Love was truly a pastor. One can see from the titles

of his sermons that he aimed at making theology useful for his parishioners. There are twenty-seven sermons on the combat between the flesh and the spirit; seventeen sermons on the Christian's growing in grace, and that there are degrees of grace and growth in Christians; numerous sermons on dealing with sin and its guilt. While his works attest to his grasp of deep theological truths, the application reveals the pastor's heart of Christopher Love.

In the collection of books that once belonged to Jonathan Edwards, and now housed in the library at Princeton University in America, there is a copy of Love's work on hell, *Hell's Terror.* Comparing Edwards' sermons on hell and Love's sermons on hell, one can see that Edwards was impressed with the keen insights of Love into this ominous subject. There is also a reference to Christopher Love in John Gerstner's *Rational Biblical Theology of Jonathan Edwards,* in the footnotes at the end of volume three. When one remembers that Love's ministry was confined to a space of only about six years, the amount of material he produced is quite astounding.

Christopher Love was also a pastor to his family. His wife states in her memoirs of him that he was very strict not only in his observance of the Sabbath, but in his preparation for the Sabbath on Saturday evening. He was a lover of children, having told Mary that if he had been unable to secure ordination he would have been content to be a teacher of children all his life. His wife remembered him this way: "Now, after he had a family of his own, he made it a little nursery for God, resolving that whatever others did, yet that he and his house would serve the Lord, and that his family should be among the number of those that know God and call upon His name."

Christopher Love knew that the work of preaching was the main task to which a minister of the gospel was called. Mary wrote, "It is hard to say whether his studying or preaching did most waste his strength, for he never thought that he had time enough for his studies, and diversions from them was very troublesome to him. And this was a main inducement unto him as well as for his health to take a little house in the country that he might have more freedom for his studies than he could have in the city. He took more usually in the morning, before dinner, and in the evening until going to bed (which would have been very late, for of all times he liked that best for his studies)."

St. Mary Aldermanbury Church
(Where Christopher Love was ordained)

7

My Dear Friend

August 19, 1651

The loss which the church of God will sustain by your death is a very great trouble to me, and I doubt not but a far greater to others whose hearts God hath made more sensible to feel His hand. This stroke I am confident will be your happiness, but a great misery, a sad punishment, to many. When God hath a purpose to punish many at once, He useth to take this course. The extinguishing such a star (I do not flatter you, God knows) cannot but greatly afflict the whole world. I wish heartily God would grant me the favor to see you before your "wedding day," for I dare not call it a dying day. I hope I shall be in your thoughts when you are at the throne of Grace. Good sir, heap up as many prayers as you can for the poor church of God before you leave us; it shall be the best legacy you can bequeath. What you shall sow, some will live to reap, and you shall not be unrewarded. Jesus Christ had his thoughts on the Church even to His dying hour; good sir, imitate your Master.

I need not say anything to strengthen you against the fear of your approaching day; I doubt not but you have often overcome that fear through Jesus Christ. What you think is death is a journey; 'tis but the taking of a journey, and, though the way be deep, yet it's but short. God brings you the nearest way. A shorter cut never had any to rest.

I know you have been upon Mount Nebo, where you have seen Canaan, wither you are going. The mystical head cannot be cut off; you have finished your testimony and fear not to receive your recompense. Christ hath transformed this black messenger to you into an angel of light. How soon others may follow you is known only to God; if we stay longer, it is but to row in a stormy sea.

Moses was very willing to die. God said, "Go up and die," and he went up and died. Let not the care of your relations afflict you. "The earth is the Lord's and the fullness thereof. Leave your fatherless children, God will provide for them. Let your widow trust in God." Your dear yoke-fellow is a partaker of that same grace with you; how rich are they that are heirs to the promises? You can commend your spirit into God's hands, much more your wife and children. Remember that promise: "I will be thy God, and the God of thy seed." Sir, it is a richer portion than the mines of India. You were but a cistern to them; the fountain lives, and will live when you are dead. God can provide without you, you cannot without God.

Good sir, cheer up. I hear how full of joy you are, blessed be God; all these are but little drops to the ocean. I have written this to fill you up more and more. An ax and a fever are all one; you shall die without sickness. When you think of the present ignominy, look on the future glory. You shall be with God, Christ, angels, and the souls of just men made perfect, in a short time. What a happiness is it to have grace in perfection! To see God face to face, to be freed from the being of sin, temptations of devils, and the society of wicked men!

You have fought a good fight; you have finished your course; you have kept the faith, and you are going to receive your crown, a crown of glory that fadeth not away. You are now going to that place where the voice of the oppressor shall never be heard. You are going to your best, the best and safest you ever slept on. The steps of the scaffold will be a Jacob's ladder, upon which you shall ascend to your loving Father. The scaffold will be as Mount Nebo; the ax of the executioner will cut off the head of sin and put an end to all misery.

Be sure, sir, not only the angels of God but the God of the angels Himself will mightily strengthen you. If your death, and this kind of death, were not most for the glory of God and the benefit of the Church, I am confident, sire, God would have saved you from this hour.

I have written this not because you want advice, but to testify my love, my dear love, to you, and to give you a remembrance of me and mine before your departure hence. Good sir, accept it as my last farewell. Farewell, farewell, dear friend. God, that hath bound up your soul in the bundle of life, be your comfort, joy, hope, peace, confidence in life and death to all eternity. Yea, He will be your guide unto death. He will be a Husband and head to your dearest wife; He will be a tender Father to your little babes. This is the confidence, this shall be the prayer of, sir, your dear friend.

Ralph Robinson

St. Anne's Church
(Where Christopher Love was lecturer)

8

Love's Plot

Christopher Love seems to have always been politically active. As early as 1642, he co-wrote a brief tract comparing the Cavaliers of England with the Midianites of the Old Testament. The full title was "The Debauched Cavalier: or the English Midianite. Wherein are compared by way of parallel the carriage, or rather miscarriage of the Cavaliers in the present reign of our King Charles with the Midianites of old. Setting forth their diabolical, and hyper-diabolical blasphemies, execrations, rebellions, cruelties, rapes, and robberies."

Love, with co-author George Lawrence, laid down six characteristics of the Old Testament Midianites which, they felt, corresponded to the character of King Charles' Cavaliers.

1. They were full of rage and blasphemy.
2. They were men of cruelty and oppression.
3. They were rambling renegades.
4. They were a crafty and subtle generation.
5. They were unclean both in body and in spirit.
6. They were frequent in plotting combinations with the children of the East.[1]

---

[1] Christopher Love, *The Debauched Cavalier* (London: L.N. for Henry Overton, in Pope's Head Alley, 1642).

Before the death of Charles I, his commissioners proposed to the parliament that there be a treaty of peace at Uxbridge, commencing January 30, 1645 and continuing for twenty days. The propositions to be treated were religion, the militia, and Ireland, each of which were to be debated for three days successively until the twenty days had passed

The treaty was preceded by a day of fasting and prayer on both sides for a blessing, but this was interrupted the very first day by a sermon preached in the church at Uxbridge by Christopher Love, who was at that time the preacher to the garrison at Windsor Castle. The sermon was entitled "England's Distemper, having Division and Error as its Cause: Wanting peace and Truth for its Cure." Love stated in the vindication of his sermon that he would prefer a just war to a wicked peace: "By a just war we have only man for our enemy, but God our real friend; by a wicked peace we shall have God our real enemy and men but our seeming friends." In this sermon Love denounced the king's commissioners saying that they were "not lovers of peace, but still carry blood and revenge in their hearts against us." He also stated that "we can as soon make fire and water to agree, yea, reconcile heaven and hell, as their spirits and ours. Either they must grow better or we must grow worse before we can agree."

Love referred in this sermon to "the blood-thirsty rebels of Ireland, the idolatrous papists of England, the pompous prelates, the rest of the corrupt clergy, and the profaner sort among the nations who join hand in hand together." He had sufficiently offended nearly everyone.

Having greatly offended the royalists, Love was

called to London to give an account of this affair. His explanation was that he had been unexpectedly called upon to give a sermon, which was the same one he had given just a day before.

For his invectives, Love was confined to his house during the treaty and then discharged. He had been no less optimistic, however, than the king himself, who, in a letter to the queen dated January 22, 1645, said of the stances of the opposing groups, "I cannot alter mine, nor will they ever theirs, till they be out of hope to prevail with force. . . ."

King Charles I was beheaded by Parliament for crimes of treason against his own people. Oliver Cromwell, a Presbyterian who turned Independent, became Lord Protector of the Commonwealth; but there were many who still believed that God has appointed kings and man could not dethrone them. Christopher Love was among those, as would be expected of a staunch Presbyterian. While Cromwell ruled England, the Scots courted Charles I's son, Charles II, and sought to re-establish him as ruler of all the British Isles. If that meant building an army to take England back, so be it.

The coronation of King Charles II by the Scots was held on New Year's Day in 1651. On that occasion, Charles took the following oath:

> I Charles, king of Great Britain, France, and Ireland, do assure and declare by my solemn oath, in the presence of Almighty God, the searcher of all hearts, my allowance and approbation of the national covenant, and of the solemn league and covenant; and faithfully oblige myself to prosecute the ends thereof in my station and

> calling; and that I myself and successors shall consent and agree to all the acts of parliament enjoining the national covenant, and the solemn league and covenant, and fully establish Presbyterian government, the directory of worship, confession of faith, and catechisms, in the kingdom of Scotland, as they are approved by the general assembly of this kirk, and parliament of this kingdom; and that I will give my royal word and assent to all acts of parliament passed, or to be passed, enjoining the same in my other dominions; and that I shall observe these in my own practice and family, and shall never make opposition to any of these, or endeavour any change thereof.

This oath was annexed to the covenant itself, drawn up on a roll of parchment, and subscribed by him in the presence of the nobility and gentry. He also signed a declaration in which he acknowledged the sin of his father in marrying into an idolatrous family, and that the blood shed in the recent war lay at his father's door. He expressed a deep sense of his own poor education against the cause of God, of which he was now sensible. He confessed all the former parts of his life to have been a course of enmity to the Word of God. He acknowledged his own sins and the sins of his father's house. He stated that he would count those to be his enemies who opposed the covenants, both which he had taken without any sinister intention of attaining his own ends. He declared his detestation and abhorrence of all popery, superstition, idolatry, and prelacy, and resolved not to tolerate them in any part of his dominions. He acknowledged his great sin in making peace with the Irish rebels and allowing them the liberty of their religion, which he made void, resolving for the future to choose affliction rather than sin. He promised not to employ anyone in the future until they had taken the covenant.

The king took the covenant three times with a tremendous oath, "By the Eternal and Almighty God, who liveth and reigneth forever, I will observe and keep all that is contained therein."

With a king like this, the Scots could not but be opposed to Cromwell and his forces. With Samuel Rutherford, they believed in "the divine right of kings," particularly a king who was for Presbyterianism and opposed to anything that reeked of popery. Additionally, this king was from Scotland. And not only this, but such a king must have an army if he is to reclaim his rightful place on the throne of all his subjects.

In 1651, while the Scots were raising forces for the King's service, private correspondence was carried on with a group of English Presbyterians. Letters were written and messengers sent from London to the king and queen-mother in France to hasten an accommodation with the Scots, assuring them that the English Presbyterians would side with the King at the first opportunity. Considerable sums of money were collected privately to forward an expedition into England, but the vigilance of the commonwealth discovered and defeated their designs.

Love and others had stated their opposition to the death of Charles I at the hands of Cromwell. A number of gentlemen and ministers attempted to raise money by private contribution to finance Charles II's return. There were several disbanded officers who had served parliament in the wars involved. The ministers implicated were Dr. Roger Drake, Thomas Case, Thomas Watson, Richard Heyrick, William Jenkyn, Arthur Jackson, Ralph Robinson, Thomas Cawton, Mr. Nalson, Matthew Haviland, William Blackmore, and Christopher Love.

The whole affair came to be known as "Love's Plot," although Love appears to have been one of the lesser players. Thomas Coke, the son of Charles I's secretary of state, was captured in London. Offered his life in exchange for information, Coke revealed that well-known people in nearly every county were involved, including the popular Presbyterian ministers previously listed.[1]

This was no insignificant group of political malcontents. Thomas Case was a member of the Westminster Assembly. He pastored St. Mary Magdalene Church in Milk-street, London, just yards from St. Lawrence Jewry. He initiated the Morning Exercises while ministering at St. Giles, Cripplegate and often preached before Parliament. For his part in Love's Plot, he spent six months in the Tower of London.[2] Soli Deo Gloria has published a volume of his selected works.

Thomas Watson was (and continues to be) one of the most popular Puritans. He ministered at St. Stephen's in the ward of Walbrook. After his arrest in 1651, he was imprisoned for several months. He petitioned for mercy and, on June 30, 1652, was reinstated as vicar of St. Stephen's. Watson was one of

---

1 Robert S. Paul, *The Lord Protector*, (London: Lutterworth Press, 1955), 236.
2 Brook, 3:153.

the thousands of ministers ejected for non-conformity in 1662. He preached privately thereafter in London and retired in 1686 to Essex where he died in July and was buried in Barnston. Soli Deo Gloria has reprinted many of Watson's scarcest works.

William Jenkyn is best known for his commentary on Jude. In 1641, he was minister of Christ-Church and lecturer at St. Anne's, Blackfriars. He continued there until the death of William Gouge, at which point he assumed the pastorate. He, too, spent six months in the Tower for his part in Love's Plot.

Dr. Roger Drake, who has several letters to Love printed in this book, was one of the commissioners to the Savoy Conference. Richard Baxter and Samuel Annesly, grandfather of John Wesley, both spoke highly of his character and ministry.

Ralph Robinson was a highly-esteemed preacher whose book *Christ All in All* is still in great demand (it also has been reprinted by Soli Deo Gloria). Thomas Cawton, minister of St. Bartholomew's behind the Royal Exchange, was forced to escape to Holland. Arthur Jackson was a noted Bible commentator. While the others are lesser known today, their association with men of such renown speaks highly of their character.

All of these men were charged with corresponding with Charles Stuart and the prince's mother (Henrietta Maria) between October 1649 and June 1651. A Colonel Titus had been commissioned by certain Presbyterians to carry several letters to the queen-mother in France. The queen's replies were conveyed by a

Colonel Ashworth, and were read in Love's house.[3]

Other meetings were held at the houses of Major Adams, Colonel Barton, and Christopher Love. The king desired them to send commissioners to moderate the Scots' demands, promising to reward them all when God restored him to his throne. On December 18, 1650, Mary Love obtained a pass to travel to Amsterdam, which the Dictionary of National Biography asserts was in connection with these negotiations.

Christopher Love was arrested on May 2, 1651. Two priors and three soldiers came to take him at four o'clock in the morning. Mary Love remembers that they would not even allow her husband to get dressed, and that they overturned the house looking for papers. She recalled, "Such was their severity that they would not suffer him to pray in private nor in his family nor take his leave of his wife, but at a distance, calling to her desiring her not to be troubled, telling her that this was no strange thing to him."

Love was committed to the Tower of London on a charge of high treason and was kept as a "close prisoner" for a few weeks. On May 10, 1651, the State Papers of England record that Elizabeth Jenkyn, Ann Case, Mary Love, and Susan Drake were to be permitted to come and abide with their husbands who were now prisoners in the Tower. Their close imprisonment would normally have excluded visitors. The records of May 12 show that these wives were to be given liberty to visit their husbands, provided they did not speak to them unless they were in the presence and hearing of the Lieutenant of the Tower.

---

[3] *Dictionary of National Biography,* 12:156.

Mary Love remembered her husband writing two sermons a week, as if he were going to preach them, but soon the guards took away his pen and paper which prevented him from penning his prison experience. Yet Love told her that he never enjoyed more of God than when he was in close confinement. He told friends that his comfort was that though they could shut him up from his relations, they could not imprison him from his God.

All the other ministers petitioned parliament for mercy and promised submission to the government in the future. Only Christopher Love, among the ministers, was executed.

St. Lawrence Jewry
(Where Christopher Love ministered)

9

My Dear, Dear Heart

Thou art very near to my soul. The Lord Jesus Christ smile with the pleasantest face upon thee, that ever He did upon any sufferer. I here send thee a book that I have been much relieved in by my imprisonment. What are ten thousand deaths where Christ is apprehended by faith! These considerations, where the leaf is turned down, page 335, do sweetly support faith. I am afraid almost to send these thoughts for fear many notions may disturb thee. I judge these more profitable than speculative discourses of death. The great God, that hangs the earth upon nothing but His Word, bear up thy soul on His promises. Oh sweet, most sure, sure, sure (oh, remember, "sure"!) promises; as stable as the very essence of God, for the performances whereof God hath pawned His being. "As I live. . . ."

My heart, I love thee, I kiss thee, I weep upon thee, I rejoice for thee. I shall see thee in glory. The Lord Jesus strengthen thee. He will.

Blame me not of this backwardness to cast in this mite. I was hardly persuaded of the fitness thereof. Your greater danger is in the plenty of these tokens, considering your own store. Though your appetite be never so good, it's impossible you should concoct all the food dished up in books, friend's papers, and your own meditations by and for you. I shall desire to make up my paper defects by fervent prayer; and, oh, that I could pray so this once as if I were not to do it a second time.

My only counsel must be that which I know hath been your only care and will be your only comfort, namely, that you sleep in Jesus. Thou shalt not sleep (though that were much) in the lap, bosom, and arms of Jesus; but in this sleep He looks upon thee as a piece of Himself, even as a member, a dear limb. In dying thou shalt not die. They who are fallen asleep in Jesus perish not. Christ, the first fruits (a most sweet resemblance), the happy hansell of the grave, the first born from the dead, the Head of the body, did rise from the dead as such, and not as a private person. So that our resurrection is, even now, in its cause.

The union between Christ and thee (and this union is not only between Christ and thy soul, but thy body also; and, therefore, He is the first fruits of the dead) cannot be broken off by death. Christ should rebel against the will of His Father (which were blasphemy to think) if He should lose anything which His Father hath given Him; as He should, were it not to be raised up at the last day. Christ is the very resurrection, and he that believeth in Him, though dead, yet shall live.

Oh, how hath Christ perfumed the grave and beautified the grisly face of death! Death is now a privilege, our best friend next to Christ, and the truth is, all our moans and sorrows in this life are for want of that which we so much fear: death; as the child that cries for want of sleep and yet cannot endure to undress and go to bed.

My dear heart! Thou hast better clothes to put on in the morning of the resurrections. "This mortal shall put on immortality." Thy garment of grace hath had many spots, perhaps; this day thou shalt take thy leave of mourning for them, and, therefore, the Lord help thee to mourn more holily and meltingly than ever; but the garment of glory shall not have one. Lord, is there a condition wherein I shall never sin more, wherein I shall have as much grace as I can hold, and wish, and will desire, wherein I shall no more wash the feet of Jesus Christ, and now and then be suffered to give them a kiss, but shall lie in His blessed bosom and be clasped in His glorious arms to eternity! This is thy approaching happiness, and every comfort, by how much the nearer, is the sweeter. Now is thy salvation nearer than when thou first believed.

Oh, dear heart! Now for a strong faith! Oh, wrestle mightily with the great God for strength to overcome Him; cling about the promises, precious promises, not only for their fullness but infallibility. Adventure thy soul upon them. The faithfulness of God is a foundation which bears the heaviest structure and the greatest load of sin and expectation. Jesus Christ calls, beseeches, commands, threatens, and all to make thee believe. The Lord increase thy faith; thou art to go through a very great work, but Christ hath labored, and thou art but to enter into His labors. Death is but a nominal enemy when Christ hath disarmed it! There is more terror in the pomp of it (as Seneca said), the scaffold, the ax, spectators, reports, than in the thing itself. Oh, how may a Christian insult over it! Oh, death, where is thy sting! Christ hath spoiled principalities and powers, disarmed, disrobed them. His death is the death of death; all its stings are left in His side. Say not, therefore (dear heart), who shall roll away the stone from the mouth of the sepulcher? When thou comest hither, thou shalt find it rolled away to thy hand. Its difficulties and distresses are taken away in Christ.

To this dear Lord Jesus I commit thee, who, in His due time, will wipe away all tears from the eyes and sin from the souls of His poor servants, and, out of all our storms, bring us to that haven where we would be. I know not where to break off, and yet not where to leave thee so well as there.

Thine in the bowels of this Saviour,

William Jenkyn

Thomas Watson
(Rector of St. Stephen's Walbrook, London;
arrested in Love's plot and imprisoned for six months)

10

Love on Trial

Christopher Love was brought before a new high court of justice erected for this purpose, as was the custom of these times for state criminals. On June 20, the court being set and called over, the Lieutenant of the Tower was commanded to bring forth his prisoner, and Love was brought to the bar.

After the reading of various acts of Parliament concerning treason, Attorney General Edmond Prideaux spoke, "My Lord, you have heard several acts of Parliament read and the offenses therein mentioned. My Lord, I have here a charge against Mr. Love, the prisoner at the bar, and I humbly desire that it may be read likewise; and you may please to take his reply to it whether by confession or otherwise."

At that point, the clerk was commanded to read the charge. "A charge of high treason, and other high crimes and offenses, exhibited to the high court of justice by Edmond Prideaux, Attorney General for the Commonwealth of England, for and on the behalf of the keepers of the Liberties of England, by authority of Parliament, against Christopher Love, late of London Clerk, by him preferred and commenced against the said Christopher Love. That is to say that the said Christopher Love, as a false traitor and enemy of this Commonwealth and free state of England, and out of a traitorous and wicked design to stir up a new and bloody war, and to raise insurrections, seditions, and rebellions within this nation, did in several days and times, that is to say, in the years of our Lord, 1648, 1649, 1650, 1651, at London, and at divers other places within this Commonwealth of England, and elsewhere (together with William Drake, late of London Mercer, Henry Jermin, late of London Esquire, Henry Piercy, late of London Esquire, John Gibbons, late of London Gentleman, Edward Massey, late of London Esquire, Richard Graves, late of London Esquire, Sylas Titus, late of London Gentleman, James Bunce, late of London Alderman, and other accomplices yet unknown traitorously and maliciously combine, confederate, and complot, contrive and endeavor to stir up and raise up forces against the present government of this nation, since the same hath been settled in a Commonwealth and free state without a King and House of Lords, and for the subversion and alteration of the same."

Further, the charges stated that these men "had declared and published Charles Stuart, eldest son of the late king, to be king of England, without consent of parliament; that they had aided the Scots to invade this commonwealth; that the said Christopher Love, at divers times between the 29th of March 1650 and the first of June 1651, at London and other places, had traitorously and maliciously maintained correspondence and intelligence by letters and messages with Charles Stuart, son of the late king, and with the queen his mother, and with sundry of his council; that he did likewise hold correspondence with divers of the Scots nation, and had assisted them with money, arms, and other supplies, in the present war, as well as Colonel Titus and others of the English nation, in confederacy with them, to the hazard of the public peace, and in breach of the laws of this land."

The complete charge is quite lengthy, but very thorough in its indictment. Love was said to be "a traitor and public enemy to this Commonwealth and free state of England."

To Love himself the clerk said, "Christopher Love, you stand charged on the behalf of the Keepers of the Liberties of England, by authority of Parliament, of high treason and other high crimes and offenses against the Parliament and people of England; this high court therefore requires you to give a positive and direct answer whether you are guilty or not guilty of the crimes and treasons laid to your charge."

At this point, Love began to speak in a manner that would not endear him to the high court. Several times he had to be interrupted to make his point with more brevity. He began to make emotional appeals, "I do earnestly beg the prayers of them that have an interest in God, that He would carry me through this whole trial with such gravity, godliness, and meekness of wisdom as becomes a professor and preacher of the gospel, and that He would keep me in this hour of temptation rather from sin than from suffering. Sir, I am this day made a spectacle unto God, angels, and men, singled out from among my brethren to be the object of some men's indignation and insultation. By my appearing in this place, I am made a grief to many that are godly, and a laughing stock to the wicked."

At this point he was interrupted by the court, "Mr. Love, how long a time do you intend to take up?"

Though Love promised to be brief, he stated that a certain John Lilburn had been allowed to speak for two hours before pleading guilty or not guilty. Evidently, Lilburn had come to visit Love in the Tower and had advised him on some legal matters. To this the court replied that Lilburn's case was no precedent in this one. Again Love was asked to make his plea of guilty or not. Again he asked permission to speak, citing his position as a minister of the gospel.

Frustrated, the Attorney General said that "if he had applied himself to God as he might have done, he need not have been brought thither." Prideaux also pointed out that the laws of England stated that one was not to speak out until he had pleaded guilty or not. Immediately there was an impasse. The court would not allow him to speak until he had pleaded; Love refused to plead until he had been allowed to speak.

The court cited legal standards and Love, though he pleaded ignorance in legal matters, was ready with other court rulings that seemed to contradict the course they were taking with him, appealing to Judge Cook's Institutes. He also questioned the legality of the trial since the Act of 1650, by which he was being charged, did not specify Scotland. At this point, the Attorney General asked if he was admitting that he had received or sent letters to Scotland. Love admitted nothing of the kind, stating, "I have so much of a Christian in me that I will deny nothing that is proved to be true, and so much of an Englishman that I will admit nothing that is seemingly criminal."

Love appealed to Christ Himself as a model. As the members of the high court grew more impatient with his refusal to plead, Love cited that Christ did not answer a word before His judicatory. Further, Love questioned how he could be charged with violating the act of Parliament of 1650 when his charges included supposed crimes committed in 1648 and 1649. Surely the high court realized that crimes could not be made retroactive!

Love also requested counsel before making his plea. The court demanded his plea before granting counsel, and another impasse had been reached. Soon after, Love declared that he believed the trial to be illegal and that, if he were to plead, it would be the same as admitting the legality of the trial.

Finally, the Lord President of the court threatened Love, ". . .now plead or you shall have judgment."

At last Love pleaded, "Not guilty," at which point the high court began to call its witnesses, each of whom was challenged by Love as either having been paid to lie against him or having been promised death if they did not testify against him. Several members of the court stated that this behavior on Love's part made him appear guilty, for an innocent man would not have carried on in such a manner. Love replied that he was fighting for his life.

During the proceedings, Love emphatically denied that he had ever sent or received any letters to or from Scotland, that he had ever raised or lent any money for Scotland, and that he had never carried on any correspondence with anyone in Scotland since the time the wars began.

On the second day of deliberations, John Jacquel, who would later write Love a letter of repentance (see chapter 19 of this book), implicated the other Puritan ministers, Thomas Watson, Nalton, Jenkyn, Case,

Cawton, Robinson, Drake, and others.

A later witness, Arthur Jackson, refused to swear testimony against Love, because he looked on him to be "a man very precious in God's sight." He said that he would have a hell in his conscience to his dying day if he should speak anything that would be prejudicial to Christopher Love's life. The court reminded him of his obligation to the public and that the very safety of all government depended upon it, but he refused to be sworn. For this, he was accused of being "worse than a Jesuit." The court sent him to be imprisoned indefinitely, and fined him £500.[4]

On the third day, Love made his defense. He did not call any witnesses, but attempted to show how the witnesses called by the high court had contradicted themselves in many places and were, therefore, without credibility. He stated that none of them had shown that he had written any letters contrary to law, that he had only been present where some letters had been read, and that, surely, it could not be a crime to be present where letters are read! He pointed out that one witness had mentioned a sum of £400, whereas other witnesses had said £200 or £300. One witness said this, but it was contradicted by the next witness. And Love, therefore, questioned how anything could have been proven against him when the testimony of the witnesses was so contradictory. Love pointed out that Jacquel's testimony was inadmissible since he had refused to take the oath before testifying.

He did admit that "I was present at the reading of letters. . . . And this I say, that I was ignorant of the

---

4 Brook, 3:582.

danger that now I see I am in." Love spoke, according to the Lord President, for nearly two hours in his own defense. At that point, the court adjourned for the day.

Love requested the celebrated Matthew Hale to be his counsel at that point, a request which was granted. But after all Hale's advocating, Love was pronounced a traitor after five days of trial and sentenced on the sixth day, July 5, 1651, as follows: "Whereas Christopher Love, the prisoner at the bar, stands charged (on behalf of the Keepers of the Liberties of England) of high treason, and other high crimes and offenses, for all which treasons and traitorous and wicked practices of him, the said Christopher Love, this court doth adjudge him to suffer the pains of death by having his head severed from his body."

"My Lord, I would speak a word," said Love.

"You cannot be heard now, Mr. Love," said the Lord President of the high court of justice.

"But a word, my Lord, and 'tis this, in the words of the Apostle. 'I have received the sentence of death in myself, that I should not trust in myself, but in God which raiseth the dead.' And my Lord, though you have condemned me, yet this I can say, that neither God nor my own conscience doth condemn me."

At that point, Love withdrew and the Lieutenant of the Tower took him into custody.

On Friday night, the 4th of July, 1651, twenty-four men voted to pass sentence on Christopher Love for his execution. Originally, his execution was to take place on July 16. He was reprieved for a month, and then again for a week while petitions were read before Parliament for his life, and letters were sent to Cromwell to see if he would stay the sentence. Love himself wrote four petitions to Parliament dated July 9, July 11, July 15, and August 14. In the very first petition he acknowledged that "he hath offended against the Acts of this Commonwealth, and thereby is fallen under your sore displeasure, of which he is very deeply sensible and sorrowful also." In his second petition, he promised "neither to plot, contrive or design anything to the hurt of this present government." He also asked to be banished to "some strange land, where he may sit alone, lamenting his sad and deplorable condition," rather than to be executed.[5]

The affairs of the Commonwealth, however, were at a crisis, and Charles II had entered England at the head of 16,000 Scots. It was therefore thought necessary to strike some terror into the Presbyterian party by making an example of one of their favorite clergymen.[6]

Two historians, Kennet and Echard, say that Cromwell sent a letter of reprieve and, if he would guarantee good behavior in the future, agreed to pardon Love. The courier, however, was stopped by some cavaliers who belonged to the late king's army. Searching the courier's packet, they found the letter of reprieve and tore it up, still angry over Love's sermon at Uxbridge.

When no letter arrived from Cromwell, Parliament had no choice but to read this as Cromwell's refusal to grant the petitions. Execution was set for August 22, 1651, the very day the king entered Worcester at the

---

[5] *Mr. Loves' Case.* (London: Printed for R.W. and Peter Cole, 1651).
[6] Daniel Neal, *History of the Puritans,* (London: Thomas Tegg, 1837) 2:585.

head of his Scottish army.

Mary Love wrote that "he was continually. . . laboring after further manifestation of the love of God in his vocation, and wherein he gave all diligence in making his calling and election sure, which God kept to the last for him, this refreshing cordial reserved for a fainting time, for he said himself that he did never know what it was to have full assurance of faith till he had received that sentence of death at the bar, and at that very minute he said to his wife that 'God came in with such ravishing manifestations of love upon my soul that I feared it was to discovered in my countenance and may be so interpreted if I smiled in a contemptuous way upon my judges.' "

The names of those who, on Friday night, the 4th of July, passed sentence on Christopher Love for his execution are:

Lord President Keeble	Matthew Shepheard
Sir John Thorowgood	John Harrison
Mr. Shuite	Col. Roe
Col. Ralph Harrison	Mr. Manley
Col. Whetham	Mr. Wyburn
Josias Barners	Mr. Steel
Alderman Estwick	Mr. Hurst
Cornelius Cook	Mr. Ayers
Alderman Hayes	Mr. Cooper
Mr. Sadler	Mr. Martin
Mr. Graves	Mr. Warcupp
Mr. Moyer	Sheriff Tichburn

Matthew Hale
(Christopher Love's attorney before the High Court)

11

Heavenly Saint

Thou art now awakened out of thy last natural rest to go to thy eternal rest. The night is past, thou shalt never know night any more, but God shall give thee light and thou shalt reign forever and ever, Revelation 22:3-5. Thou art now going where thou shalt be, in a true sense, above ordinances and above Scripture, 2 Corinthians 13:12-13; where God in Christ shall be thy all in all. Thy prison shall be turned into a palace, and thy filthy garments shall be taken away, and thou shalt be clothed with long white robes, and in the moment when thy body and head shall be severed thou shalt be united to Christ thy Head. In Him thou shalt be crowned, and with Him thou shalt reign to eternity.

It is finished, John 17:1, 4, 5, 6, 11, 13, 24. Let me see that face once more which I shall see no more till the last day. Send up one sight before thee for thy following brother and companion in tribulation, and in the kingdom and patience of Jesus Christ.

Dear soul, thou art now going to heaven. To quicken thy desires, put it into these notions that are most suitable to thy condition.

To the weary it is rest, Isaiah 57:2, Revelation 14:13.

To the banished it is home, 2 Corinthians 5:6.

To the reproached it is glory, Romans 5:2.

To the molested and captived with corruption it is

the glorious liberty of the sons of God, Romans 8:21.

To the resister to blood it is conquest, Romans 8:37.

To the vexed with sin and sorrow it is the extinction of both.

To the hungry soul it is the hidden manna, Revelation 22:17.

To the thirsty it is rivers of pleasure, water of life, fountain of life, Revelation 22:17, Psalm 36:8-9.

To the grieved soul it is fullness of joy, and to the sorrowful heart it is pleasures forevermore, Psalm 16:8.

In a word, to them that have lain upon the dunghill here and kept their integrity it is a throne upon which they shall sit and reign with Christ forever and ever, Revelation 3:31 and 22:5.

Dear heart, cheer up. A sharp breakfast, but a blessed supper, the supper of the Lamb. The Bridegroom saith, "Lo, I come quickly." Let thy rejoiced soul echo back again, "Even so, come Lord Jesus."

There is but a little time for prayer left; in that, remember me, and then everlasting hallelujahs will be thy work and rest. Live forever with thy God.

I shall accompany thee with my prayers, though I cannot with my person.

Roger Drake

Thomas Case
(Minister of St. Mary Magdalene, London,
and arrested in Love's Plot)

12

A Plea for Love

[After the sentence of death was given to her husband, Mary Love petitioned Parliament four times regarding her husband. The first petition asked for a pardon; she cited friends and admirers who would guarantee that her husband would live a peaceable life from there on. In the second petition she asked for banishment instead of death. Her third petition specifically asked that he be banished to New England so that he might be used of God in the conversion of the Indians. Lastly, in desperation, she offered to give her life on the scaffold in place of her husband's, though she was at least eight months pregnant at the time. The four petitions follow:]

To the Supreme Authority, the Parliament of the Commonwealth of England,

The humble petition of Mary, the distressed wife of Christopher Love, showeth that whereas the high court of justice hath lately sentenced to death her dear and tender husband, in whose life the life of your petitioner is bound up, in the execution of which sentence your poor handmaid should become an unhappy widow and the miserable mother of two young fatherless children. And she being so near to her appointed hour, having sorrow upon sorrow, be forced, through unexpressable grief, to bow down in travail and give up the ghost; and so with one blow there be destroyed both father and mother and babe in one day.

Yet her spirit is somewhat revived with the thought that there is hope in Israel concerning this thing when she considers that her humble petition is this day presented before so many professing godliness, who have tasted abundantly how gracious the Lord is, and who through mercy are called of God to inherit a blessing, and to be a blessing to the afflicted in the midst of the land.

Therefore, your distressed handmaid, throwing herself in all humility at your feet, beseecheth you by the womb that bare you and the breasts that gave you suck, in the bowels of the Lord Jesus Christ, mercifully to interpose that this fatal blow may be prevented, which act of compassion in you will be to your poor handmaid as resurrection from the dead; and not only all the tender-hearted mothers in England, but even the babe yet unborn shall rise up and call you blessed. And this will be to you a glory and crown of rejoicing in the sight of the nation, when the blessing of them that are ready to perish shall come upon you. And your poor handmaid humbly conceives that your mercy herein will be no danger to the state, for your poor petitioner's friends are willing to give all sufficient security that her husband shall live peaceably and quietly for the time to come, and never act anything to the prejudice of this Commonwealth and present government. Now the God of heaven bow your hearts to show mercy, and your petitioner shall pray, etc.

Mary Love

To the Supreme Authority, the Parliament of the Commonwealth of England,

The humble petition of Mary, the wife of Christopher Love, condemned to die, showeth that whereas your distressed handmaid hath in all humility in the exceeding great bitterness of her spirit, poured out her very soul to this honorable house for the life of her condemned husband: which petition was mercifully received and read in Parliament (as your petitioner is informed).

For which high favor she desireth to bless God and be thankful to your Honors. And although she hath great cause to be very sensible of your high displeasure against her husband, for which she is heartily sorry, nevertheless she, hoping that your bowels yearn towards her in this her sad condition, ventures once more to make her humble supplication and doth pray that, if your poor petitioner's husband hath provoked you so far as to render him utterly incapable of your full pardon, yet you would graciously be pleased to let your handmaid find so much favor in your eyes that you will say of your petitioner's dear husband as Solomon said of Abiarthar, "though thou art worthy of death, we will not at this time put thee to death." Oh, pardon your perplexed handmaid, if she again beseech you by the wombs that bare you and the breasts that gave you suck, in the bowels of the Lord Jesus Christ, reprieve him for a time, till she may recover her strength, before he depart hence and be seen no more; lest at one terrible stroke in his execution, the lives of him, her, and the tender babe in her womb be cut off, and two poor innocent orphans be left behind to begin and end their days in misery. And though he may not be thought worthy to breathe English air (which God forbid), yet give him, oh, give him leave to sigh out his sorrows under your displeasure in the utmost parts of the earth, wheresoever you shall think fit to banish him. Which, although it be a very great punishment in itself, yet your handmaid and her dying husband shall acknowledge even this to be a great mercy, and shall thankfully receive it at your hands, and shall pray, etc.

Mary Love

To the Supreme Authority, the Parliament of the Commonwealth of England

The humble petition of Mary, the distressed wife of Christopher Love, humbly showeth that your sad and sorrowful petitioner, in the multitude of her fears wherewith her spirit is overwhelmed within her, after sundry applications and grievous disappointments, more bitter than death, cannot cease to follow your Honors with strong cries and supplications, as the importunate Canaanitish woman did the Lord Christ. And O that now at last you would suffer yourselves to be entreated and let your bowels yearn within you that so root and branch may not be cut off in one day! The great God hears the cries of ravens. O that God would open your hearts to hear the cries and heart-breaking groans of the mother with the tender babes that cannot keep silence whilst there is any hope!

Your desolate handmaid waiteth with all humility and earnest expectation (at your doors), beseeching you not to forget to show mercy to your poor petitioner and her tender babes. O make not your handmaid a widow, and her children fatherless! But be graciously pleased to prevent this dreadful blow, which your petitioner trembleth to think upon, and earnestly beseeches you to change the sentence of death into a sentence of banishment; and whilst you are propogating the gospel in New England, let her dying husband, as a prophet from the dead, be sent to endeavor the conversion of the poor Indians, that so many souls may bless God in your behalf; and she shall receive it from your hands as a signal favor. And your petitioner shall pray, etc.

Mary Love

To the Supreme Authority, the Parliament of the Commonwealth of England,

The humble petition of Mary, the wife of Christopher Love, showeth that your poor petitioner hath great cause to say "Blessed be God," and blessed be you for your merciful vote of the 15th of July (a day never to be forgotten) in adding a month to the life of her dear husband, which hath opened a door of hope to her in the midst of the valley of Achor, and made her glad, though she be a woman of sorrowful spirit. Yet your distressed handmaid is overwhelmed with grief and anguish of soul, and cannot be comforted when she remembers the doleful day, the 15th of August, so near approaching; her heart doth almost die within her, and she is as one giving up the ghost before she is delivered of the fruit of her womb.

Wherefore, your greatly distressed handmaid doth again pour out her soul with renewed and importunate requests, beseeching your Honors to commiserate her deplorable condition by putting on bowels of pity and compassion towards her dear condemned husband, that she may not grapple with the intolerable pains of travel and the insupportable thoughts of her husband's death in one day. Oh, that the life of your handmaid and her babe might be ransom for the life of her condemned husband; she had rather choose out of love to die for him than for sorrow of heart to die with him! Now the good Lord incline your hearts to give him his life for a prey, wheresoever it shall please your Honors to cast him, and your petitioner shall ever pray, etc.

Mary Love

Mary Love was not alone in pleading for the life of Christopher. Various ministers in and about the city of London signed a petition asking for a pardon. Obadiah Sedgwick, another member of the Westminster Assembly of Divines, and an influential preacher in London, presented this petition, which had fifty-four signatures on it,[1] beseeching Parliament "earnestly, and in the bowels of Jesus Christ, who when we were sinners died for us, if not totally to spare the life of our dear brother, that yet you would say of him as Solomon of Abiathar, that at this time he should not be put to death."[2]

After Mary had one of her petitions rejected, Christopher said to her, "Well, my dear, didst thou not promise me this morning that thou wouldest endeavor to be satisfied, and submit unto the will of God, whatever this effect of my petition should be this day?"

He told her, "After thou went from me this morning, I took my Bible in my hand and begged of God that when I opened the book He would by the first place that I should cast my eyes upon declare unto me His mind concerning me whether for life or death. The first place I cast mine eyes upon was in the 116 Psalm, 15 and 16 verses: 'Glorious in the sight of God is the death of His saints.' "

Parliament granted a one month reprieve to Love, waiting to hear from Cromwell. On August 16, a petition from Love himself and a narrative of the entire affair were read before Parliament. Also read was "the Humble Petition of divers well-affected citizens of the city of London" and "the Humble Petition and acknowledgment of divers ministers of the Word, in the county of Worcester." But when it came to whether or not Parliament would grant a stay of execution, they voted negatively 27-16. Christopher Love was to die.

---

[1] Rev. James Anderson, *Memorable Women of the Puritan Times*, (London: Blackie and Son, 1862), 1:343.

[2] Whitelocke, *Memorials*, 471, quoted in Anderson.

William Jenkyn
(Minister of Christ-Church, Blackfriars,
London, and arrested in Love's Plot)

13

My Heavenly Dear

August 21, 1651

I call thee so because God hath put heaven into thee before He hath taken thee to heaven. Thou now beholdest God, Christ and glory, as in a glass; but tomorrow, heaven's gates will be opened and thou shalt be in the full enjoyment of all those glories which eye hath not seen, nor ear heard, neither can the heart of man understand. God hath now swallowed up thy heart in the thoughts of heaven, but ere long thou shalt be swallowed up in the enjoyment of heaven. And no marvel there should be such quietness and calmness in thy spirit while thou art sailing in this tempestuous sea, because thou perceivest by the eye of faith a haven of rest where thou shalt be richly laden with all the glories of heaven. O lift up thy heart with joy when thou layest thy dear head on the block in the thought of this: that thou are laying thy head to rest in thy Father's bosom which, when thou dost awake, shall be crowned not with an earthly fading crown but with a heavenly eternal crown of glory.

And be not discouraged when thou shalt see a guard of soldiers triumphing with their trumpets about thee, but lift up thy head and thou shalt behold God with a guard of His holy angels, triumphing to receive thee to glory. Be not dismayed at the scoffs and reproaches that thou mayest meet with in thy short way to heaven, for be assured that God will not only glorify thy body and soul in heaven but He will also make the memory of thee to be glorious on earth!

O let not one troubled thought for thy wife and babes arise within thee. Thy God will be our God and our portion. He will be a husband to thy widow and a father to thy children; the grace of thy God will be sufficient for us.

Now, my dear, I desire willingly and cheerfully to resign my right in thee to thy Father and my Father, who hath the greatest interest in thee. And confident I am, though men have separated us for a time yet our God will ere long bring us together again where we shall eternally enjoy one another, never to part more. O let me hear how God bears up thy heart, and let me taste of those comforts that support thee, that they may be as pillars of marble to bear up my sinking spirit. I can write no more. Farewell, farewell, my dear, till we meet there where we shall never bid farewell more; till which time I leave thee in the bosom of a loving, tender-hearted Father, and so I rest till I shall forever rest in Heaven,

Mary Love

Obadiah Sedgwick
(Westminster Divine who petitioned
Parliament for Love's release)

14

Love's Last Visitors

A few nights before he was sentenced to be beheaded on Tower Hill, ten days before his appointed time by the sentence he received, Christopher Love was visited by two of his intimate acquaintances, or "bosom friends," as he called them. They began to complain of the cruelties of the times and "the malice and usage of time-serving brethren."

To this Love answered, "And think you this is an evil time? No, no; this is the very time when grace and true godliness can be distinguished from hypocrisy. Many have followed Christ hitherto for the loaves, and are not turned back for the roughness of the way, and the sore trial and tribulation which others met with who are gone before them.

"There are many in London at this very day who think to go to heaven in their gilded coaches, and have denied Christ's cause before men, against whom I now witness, and Christ in His never-failing Word has promised to deny all such before His Father and the holy angels. This is the time to discern between him who serves God and him who serves Him not. They formerly were my familiar acquaintances in fellowship and sweet converse. I sent this day to have a few words with them here in the prison, but they would not come for their countenances are fallen; their consciences are wounded and they cannot look me in the face because I knew of their resolution and was a witness to their perjuration. But, ah, how will they look the blessed Jesus in the face in the morning of the resurrection? What answer or excuse will they have for what they have done? O foolish people, who think to escape the cross and come to the crown! I tell you, nay, you must all suffer persecution who follow the Lamb; we must be hated of all nations for Christ's sake; we must come through great tribulation before we can enter the land of joy and felicity. Know ye not that the souls that were slain for the testimony of Jesus are placed under the altar? Happy, happy are those men at this day, and ever shall be happy, who suffer for Christ's sake in a right and charitable way through love to His cause and honesty of heart, not through pride and hypocrisy, without the root of the matter, to have it said they died martyrs. These are they who will miss their mark, and those who denied the call and looked back shall never have the honor to find it.

"I am now pointed out by many to be in a destitute and forlorn condition, but I would not exchange my state, no, not for all the glory that is on the earth. I find my Redeemer's love stronger in my bonds than ever I did in the days of my liberty. Therefore, I hold living here as death itself. I am as full of love and joy in the Holy Spirit as ever bottle was filled with new wine. I am ready to cry out, 'The Spirit of the Lord God is upon me.' I will not take upon me to prophesy, nevertheless the Spirit of the Lord causeth me to utter:

1. This usurped authority, now in the hands of Cromwell, shall shortly be at an end.

2. England shall be blessed with meek kings and

mild governments.

3. Powerful preachers and dull hearers, good sermons to them will be as music to a sleepy man. They will hear but not understand, nor lay the Word to heart to practice it in their lives, to walk by it.

4. O England, thou shalt wax old in wickedness. Thy sins abound like those of Sodom, thy voluptuousness shall cry aloud for vengeance.

5. The Lord shall threaten and chastise thee, yet in mercy and love will He look on those that fear Him and call upon His name. He will spare and save them alive in the day of His anger, when the wicked shall be sifted from amongst you as the chaff is sifted from among the wheat.

6. For out of thee, O England, shall a bright star arise, whose light and voice shall make the heathen to quake and knock under with submission to the gospel of Jesus. He shall be as a sound of thunder in the ears of the wicked, and as a lantern to the Jews to lead them to the knowledge of Jesus, the only Son of God, and the true Messiah, whom they so long mistrusted.

7. For the short work spoken of by the apostle, which the Lord is to make upon the earth in the latter age of the world cannot be far off. Observe, my dear friends, while you live, my calculations of the dates in the book of Revelation, and in Daniel, which the Spirit of the Lord led me into, for the Lord will reveal it to some of His own ere that time come. For the nearer the time is, the seals shall be taken away, and more and more shall be revealed to God's people, for the Lord doth nothing without He reveals it by His Spirit to His servants, the prophets. He destroyed not the old world without the knowledge of Abraham. I do not mean

now that any new prophet shall arise, but the Lord by His Spirit will cause knowledge to abound among His people, whereby the old prophecies shall be clearly and perfectly understood."

Christopher Love was a Covenanter. One of the things that makes them unique is their commitment to exclusive psalmnody, and their strict keeping of the Sabbath. In other words, covenanters will sing only the divinely-inspired psalms of Scripture in their worship services, and they sing them without musical accompaniment. Since God wrote the psalms, they reason, why sing hymns written by fallible men?

Mary Love remembered this about her husband's days in the Tower of London: "He was observed many times to sing the 56th Psalm and the 35th Psalm, with several others which he made as his songs in the hours of his pilgrimage." The words to these psalms are worthy of note, and give us a further insight into how Love saw his plight. The text here is from the King James Version, the one Love would have most likely used, the recent "Authorized" Version having largely replaced the Geneva Bible by this time.

Psalm 35

Plead my cause, O LORD, with them that strive with me: fight against them that fight against me.

Take hold of shield and buckler, and stand up for mine help.

Draw out also the spear, and stop the way against them that persecute me: say unto my soul, I am thy salvation.

Let them be confounded and put to shame that seek after my soul: let them be turned back and brought to confusion that devise my hurt.

Let them be as chaff before the wind: and let the angel of the LORD chase them.

Let their way be dark and slippery: and let the angel of the LORD persecute them.

For without cause have they hid for me their net in a pit, which without cause they have digged for my soul.

Let destruction come upon him at unawares; and let his net that he hath hid catch himself: into that very destruction let him fall.

And my soul shall be joyful in the LORD: it shall rejoice in his salvation.

All my bones shall say, LORD, who is like unto thee, which deliverest the poor from him that is too strong for him, yea, the poor and the needy from him that spoileth him?

False witnesses did rise up; they laid to my charge things that I knew not.

They rewarded me evil for good to the spoiling of my soul.

But as for me, when they were sick, my clothing was sackcloth: I humbled my soul with fasting; and my prayer returned into mine own bosom.

I behaved myself as though he had been my friend or brother: I bowed down heavily, as one that mourneth for his mother.

But in mine adversity they rejoiced, and gathered themselves together: yea, the abjects gathered themselves together against me, and I knew it not; they did tear me, and ceased not:

With hypocritical mockers in feasts, they gnashed upon me with their teeth.

Lord, how long wilt thou look on? Rescue my soul from their destructions, my darling from the lions.

I will give thee thanks in the great congregation: I will praise thee among much people.

Let not them that are mine enemies wrongfully rejoice over me: neither let them wink with the eye that hate me without a cause.

For they speak not peace: but they devise deceitful matters against them that are quiet in the land.

Yea, they opened their mouth wide against me, and said, Aha, aha, our eye hath seen it.

This thou hast seen, O LORD: keep not silence: O LORD, be not far from me.

Stir up thyself, and awake to my judgment, even unto my cause, my God and my Lord.

Judge me, O LORD my God, according to thy righteousness; and let them not rejoice over me.

Let them not say in their hearts, Ah, so would we have it: let them not say, We have swallowed him up.

Let them be ashamed and brought to confusion together that rejoice at mine hurt: let them be clothed with shame and dishonour that magnify themselves against me.

Let them shout for joy, and be glad, that favour my righteous cause: yea, let them say continually, Let the LORD be magnified, which hath pleasure in the prosperity of his servant.

And my tongue shall speak of thy righteousness and of thy praise all the day long.

Psalm 56

Be merciful unto me, O God: for man would swallow me up; he fighting daily oppresseth me.

Mine enemies would daily swallow me up: for they be many that fight against me, O thou most High.

What time I am afraid, I will trust in thee.

In God I will praise his word, in God I have put my trust; I will not fear what flesh can do unto me.

Every day they wrest my words: all their thoughts are against me for evil.

They gather themselves together, they hide themselves, they mark my steps, when they wait for my soul.

Shall they escape by iniquity? In thine anger cast down the people, O God.

Thou tellest my wanderings: put thou my tears into thy bottle: are they not in thy book?

When I cry unto thee, then shall mine enemies turn back: this I know; for God is for me.

In God will I praise his word: in the LORD will I praise his word.

In God have I put my trust: I will not be afraid what man can do unto me.

Thy vows are upon me, O God: I will render praises unto thee.

For thou hast delivered my soul from death: wilt not thou deliver my feet from falling, that I may walk before God in the light of the living?

In his last conversation with his wife the night before he died, Christopher told Mary, "Be not troubled to think what shall become of thee and thine after my death, for be assured that my God, and the God of the widows and fatherless, will not forsake thee, but will wonderfully provide for those and be comforted in this, that tho' men take thy husband from thee, they cannot take thy God from thee; and so do not think that thou hast lost thy husband, but only parted with him for awhile, and in the meantime thy Savior will be a husband unto thee and a father unto thy children."

Before their sad parting he said to his wife, "Come, let us once more go together to our good God in prayer," at which time his heart was abundantly enlarged in blessing God for the riches of His grace manifested to his soul through Jesus Christ.

When he rose from his knees, he said to his wife, "I beg of thee, when I am gone to heaven tomorrow, not to be troubled to hear that I shall not make mention of thee or thine in my prayers when I am upon the scaffold, for I cannot do it but natural affections do arise that will not be suitable for the place, but be assured that the last words that I shall speak in this room shall be to God for those and thine."

And after some further discourses he wished his wife not to trouble herself to send his dinner the next day, but she, desiring him to eat something that should be sent him, he said, "I shall then do it to please thee, but I shall need no dinner, for within a few hours I shall have a blessed supper, the supper of the Bridegroom where I shall sit down with Abraham, Isaac, and Jacob, and know hunger and thirst and sorrow no more.

"As soon as my head is severed from my body, it shall be united with Christ my Head in heaven, and I am persuaded that I shall tomorrow go up Tower Hill as cheerfully to be everlastingly martyred unto my Redeemer as I went to Gile's church to be married to thee."

He gave his wife directions in every particular concerning his outward affairs, what to do and how to dispose of houses and care for the children after his death. He wished her to get him into his grave as soon as she could without any funeral solemnities. He made her promise him faithfully that she would not see him after his death, nor call the soon-to-be-born child by any name that might call to her remembrance that bitter affliction, saying, "I would not have my poor wife to be mourning on earth when I shall be rejoicing and singing hallelujahs in heaven."

Edmund Calamy
(London minister responsible for seeing many of Love's sermons printed after his death)

15

Love's Letters

[Christopher Love's letters to his wife were tender and poignant. What follows are his letters written to her during his imprisonment in the Tower of London.]

July 15, 1651 [the day he expected to be executed]
From the Tower of London

My Dearest Beloved,

I am now going to my long home, yet I must write thee a word before I go hence and shall be seen no more. It is to beg thee to be comforted in my gain and not to be troubled in thy loss. Labor to suppress thy inward fears now that thou art under outward sorrows. As thy outward sufferings abound, let thy consolations in Christ also abound. I know thou art a woman of a sorrowful spirit. My time is short; I have but a few words of counsel to give thee, and then I shall leave thee to God who careth for thee and thine.

1. While thou art under desertions, labor rather to strengthen and clear up thy evidences for heaven than question them.

2. Remember a faith of adherence or reliance on the Lord Jesus brings thee to heaven, though thou want the faith of evidence or assurance.

3. Labor to find that (and more also) in God which thou hast lost in the creature.

4. Spend not thy days in heaviness for my death. If there were knowledge of things below or sorrow in heaven, I should grieve to think my beloved should mourn on earth.

5. Lie under a soul-searching ministry. I know thou art not a spongy hearer, sucking in foul water as well as fair. God hath given thee a good understanding, to be able to discern things that differ. As the mouth tastes meat, thy ear trieth words.

6. Be conversant in Christian meetings and much in the exercises of mortification, in fasting and prayers, yet have respect to the weakness of thy body and thy present condition.

7. Have a care of thyself and babes. God will take care of thee and them. I can write no more; farewell, my dear, farewell, farewell.

My dear, I beg thee to be satisfied. My heart is greatly comforted in God. I can quietly submit to the good pleasure of His will, and I hope thou dost so also. I am delivered by the determinate counsel of God; the will of the Lord be done. Read for thy comfort when I am dead and gone Jeremiah 49:11 and the beginning of 12; Isaiah 9:6-8; Psalm 5:6 and 146:9; 2 Corinthians 4:17-18; and Hebrews 12:6-7.

These are the last words written by thy dying, yet comforted husband,

Christopher Love

From the Tower on the Lord's Day

More Dear to Me than Ever,

It adds to my rejoicing that I have so good and gracious a wife to part with for the Lord Jesus. In thy grief, I have been grieved; but in thy joy I have been comforted. Surely, nature could never help thee to bear so heavy a stroke with so much silence and submission to the hand of God! Oh, dearest, every line which thou writest gladdeneth my heart. I dare not think that there is such a creature as Mary Love in the world. For Kit and Mall [the two living children], I can think of them without trouble, leaving them to so good a God and so good a mother.

Be comforted concerning thy husband, who may more honor God in his death than in his life. The will of the Lord be done; he is fully satisfied with the hand of God. Though there is but little between him and death, he knows there is but little between him and heaven, and that ravisheth his heart.

The Lord bless and requite thee for thy wise and good counsel. Thou hast prevented me; the very things I thought to have written to thee, thou hast written to me. I have had more comfort from thy gracious letters than from all the counsel I have had from any else in the world. Well, be assured, we shall meet in heaven. I rest till I rest in heaven, thy dying but comforted friend,

Christopher Love

From the Tower
August 18, 1651

My dearest delight on earth,

I was fast asleep when thy note came. I bless God, I break not an hour's sleep for all my sufferings. I know they work for me a more exceeding and eternal weight of glory. I slept this night from ten at night till seven in the morning and never waked. My dear, I am comforted in the gracious support God gives thee, that my burdens are the lighter on my shoulder because they are not too heavy on thine; or, if they be heavy, yet that God helps thee to bear them. The Lord keep it in the purpose of our hearts forever to submit to the good pleasure of God. I bless God I do find my heart in as quiet and composed a temper as ever I did in all my life. I am till I die, thy tender-hearted husband,

Christopher Love

From the Tower of London
August 22, 1651
The Day of My Glorification

My most gracious beloved,

I am now going from a prison to a palace. I have finished my work, I am now to receive my wages. I am now going to heaven where are two of my children, and leaving thee on the earth where are three of my babes. Those two above need not my care, but the three below need thine. It comforts me to think two of my children are in the bosom of Abraham and three of them will be in the arms and care of so tender a godly mother.

I know thou art a woman of a sorrowful spirit, yet be comforted; though thy sorrow be great for thy husband's going out of the world, yet thy pains shall be the less in bringing thy child into the world. Thou shalt be a joyful mother, though thou beest a sad widow. God hath many mercies in store for thee; the prayers of a dying husband for thee will not be lost. To my shame I speak it: I never prayed so much for thee at liberty as I have done in prison. I cannot write more, but I have a few practical counsels to leave with thee:

1. Keep under a sound, orthodox and soul-searching ministry. Oh, there are deceivers gone out into the world, but Christ's sheep know His voice and a stranger will they not follow. Attend on that ministry that teaches the way of God in truth, and follow Solomon's advice, Proverbs 19:27, "Cease to hear instruction that causes to err from the ways of knowledge."

2. Bring up thy children in the knowledge and admonition of the Lord. The mother ought to be a teacher in the father's absence. Proverbs 31:1, "The words which his mother taught him;" and Timothy was instructed by his grandmother Lois and his mother Eunice, 2 Timothy 1:5.

3. Pray in thy family daily, that thy dwelling may be in the number of the families that call upon God.

4. Labor for a meek and quiet spirit, which is in the sight of God of great price, 1 Peter 3:4.

5. Pour not on the comforts thou wantest, but on the mercies thou hast.

6. Look rather at God's end in afflicting than at the measure and degree of thy affliction.

7. Labor to clear up thy evidences for heaven when God takes from thee the comforts of earth, that as thy sufferings do abound, so thy consolations in Christ may abound much more, 2 Corinthians 1:5.

8. Though it is good to maintain a holy jealousy of the deceitfulness of thy heart, yet it is evil for thee to cherish fears and doubts about the truth of thy graces. If ever I had confidence touching the grace of another, I have confidence of grace in thee. I can say of thee as Peter did of Silvanus, "I am persuaded that this is the grace of God wherein thou standest," 1 Peter 5:12. Oh, my dear soul, wherefore dost thou doubt, whose heart hath been upright, whose walkings have been holy. I could venture my soul in thy soul's stead, such a confidence I have of thee.

9. When thou findest thy heart secure, presumptuous and proud, then pour upon corruption more than upon grace; but when thou findest thy heart doubting and unbelieving, then look on thy grace not on thy infirmities.

10. Study the covenant of grace and the merits of Christ, and then be troubled if thou canst. Thou art interested in such a covenant that accepts purposes for performances, desires for deeds, sincerity for perfection, the righteousness of another, that of Jesus Christ, as if it were thine own. Oh, my love! Rest, rest, then, in the love of God, in the bosom of Christ.

11. Swallow up thy will in the will of God. It is a bitter cup we are to drink, but it is the cup our Father hath put into our hands. When Paul was to go to suffer at Jerusalem, the Christians could say, "The will of the

Lord be done." Oh, say thou, when I go to Tower Hill, "The will of the Lord be done."

12. Rejoice in my joy. To mourn for me inordinately argues that either thou enviest or suspectest my happiness. The joy of the Lord is my strength; oh, let it be thine also!

Dear wife, farewell. I will call thee wife no more. I shall see thy face no more, yet I am not much troubled for now I am going to meet the Bridegroom, the Lord Jesus Christ, to whom I shall be eternally married.

Thy dying yet most affectionate friend till death,

Christopher Love

[In my research, I found two variations of this last letter. Below is the portion of the letter that differs from the one above, taken from the 1806 edition of Love's works. While most of the difference is simply in the enumeration, there *is* material in the following not included above.]

5. Pour not on the comforts you want, but upon the mercies you have. Look rather at God's end in afflicting than to the measure and degree of your affliction.

6. Labor to clear up your evidence for heaven when God takes from you the comfort of earth, so that as your sufferings do abound, your consolation in Christ may abound much more, 2 Corinthians 1:5. Though it is good to maintain a holy jealousy of the heart, yet it is ill for you to cherish fears and doubts touching the truth of your graces. If ever I had confidence touching the grace of another, I have confidence of grace in

you. As Peter said of Silvanus, I am persuaded that this is the grace of God wherein ye stand, 1 Peter 5:12.

7. Oh, my dear soul! Wherefore dost thou doubt, whose heart has been upright, whose walking has been holy. I could venture my soul this day in thy soul's stead, such a confidence I have in you.

8. When you find your heart secure, presumptuous and proud, then pour upon corruption more than grace. Then look upon your graces without your infirmities.

9. Study the covenant of grace and the merits of Christ, and be troubled if you can. You are interested in such a covenant that accepts purposes for performances, desires for deeds, sincerity for perfection, the righteousness of another, that of Jesus Christ, as if it were your own alone. Oh, my love! Rest thou in the love of God, in the bosom of Christ.

10. Swallow up your will in the will of God. It is a bitter cup we are to drink, but it is the cup our Father hath put into our hands. When Paul was to suffer at Jerusalem, the Christians said, "The will of the Lord be done." Oh! Say ye so when I go to Tower Hill, "The will of the Lord be done!"

11. Rejoice in my joy. To mourn for me inordinately argues that you either envy or suspect my happiness. The joy of the Lord is my strength. Oh! Let it be yours also! Dear wife, farewell. I will call thee wife no more. I shall see thy face no more; yet I am not much troubled, for now I am going to meet the bridegroom, the Lord Jesus, to whom I shall be eternally married.

12. Refuse not to marry when God offers you a fair opportunity; but be sure you marry in the Lord, and

one of a good disposition, that he may not grieve you, but give you a comfortable livelihood in the world.

Farewell, dear love, and again I say, farewell. The Lord Jesus be with your spirit, the Maker of heaven and earth be a husband to you; and the Father of our Lord Jesus Christ be a Father to your children.

So prays your dying, your most affectionate friend till death,

Christopher Love

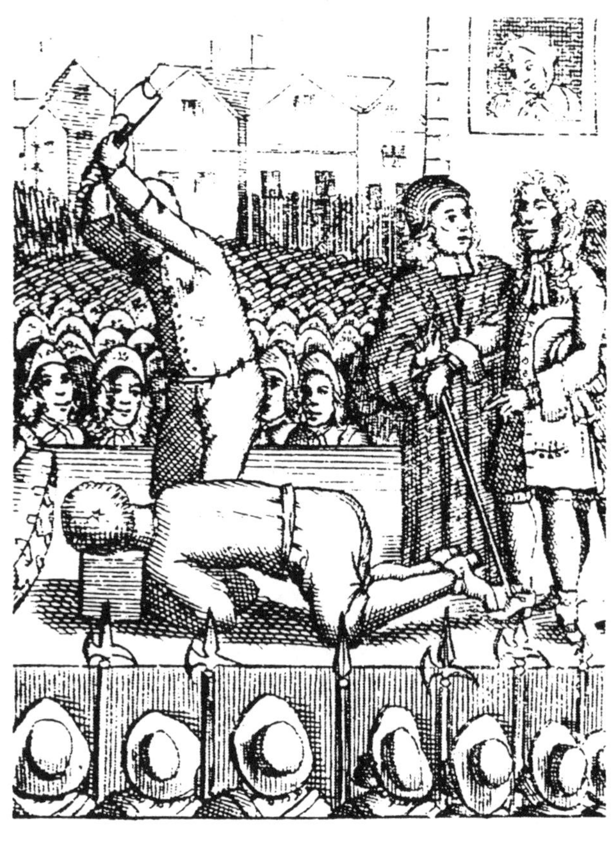

An artist's engraving of a beheading
on Tower Hill from 1685

16

The Death of Love

Christopher Love was brought from the Tower by the Sheriffs of London to the scaffold on Tower Hill about two o'clock in the afternoon on Friday, August 22, 1651. He left his chamber at the Tower carrying his Bible in one hand. The ministers who accompanied him were Simeon Ashe, Edmund Calamy, and Thomas Manton.

Mary Love wrote: "When he came through the gates of the Tower, many thousands of spectators and friends made the hill ring with their bitter weeping and lamentations, pressing upon him that they might but touch him and see his face which they should see no more. There was one among the crowd who had said to his neighbor earlier in the day, 'Let us go and see what a spot Love's blood will make on Tower Hill.' But when he saw him, and heard him speak and pray, he cried out and lamented that he had thirsted for his blood, and was thought with some others to have been converted by this martyr's death."

When he arrived on the scaffold, Sheriff Tichburn showed him the warrant for his suffering, telling him that he took no pleasure in it, but it was a duty laid upon him.

"I believe it, sir," said Love.

"I have done my duty for you," said Tichburn.

"The Lord bless you," was Love's reply.

At that point, the Lieutenant of the Tower said, "The Lord strengthen you in this hour of your temptation."

To which Love replied, "Sir, I bless God, my heart is in heaven. I am well." Then, turning to Sheriff Tichburn, he said, "May I have the liberty to speak and pray?"

Tichburn replied, "Yes, but I desire you to consider that we have the other [Mr. Gibbons] to execute afterwards, and six o'clock is our hour; but we will give you as much time as we can."

"I shall be the briefer," said Love. Then he put off his hat two times to the people and spoke as follows:

"I am made this day a spectacle unto God, angels, and men; and among men I am made a grief to the godly, a laughing stock to the wicked, and a gazing stock to all, yet, blessed be my God, not a terror to myself. Although there is but little between me and death, yet this bears up my heart: there is but little between me and heaven. It comforted Dr. Taylor, the martyr, when he was going to execution, that there were but two stiles between him and his Father's house. There is a lesser way between me and my Father's house, but two steps between me and glory. It is but lying down upon the block, and I shall ascend upon a throne.

"I am this day sailing towards the ocean of eternity, through a rough passage to my haven of rest, through a Red Sea to the promised land. I think I hear God say to me as He did to Moses, 'Go up to Mount Nebo, and die there.' So to me, 'Go up to Tower Hill and die there.' Isaac said of himself that he was old and yet he knew not the day of his death, but I cannot say so. I am young, and yet I know the day of my death, and I know the kind of my death and the place of my death also. I am put to such a kind of death as two famous preachers of the gospel were put to before me: John the Baptist and Paul the Apostle. They were both beheaded. You have mention of the one in Scripture story, the other in ecclesiastical history. And I read in Revelation 20:4 that the saints were beheaded for the Word of God and for the testimony of Jesus. But herein is the disadvantage which I lie under in the thoughts of many: they judge that I suffer not for the Word of God or for conscience but for meddling with state matters.

"To this I shall briefly say that it is an old guise of the devil to impute the cause of God's people's sufferings to be contrivements against the state, when in truth it is their religion and conscience they are persecuted for. The rulers of Israel would have put Jeremiah to death upon a civil account though, indeed, it was only the truth of his prophecy that made the rulers angry with him. And yet, upon a civil account, they pretended he must die because he fell away to the Chaldeans and would have brought in foreign forces to invade them.

"The same thing is laid to my charge, of which I am innocent as was Jeremiah. Yea, I find other instances in Scripture where in the cause of the saints' sufferings were still imputed to their meddling with state matters. Paul, though he did but preach Jesus Christ, yet must die, if the people had their way, under pretense that he was a mover of sedition. Upon a civil account, my life is pretended to be taken away, whereas indeed it is because I pursue my covenant and will not prostitute my principles and conscience to the ambition and lusts of men.

"Beloved, I am this day making a double exchange. I am changing a pulpit for a scaffold and a scaffold for a throne; and I might add a third: I am changing this numerous multitude, the presence of this numerous multitude on Tower Hill, for the innumerable company of saints and angels in heaven, the holy hill of Zion; and I am changing a guard of soldiers for a guard of angels which will receive and carry me into Abraham's bosom. This scaffold is the best pulpit that ever I preached in. In my church pulpit, God, through His grace, made me an instrument to bring others to heaven, but in this pulpit He will bring me to heaven. These are the last words that I shall speak in this world, and it may be I shall bring more glory to God by this one speech on a scaffold than I have done by many sermons in a pulpit.

"I shall divide my speech into three parts. I shall speak something concerning my change, a word concerning my accusers and touching my judges, without any animosity at all, and then a word of exhortation, and so I shall commit my soul to God.

"Concerning my charge, it is black and hideous, many things falsely suggested, hardly a line of it true, and nothing capital sufficiently proved against me by any one act that I am conscious to myself I did. The charge is high and full, but the proof empty and low. Though there were eight witnesses that came in against me, yet none of them proved that ever I wrote any letter, or directed any man to write a letter into Scotland or into foreign parts. No man proved that I sent away any letter, that I received any letter, that I collected, gave, or lent any money to assist or promote the

Scottish war. This is all that is sworn against me: that I was present where letters were read, and that I made a motion for money to give to Massey; so that (beloved) my presence at, and concealment of, letters that were received and sent from foreign parts is that for which I must die.

"As concerning my accusers, I shall not say much. I do forgive them with all my heart, and I pray God forgive them also. Yet, what the Evangelist said concerning Christ's accusers, I may (without vanity or falsehood) say of mine, that they did not agree amongst themselves. One witness swears one thing and another quite the contrary. Yea, not only did they contradict one another, but sometimes a single witness contradicted himself. And though their testimony condemned my person, yet I have condemned their testimony. And truly there are many remarkable circumstances that I might take notice of either in or before or since the trial that might be worthy of observation, but I will not insist upon it, only in the general (for I shall name none of my accusers); some of them have sent to me to pray me to forgive them the wrong they have done me. And one of them has written to me under his own hand to pray me to forgive him the wrong that he has done me, and told me that the day I should die a violent death his life would be no comfort to him because he was an instrument in taking away mine. Other witnesses were terrified before they could testify; some were hired, some fined before they bore witness against me. But I will be off of this. Concerning my judges, I will not judge them and yet I will not justify them. I will say but this of them. I believe that what moved Herod to cut off John the Baptist's head moved them to cut off mine, and that was for his oath's sake. Herod, to avoid perjury, would commit murder; whereas, if John's head had been upon his shoulders, he would have been guilty of neither.

"I have something in the second place to speak concerning myself, and then I shall come briefly to a conclusion. Concerning myself, I have gone through various reports. There are many sons of slander whose mouths are as open sepulchers in which they would bury my name before my friends can bury my body, but my comfort is this: there will be a resurrection of names as well as the bodies at the last day. God will not only wipe off all tears from my eyes this day, but He will also wipe off all blots and reproaches from my name before many days are over; and though my body will soon rot under ground, yet my hope is my name will not rot above it. I am not ignorant what calumnies are cast upon me, and more likely to be after I am dead and gone. The very night before my intended execution last month, there was an insulting letter written to me to tell me that, after my death, there should be something published against me to my shame. I hope you will have so much charity as not to believe reproaches cast upon a dead man who will be silent in the grave and not able to speak a word in his own justification. I am aspersed both as to my practice and as to my principles. I shall begin with the first.

"There are five aspersions as to my practice that are laid upon me: That I am a liar, that I am an extortioner, that I am an adulterer, that I am a murderer, and that I am a turbulent person. Crimes scandalous in any man, but much more abominable in a minister. Now, I hope you will believe a dying man who dares not look God in the face with a lie in his mouth.

"I am accused of lying, that what I denied before the High Court of Justice afterwards I confessed, or else was proved against me. Now, in the presence of God, I tell you as I would confess nothing that was criminal, so I denied nothing that was true; and that I may seal it to you with my blood, the same protestations I made before the High Court, I make briefly now:

1. I never wrote letters to the King, Queen, Church or State of Scotland, or to any particular person of the Scottish nation, since the wars began to this day.

2. I never received any letter written to me either from the King, or from the Queen, or from the Church or State of Scotland, or from any particular person of the Scottish nation since the wars began to this day.

3. I never collected, gave, or lent one penny of money either to the King, Queen, Church or state of Scotland, or to any particular person to send into Scotland, to any person of the Scottish nation to this day. It is true, I did confess, though it was not proved (and haply upon that ground the mistake might arise) I did give money to Massey, and I did also write a letter to him, but he is of the English not of the Scottish nation. That for which I come here is only for moving for money for him, and that not upon a military account, but merely to relieve his personal necessities and for being present where letters were read from him and others. And although man has condemned me, yet I am so far from thinking that either God or my own conscience condemns me as sinning in what I am condemned for that both God and my own conscience ac-

quit me. And what I said at the bar when I received my sentence I shall say upon the scaffold, that for those things for which I am condemned, neither God nor my own conscience condemns me.

"Again, I am accused to be an extortioner, and this in the mouths of. . .I am loathe to name them because I will avoid all rancor. But I am charged as if I should be a grievous extortioner, to receive thirty pounds for the loan of three hundred pounds besides eight pounds per cent for interest. In the presence of God and of you all, I declare to you this is a most notorious and abominable falsehood.

"I am accused likewise of being an adulterer[1] , and this report is not in the mouths of mean men, but in the mouths of those that sit at the stern: as if I were a debauched person and were guilty of uncleanness. Now, I tell you, as Luther said of himself in another case, that he was not tempted to covetousness so, through the grace of God, I can say I have not been tempted in all my life to uncleanness. It does not much grieve me, though these slanders are cast upon me. I know my betters have been worse accused before me. Athanasius was accused by two harlots that he had committed folly with them, and yet the man was chaste and innocent. Beza was charged not only with drunkenness but with lasciviousness also, and many others have been accused with the same, if not worse, slanders than I have been.

"But that which goes nearest my heart is that I am

---

[1] An Edward Love had been charged with visiting a prostitute, but Love's enemies had used this against him by spreading the rumor that "Mr Love" had been arrested for visiting prostitutes.

accused of being a murderer also, and this is a high charge indeed. I am charged with the guilt of all the blood of Scotland; whereas, did I lie under the guilt of one drop of blood I could not look upon God with so cheerful a countenance, and I could not be filled with so peaceable a heart and conscience as I have at this day. I bless my God, I am free from the blood of all men. Those who lay this to my charge, they do to me as Nero did to the Christians. He set Rome on fire and then charged the Christians with it; so they put England and Scotland into a flame to quench the burning which these men's ambitions and lusts have kindled. And I would fain know of any man, what act is it that I have done? What is it that was proved in the High Court against me that makes me guilty of Scotland's blood? Did I ever invite the Scots to invade England? What man lays that to my charge? Did I ever encourage the English army to invade Scotland? What action is it that I have done that makes me guilty of that blood? Indeed, this I have done, and this I have, and this I stand to. I have, as a private man, prayed unto God many a day and kept many a fast wherein I have sought God that there might be an agreement between the King and the Scots upon the interest of religion and terms of the covenant. Now, by what consequence can this be strained to charge me with Scotland's blood? For my part, I was but only at one meeting where the question was proposed (fasts only excepted) what should be thought fit to be done to promote the agreement between the King and the Scots. And that was moved in my house. And to that end, when there were some things there proposed which they called a commission or instructions to send to Holland, as soon as ever I heard them I declared against them. I declared that it was an act of high presumption for private persons to commissionate, an act of notorious falsehood to say it was in the name of the Presbyterian party when none knew of it (that I know of) but only those few then present. Now, this is only a political engine to make the Presbyterian party odious, who are the best friends to a well-ordered government of any sort of people in the world.

"I am accused likewise to be a man of turbulent spirit, to be an enemy to the peace and quiet of the nation. Now, as to this, let my congregation and my domestic relations judge for me whether I am not a man who would fain have lived quietly in the land. I am as Jeremiah was, born a man of contention; not actively, I contend (I strive with none), but passively; many strive and contend with me. God is my witness, my judgment has put me upon endeavoring after all honorable and just ways for peace and love among the godly. The grief of my heart has been for the divisions, and the desire of my soul for a union among God's people. But when I speak of a union, I would not be misunderstood. I do not mean a state union, to engage to the present power; that is against my principles. That is to say, "A confederacy with them that say, 'A confederacy.' " That is rather a combination than a gospel union. O join not with them lest ye be consumed in their sins. They who get power into their hands by policy and use it with cruelty will lose it with ignominy. It was said of Pope Boniface that he entered into the popedom like a fox, reigned like a lion, but died like a dog. Beloved, the union for which I plead is a church union, to wit, love among the godly, for this the desires of my soul ever have been: that those who fear God might walk hand in hand in the fellowship of the gospel, both in truth and love. If this union is not, I am afraid, through our divisions, a company of loose libertines will arise who will endeavor not only to overthrow the doctrine of faith and the power of godliness but even good manners also. I remember an observation of holy [Richard] Greenham, given this judgment upon the state of England. He said, 'There is great fear that Popery is coming into England, and I fear it too; but I fear more the coming of atheism into England than the coming in of Popery.' And, truly, that is my fear also. Thus as to my practice. A word now as to my principles.

"I am accused of being an apostate, of being a turncoat, of being this, of being that, of being anything but what I am. In general, I will tell you, I bless my God, a high court, a long sword, a bloody scaffold have not made me in the least to alter my principles or to wrong my conscience. And that I might reveal to you my principles, I hope I shall do with freedom. I will irritate and provoke none; what I shall say shall not be an irritation or provocation of others, at least not intended by me, but only as a genuine and clear manifestation of my own principles and how they stand.

"First, then, my principles as to civil and religious affairs. I declare that I die with my judgment set against malignity. I hate both name and thing. I still retain as vehement a detestation of a malignant interest as ever I did, yet I would not be misunderstood. I do not understand, nor count the godly party, our covenanting brethren in Scotland, to be a malignant party, nor the Scots defending their nation and title of the King to be a malignant interest but an honest and justifiable cause.

"Second, though I am against malignity, yet I am not against but for a regulated monarchy; a mixed monarchy, such as ours is, I judge to be the best government in the world. I did, it's true, in my own place and calling oppose the forces of the late King, but I was never against the office. I am not only against court parasites, who would screw up monarchy into tyranny, but against those who pull down monarchy to bring in anarchy.

"Third, I was never for putting the King to death, whose person I promised in my covenant to preserve. It is true, I did, in my place and calling, oppose his forces, but I never endeavored to destroy his person. There is a scandal raised of me that, in a sermon at Windsor, I was to have said these words, 'It would never be well with England till the King were let blood in the neck vein,' which speech I utterly detest, professing as a dying man, in the presence of God and you all, I never spoke such words as relating to him. Though my judgment was for bringing malignants, who seduced him and drew him from his parliament, to condign punishment, yet I deemed it an ill way to cure the political body by cutting off the political head.

"Fourth, I die with my judgment absolutely set against the engagement. I pray God forgive them that impose and subscribe it, and preserve those that refuse it.

"Fifth, I would not, in the next place, be looked upon, now that I am a dying man, as a man owning this present government. I die with my judgment against it.

It is true, in a case of life, I did petition the present power and give them the titles they take to themselves and that others give them; but herein I did not wrong nor thwart my principles. There are many instances in Scripture to justify this. Hushai gave the title of King to Absalom, though Absalom had no right to that title, for David was the lawful king. And David himself gave him that title as well as Hushai. And Calvin gave the title to the French King, calling him 'the most Christian King,' yet we know he was a Papist. And we give a title to King Henry VIII and call him 'the Defender of the Faith,' and yet he had no right to that title for he was an opposer not a defender of the faith. That title was given him upon an evil ground because he opposed the faith. He opposed the doctrine of Luther, therefore the Pope gave him that title 'Defender of the Faith;' and yet none scrupled to give him that title that was then commonly given him.

"Sixth (I reveal my judgment, I provoke none, only tell you what my own thoughts are so that after I am dead and gone I might not be belied, for I dare not now belie my principles), my judgment is against the invasion of the Scottish nation by the English army. They who gave us a friendly assistance, who are joined with us in the same covenant, who drew a sword with us in the same quarrel, should I live a thousand years I should never draw sword against them. But the English army has forgotten the brotherly covenant, so that Scotland may say as Edom, 'The men of my confederacy, who were at peace with me, have risen up and prevailed against me.' Because Scotland will not be a commonwealth, they shall not be a people. Because they will not break covenant, some men would have them broken. Because they will not lay their conscience to waste, their land must be laid to waste.

"Lastly, and so I have done (only with a word of exhortation), I die cleaving to all those oaths, vows, covenants, and protestations that were imposed by the two houses of Parliament, as owning them, and dying with my judgment for them, to the protestation, the vow and covenant, the Solemn League and Covenant. And this I tell you, I would rather die a covenant keeper than live a covenant breaker."

"I am now come to the third and last part of my speech, and so I shall have done and commit my soul to God who gave it. My exhortation shall be to this great city, unto the godly ministry of it, and unto my own congregation from whom death parts me, which nothing else could.

"To the city, I wish an affluence and confluence of all blessings upon it, and yet I fear gray hairs, as the sad symptoms of a declension, are here and there upon London, and yet she knows it not. O London, London, God is staining the pride of all thy glory! Thy glory is flying away like a bird. A contempt of the ministry, opposition against reformation, general, covenant-breaking have brought London low and, I fear, will yet bring it lower. I tremble to think what evils are coming upon it. This city is the receptacle of all errors. As your commodities are vented and spread from hence to every corner of the land, so have heresies and blasphemies had their first rise from this great and populous city and, from hence, are spread into all countries.

"To the inhabitants of this city I commend but

these few particulars:

1. Let me beg you to love your painful and your godly ministers. If they are taken away, you are likely to have worse come in their rooms. I know the Presbyterian ministers are the great eyesore, who have formerly been counted the chariots and horsemen of Israel. But I will say of London as was said of Leyden, that after Junius, an orthodox minister, was taken away, Arminius, that pestilent heretic, came in his room. If your godly ministers (and there have been ten already at one blow taken away from you) are taken away, Arminians, Anabaptists, nay, Jesuits are likely to supply their rooms, if God in mercy prevents not.

2. Submit yourselves to church government; that would lay a curb and restraint upon your lusts. It is a golden and easy yoke to which, if you do not submit, God may lay a heavy and iron yoke upon your necks.

3. Take heed of those doctrines that come under the notion of "new light." Those doctrines you ought to suspect as to whether they are true, which the broachers of them say are new, for truth is as old as the Bible. A remarkable passage I would suggest to you in Deuteronomy 32:17. It is said there, 'They chose them new gods that were newly come up;' and what were these new gods? The next verse tells you that they were old devils: 'for they sacrificed to devils and not to God.' Now, their sacrificing to old devils is called a sacrificing (to deceive the people) to new gods that were newly come up; yet their new gods were but old devils. Why, so I say, though many things go under the notion of new light, yet they are but old darkness, old heresies raked out of the dunghill, and which were buried in former ages of the Church with contempt and re-

proach many hundreds of years ago.

4. Bewail your great loss which you have in the taking away of so many ministers out of your city. There are ten ministers (if I mistake not) who have been taken away and removed at one blow who were burning and shining lights in their several candlesticks, and bright stars in their several orbs. Though I am not worthy of the world, and therefore am taken out of it, yet, as for my suffering brethren who are now in bonds and banishment, the world is not worthy of them.

5. Again, in the next place, take heed of engaging in a war against your brethren of the Scottish nation. For my part, I have opposed the tyranny of a King, but I never opposed the title. Take heed what you do.

"I have something to speak in the next place to the godly ministry of this city. Were it not that I am a dying man, I would not speak to such reverend and grave men. I would say as Elihu did (being but a young man) 'multitudes of years should teach wisdom,' and I would hold my tongue; but the words of a dying man take, whether they are discreet or not, or so well-ordered or managed or not. As to them, I would first desire God to show them mercy who have begged mercy for me. Now at the day of my death, I would beg but this of them, that as they have not been ashamed of my chains, so they would now wax confident by my bonds and by my blood. I know they are maligned and threatened, yet my prayer for them is that in Acts 4:29, 'And now, O Lord, behold their threatenings, and grant that Thy servants may preach Thy Word with all boldness.' Though I am but young, yet I will offer my young experience to my grave fathers and brethren, and that is this: Now I am to die. I have abundance of peace in my own conscience that I have set myself against the sins and apostasies of this present age. It is true, my faithfulness has procured me ill will from men, but it has purchased me peace with God. I have lived in peace and I shall die in peace. That which I have to beseech of the ministers is this: to beg them to keep up church government. Whatever God does with the governments of the world, turning kingdoms upside down, yet the government of the Church shall stand; and of all governments I die with this persuasion, that the presbyterial government makes most for purity and unity throughout the churches of the saints. I would beg them, therefore to keep up church government, that they would not let their elderships fall, that they would take heed of too general admissions of men to the Supper of the Lord, that sealing ordinance.

"And now I am done speaking to them, I shall speak a word *of* them, and so I have done. I have heard many clamors since I came to prison, as if all the city ministers were engaged in the 'Plot' (as it is called) that I am condemned for. Now as a dying man I tell you that all the ministers that were present at the meetings and had a hand in the business for which I am to be put to death are either in prison or they are discovered already. And therefore I do here upon my death free the ministers of the city who are not yet in trouble nor discovered to the committee of examinations. None of them had a hand in the business in which I was engaged, in which my conscience tells me I have not sinned. I have done immediately, for I would fain be at my Father's house.

"I have but a word to speak to my own congregation. I return praises unto God and thankfulness to them for the life I have had from them. I found them a solid, judicious and, many of them, a religious people. The ministry of that learned man, Mr. Anthony Burgess, did much good amongst them, though I have cause to be humbled that my weak ministry did but little. They afforded me a great deal of love and a liberal maintenance, and this is all I desire of them: that they would choose a godly, learned, and orthodox minister to succeed, such a one as may keep up and carry on church government. It would be a great comfort to me before I go to heaven if I had but this persuasion, that a learned, orthodox, godly man should fill that pulpit. And for encouragement to any godly minister whose lot may be to succeed me, I will say this, that he will have as comfortable a livelihood, and as loving a people, as are any people in London, only a few excepted. I had as much satisfaction among them as ever I had in any condition in all my life, and should never have parted from them had not death now parted us, to which I do submit with all Christian meekness and cheerfulness. I am now drawing to an end of my speech and to an end of my life together, but before I expire my last breath, I shall desire to justify God and to condemn myself in all that is brought upon me.

"Here I come to that which you call an untimely end and a shameful death, but (blessed be God) it is my glory and it is my comfort. I shall justify God; He is righteous because I have sinned. He is righteous, though He cuts me off in the midst of my days and in the midst of my ministry. I cannot complain that complaint in Psalm 44:12, 'Thou sellest thy people for nought, and dost not increase thy wealth by their price.' My blood shall not be spilt for naught. I may do more good by my death than by my life, and glorify God more in dying upon a scaffold than if I had died of a disease upon my bed.

"I bless my God I have not the least trouble upon my spirit, but I do with as much quietness of mind lie down (I hope I shall) upon the block as if I were going to lie down upon my bed or take my rest. I see men hunger after my flesh and thirst after my blood. Let them have it; it will hasten my happiness and their ruin, and greaten their guiltiness. Though I am a man of an obscure family, of mean parentage, so that my blood is not as the blood of nobles, yet I will say it is a Christian's blood, a minister's blood; yea, it is innocent blood also. My body, my dead body, will be a morsel which I believe will hardly be digested, and my blood will be bad food for this infant commonwealth (as Mr. Prideaux called it) to suck upon. Mine is not malignant blood, though here I am brought as a grievous and notorious offender.

"Now, beloved, I shall not only justify God (as I do without a complement, for He would be very just if my prison had been hell and this scaffold the bottomless pit, I have deserved both) so that I do not only justify God, but desire this day to magnify God, to magnify the riches of His glorious grace that such a one as I born in an obscure country (in Wales), of obscure parents, that God should look upon me and single me out from amongst all my kindred to be an object of his everlasting love. When as in the first fourteen years of my life I never heard a sermon, yet, in the fifteenth year of my life God (through His grace) converted me. And here I speak it without vanity (for what should a dying man be proud of?), though I am accused of many scandalous evils, yet (I speak to the praise and glory of my God) for these twenty years God has kept me so that I have not fallen into any scandalous sin. I have labored to keep a good conscience from my youth up, and I magnify His grace that He has not only made me a Christian but a minister, and judged me faithful to put me into the ministry. And though the office is trodden upon and disgraced, yet it is my glory that I die a despised minister. I would rather be a preacher in a pulpit than a prince upon a throne. I would rather be an instrument to bring souls to heaven than to have all the nations bring in tribute to me. I am not only a Christian and a preacher, but, whatever men judge, I am a martyr too. I speak it without vanity. If I had renounced my covenant and debauched my conscience and ventured my soul, there might have been hopes of saving my life so that I should not have come to this place. But blessed be my God, I have made the best choice. I have chosen affliction rather than sin and, therefore, welcome scaffold and welcome axe and welcome block and welcome death and welcome all, because it will send me to my Father's house.

"I have great cause to magnify God's grace that He has stood by me during mine imprisonment. It has been a time of no little temptation to me, yet (blessed be His grace) He has stood by me and strengthened me. I magnify His grace that though now I come to die a violent death, yet that death is not a terror to me. Through the blood of sprinkling, the fear of death is taken out of my heart. God is not a terror to me, therefore death is not dreadful to me. I bless my God, I speak it without vanity, I have formerly had more fear in the drawing of a tooth than I now have at the cutting off of my head. I was for some five or six years under a spirit of bondage and feared death exceedingly, but when the fear of death was upon me, death was not near me. But now death is near me; the fear of it is far from me, and blessed be my Saviour that has the sting of death in His own sides, and so makes the grave a bed of rest to me, and makes death (the last enemy) to be a friend, though he is a grim friend.

"Further, I bless my God that, though men have judged me to be cast out of the world, yet God has not cast me out of the hearts and prayers of His people. I would rather be cast out of the world than cast out of the hearts of godly men. Some think me (it is true) not worthy to live, and yet others judge I do not deserve to die. But God will judge all; I judge no man.

"I have now done. I have no more today but to desire the help of all your prayers that God would give me the continuance and supply of divine grace to carry me through this great work that I am now about; that as I am to do a work I never did, so I may have a strength I never had; that I may put off this body with as much quietness and comfort of mind as ever I put off my clothes to go to bed.

"And now I am to commend my soul to God and to receive my fatal blow. I am comforted in this: Though men kill me, they cannot damn me; and though they thrust me out of the world, yet they cannot shut me out of heaven. I am going to my long home and you are going to your short homes; but, I will tell you, I shall be at home before you. I shall be at my Father's house before you will be at your own houses. I am now going to the heavenly Jerusalem, to the innumerable company of angels, to Jesus the Mediator of the New Covenant, to the spirits of just men made perfect, and to God the Judge of all, 'in whose presence there is fullness of joy and at whose right hand are pleasures forevermore.'

"I conclude with the speech of the Apostle, 2 Timothy 4:6-7, 'I am now to be offered up, and the time of my departure is at hand; I have finished my course, I have fought the good fight, I have kept the faith, henceforth there is a crown of righteousness laid up for me; and not for me only, but for all them that love the appearing of our Lord Jesus Christ,' through whose blood (when my blood is shed) I expect remission of sins and eternal salvation. And so the Lord bless you all."

Then, turning to the sheriff he said, "May I pray?"

Sheriff Tichburn said, "Yes, but consider the time."

"I have done, sir," said Love. Then turning to the people, he said, "Beloved, I will but pray a little while with you to commend my soul to God, and I have done." And this is the prayer he prayed:

"Most glorious and eternal Majesty, Thou art righteous and holy in all Thou dost to the sons of men, though Thou hast suffered men to condemn Thy servant, Thy servant will not condemn Thee. He justifies Thee though Thou cuttest him off in the midst of his days and in the midst of his ministry, blessing Thy glorious name, that though he be taken away from the land of the living, yet he is not blotted out of the Book of the Living. Father, my hour is come. This Thy poor creature can say without vanity and falsehood. He hath desired to glorify Thee on earth; glorify Thou now him in heaven. He hath desired to bring the souls of other men to heaven; let his soul be brought to heaven.

"O Thou blessed God, whom Thy creature hath served, who hath made Thee his hope and his confidence from his youth, forsake him not now while he is drawing near to Thee. Now he is in the valley of the shadow of death, Lord, be Thou life to him. Smile Thou upon him while men frown upon him. Lord, Thou hast settled this persuasion in his heart that as soon as ever the blow is given to divide his head from his body he shall be united to his Head in heaven. Blessed be God that Thy servant dies in those hopes. Blessed be God that Thou hast filled the soul of Thy servant with joy and peace in believing.

"O Lord, think upon that poor brother of mine, who is a companion in tribulation with me, who is this day to lose his life as well as I. O fill him full with the joys of the Holy Ghost when he is to give up the ghost! Lord, strengthen our hearts that we may give up the ghost with joy and not with grief.

"We entreat Thee, O Lord, think upon Thy poor churches. O that England might live in Thy sight! And O that London might be a faithful city to Thee! That righteousness might be among them, that peace and plenty might be within her walls and prosperity within their habitations. Lord, heal the breaches of these nations; make England and Scotland as one staff in the Lord's hand, that Ephraim may not envy Judah, nor Judah vex Ephraim, but that both may fly upon the shoulders of the Philistines. O that men of the Protestant religion, engaged in the same cause and covenant, might not delight to spill each other's blood, but might engage against the common adversaries of our religion and liberty! God, show mercy to all that fear Thee. The Lord think upon our covenant-keeping brethren of the Kingdom of Scotland; keep them faithful to Thee, and let not them that have invaded them overspread their whole land. Prevent the shedding of more Christian blood if it seems good in Thine eyes.

"God show mercy to Thy poor servant who is now giving up the ghost. O blessed Jesus, apply Thy blood not only for my justification unto life, but also for my comfort, for the quieting of my soul so I may be in the joys of heaven before I come to the possession of heaven! Hear the prayers of all Thy people that have been made for Thy servant, and though Thou hast denied prayer as to that particular request concerning my life, yet let herein the fruit of prayer be seen, that Thou wilt bear up my heart against the fear of death. God show mercy to all that fear Him, and show mercy to all who have engaged for the life of Thy servant. Let them have mercy at the day of their appearing before Jesus Christ. Preserve Thou a godly ministry in this nation, and restore a godly magistracy, and cause yet good days to be the heritage of Thy people for the Lord's sake.

"Now, Lord, into Thy hands Thy servant commits his spirit; and though he may not with Stephen see the heavens open, yet let him have the heavens open. And though he may not see upon a scaffold the Son of God standing at the right hand of God, yet let him come to the glorious body of Jesus Christ and this hour have an intellectual sight of the glorious body of his Saviour. Lord Jesus, receive my spirit and, Lord Jesus, stand by me, Thy dying servant who hath endeavored in his lifetime to stand for Thee. Lord, hear, pardon all infirmities, wash away his iniquity by the blood of Christ, wipe off reproaches from his name, wipe off guilt from his person and receive him pure and spotless and blameless before Thee in love. And all this we beg for the sake of Jesus Christ. Amen and Amen."

After he had prayed, he turned to Sheriff Tichburn and said to him, "Sir, I thank you for your kindness; you have expressed a great deal of kindness to me. Well, I go from a block to the bosom of my Saviour."

Then he asked for the executioner. When the executioner came forward he said, "Art thou the officer?"

"Yes," said the executioner. At that point, Mr. Love is said to have tipped his executioner 3 pence wrapped in a piece of white paper. [This was a common practice to encourage the man to make sure that the beheading was completed with just one blow. Many executions were not completed with a single swipe of the axe, which caused enormous anxiety and anguish to the crowd and the individual.]

Love then lifted up his eyes to heaven and said, "O blessed Jesus, that hath kept me from the hurt of death and the fear of death, O blessed be God, blessed be God."

Then taking his leave of the ministers and his other friends he said, "The Lord be with you all." Then he knelt down and prayed a little while privately. And rising up he said, "Blessed be God, I am full of joy and peace in believing. I lie down with a world of comfort as if I were to lie down in my bed. My bed is but a short sleep, and this death is a long sleep where I shall rest in Abraham's bosom and in the embraces of the Lord Jesus."

When he was preparing to lay his head upon the block, Mr. Ashe said to him, "Dear brother, how dost thou find thy heart?"

Love replied, "I bless God, sir, I am as full of joy and comfort as ever my heart can hold."

The last words he was heard to speak were these, "Blessed be God for Jesus Christ."

Love then produced a red scarf which he directed to be disposed upon the block. He then knelt down and rested his head on the scarf. When he stretched forth his hands, the executioner severed his head from his body at one blow. Mr. Dun, the attending doctor, quickly united both head and body together again. Then the body of Christopher Love was placed in a black-draped coffin which was waiting to convey the remains away from the site. His body was later carried to the vicar's house where he had lived, where it lay until his burial three days later.

Richard Baxter said of him, "He died neither timorously nor proudly in any desperate bravado, but with as great alacrity and fearless quietness and freedom of speech as if he had gone to be, and had been as little concerned as the standers by."

On the day of his execution the sky was bright and unclouded, but soon after his execution had been carried out the sky grew overcast and black, and a terrible storm with thunder and lighting broke forth, raging all that night and till the next morning. The Presbyterians saw this as a sign that God was angry at the event that had occurred. On the other side of the issue, however, the Independents, Anabaptists, and others saw it as a "just judgment of God for his implacable apostasy and enmity."[1] According to Mary Love's memoirs, Christopher himself, in their last conversation before he died, predicted that God would give a visible sign of His displeasure with the whole affair.

And so it was that on August 22, 1651 Rev. Christopher Love, age thirty-three, minister of the gospel, husband to Mary and father of two with another on the way, was executed. It was generally felt that he was harshly dealt with and that the government, for taking his life, was considered by many to be pitiless. Richard Baxter said in his *Reliquae Baxterianae* (part 1, page 67), "This blow sank deeper towards the root of the new Commonwealth than will easily be believed; and made them grow odious to almost [all] the religious party in the land, except the sectaries. . . .Men count him a vile and detestable creature, who in his passion, or for his interest, or any such low account, shall deprive the world of such lights and ornaments, and cut off so much excellency at a blow, and be the persecutors of such worthy and renowned men. . . . After this, most of the ministers and good people of the land, did look upon the new Commonwealth as tyranny, and were more alienated from them than before."

On August 25, the Council of State wrote to the Lord Mayor of London the following:

> There is an intention to make a solemn funeral for Christopher Love, lately executed for high treason; James Winstanley his brother-in-law, is a

---

[1] Rev. James Anderson, *Memorable Women of the Puritan Times*, 2 vols., (London: Blackie and Son, 1862), 1:344.

> principal person in it; he is to be carried from Merchant Tailors' Hall, one of the most public places of the city. We do not judge it fit that he who was such a notorious traitor while he lived, and died an ignominious death for the same, should have so solemn a burial. Command that Merchant Tailors' Hall be kept shut up, and send for Winstanley, and any others concerned therein, and command them to desist from any such enterprise, as they will answer the contrary at their peril; and give them charge that the body be buried privately as one in his condition deserves. We have sent you such intelligence as we have, to prevent any misinformation from other reports.

Christopher Love was buried in a private ceremony at St. Lawrence Jewry on the north side of the chancel. His dear friend Thomas Manton preached his funeral sermon. The parish records gave this brief notice, "Christopher Love, our minister, buried near the chancel near reading desk the five and twentieth day of August, 1651."

Thirteen days after the execution, on September 4, 1651, Mary Love gave birth to their fifth child, James. The parish record of St. Lawrence Jewry simply states, "James Love, son of Rev. Christopher Love, our minister, baptized the 22nd day of September, 1651."

Sometime after her husband died (presumably sometime after 1660, for she speaks of the Restoration of the Monarchy in the past tense), Mary Love wrote one hundred forty pages of hand-written memoirs recounting his life and ministry. There are few references to herself within, and always in the third person. The complete manuscript is bound in a collection of printed funeral sermons in Dr. Williams' Library in London. It is preceded by two portraits of Love. One of those is used as the frontispiece of this book. Mary Love prefaced her account of his life with these words:

"I know not how far it may work thy bowels and affections (if thou pleasest to look upon it while it weeps). Surely all mine were moved in the working of it. Yet the debt I owe unto the truth, the testimony I owe unto the grace of God, and the memory of His servant suffered me not to decline either the sorrows by which such a rehearsal were moved in me or the censure which for it and its imperfections may possibly light upon me."

On October 27, 1651, the parish minutes of St. Lawrence Jewry show that the church leaders voted to give Mary Love the sum of £75 which they owed as back pay to her late husband.

Within months, at least by March of 1652, Mary had married Edward Bradshaw, mayor in 1648 and 1653 of the city of Chester in the west near Wales. This was not an uncommon practice for men of honor and the Christian religion to accept the responsibility and care of the families of men whom they greatly admired. No marriage records have been located for the marriage, but record keeping changed during the Commonwealth period. In a will dated November 1670, an Edward Bradshaw bequeathed the sum of £50 to his daughter-in-law Mary Love. This Edward Bradshaw was the father of the Edward Bradshaw who married Mary Love. The will notes that this sum had been paid to her in his lifetime and was not to be paid again after his death. This may tell us that Mary Love's second husband had already died by this time and that the other family members had taken responsibility for her maintenance.

Mary Love's marriage to Edward Bradshaw produced several children. Parish records for St. Peter's church in Chester show that Elizabeth was born January 24, 1653; Susanna was born April 12, 1657; Edward was born May 28, 1658; Hannah was born September 26, 1659; Esther was born November 5, 1661, and Benjamin was born January 25, 1662.

There is no record of the death of Mary Love in the Chester Council records, and I have been unable to locate anything further on her. The year 1665 saw the great plague come to London and surrounding areas, and it is possible that she died during this time with so many thousands of others.

In his letters to his wife before his death, Christopher Love mentioned two sons, Kit and Mall. In one of his letters to his wife from prison, however, he alluded to the fact that two of their children had already died (their first two children, both daughters and both named Mary) and were, in Love's opinion, in heaven. Mary Love, we know, was pregnant with a fifth child, James, at the time of Christopher's death, who himself died before he was seven months old. He was buried on April 26, 1652. Their oldest living son, Christopher, whom his father nicknamed "Kit," and who was only two years of age at the time of his father's death, later matriculated at Brasenose College, Oxford on March 30, 1666 at the age of seventeen. He left July 4, 1667.[2] No further record of him can be found. Nothing is said of Mall Love, and I have been unable

---

[2] *Brasenose College Register, 1509-1909*, (Oxford: Blackwell, 1909)

to find any mention of him in parish records where the other children's christening and burial dates are given. It is possible that Mall (most likely an affectionate nickname) was born while the family was out of town and was baptized in another parish.

Rev. John Quick, whose hand-written manuscript in the Williams' Library in London is a reliable source for material on Love from one who knew him personally, gave this account of his character: "He was a florid, sententious preacher, an excellent man in prayer, of a very fervent spirit, zealous in the cause of his God, and steadfast in his covenant to death. Much sweetness and love in his nature which, with other good qualities inherent in him, endeared him to his brethren in the ministry and to his congregation."

Mary Love said of her husband, "He lived too much in heaven to live long out of heaven." And as a postscript to a letter to him dated July 11, 1651, she wrote, "One comfort I would have of thee to carry to thy grave, if ever God did good to my soul, thou wast the chief instrument of it, for I never looked after God till I saw thy face."

In her memoirs she wrote, "His family looked upon him as a Moses for meekness and a Job for patience."

Simeon Ashe
(One of the London ministers who stood on the scaffold with Christopher Love)

17

My Most Dear and Precious Friend in the Lord

July 12, 1651

My most dear and precious friend, in whom I observed great reason both of love and honor, from the first day that God blessed me with the knowledge of you, but never more than at this time when you are ascending your triumphant chariot and mounting into the cloud of witnesses, Hebrews 12:1, to guide and encourage us who are left behind to run with readiness the race that is set before us.

Sweet sir, I wonder not you are so cheerful, being so near your journey's end; steered by our great pilot out of a dangerous and troubled sea, and entering into the harbor; putting off your pilgrim's weeds that you may be clothed with the white robes as a free denizen of the heavenly Jerusalem, I mistook in dreaming of an earthly Pentecost and Jubilee. That 50th day, I now perceive, was a hint and summons to call you to the everlasting Jubilee above, Hebrews 12:22-24, a parasceve [day of preparation] to the eternal Sabbath, Hebrews 4:9-10. How much are we beholden to our very enemies (rather than to God for them) who never do us more good than when they do us the shrewdest turn! I wonder not now at that epinikium of the Apostle's,

Romans 8:23, 33 to the end, and 1 Corinthians 3:21, 23. Death is so far from separating that it brings immediately to Christ, Philip-pians 1:23, and that by a stroke so honorable, so easy, so comfortable, so speedy, that you need but wink and go to heaven. The Lord is pleased to give you a writ of ease and to pay you your penny at the sixth hour. Blessed be God, we serve a good master who puts us only upon honest and honorable employments, makes our task easy and short, does all our works for us and in us, and after all rewards us freely and richly as if we had earned our wages; better be God's hireling than the world's darling, Luke 15:17, 19.

Dear sir, I bless God for your faithfulness, patience, courage, and wisdom, whereby you have tried and discovered the policy and strength of your antagonists, and showed to your poor unworthy fellow-sufferers that by grace they are conquerable. The Lord is with thee, thou mighty man of valor. Go in this thy might and smite the host of Midian as one man, Judges 6:12, 14, 16. The Lord make you a true Samson that you may do the devil's kingdom more mischief at your death than ever you did in all your life. God is now but in His old method, to make the martyrs the seed of His Church, Colossians 1:24. Hiel deserved a curse for building Jericho, Joshua 6:26, but God deserves blessing for building the new Jerusalem, though he lay the foundation thereof in Abiram his first-born (so is Christ our high Father, compare Genesis 17:5 with Isaiah 9:6), and set up the gates thereof in his younger son, Segub, 1 Kings 16 and last. Such are we, poor contemptible creatures, exalted and strengthened by God not only to do but also to suffer for His name, cause, church, and covenant, Acts 5:41 and Philippians 1:29. The Lord is making you such a blessed Segub, making that to be your honor, strength, and safety which many judged to be your shame, weakness, and danger.

Dear sir, God honors you to be the Elijah, and first to ascend the fiery chariot. May I, without presumption, be the Elisha and make two or three bold requests of you? And first let me beg your prayers for a double portion of your spirit. Second, let me see you, if possible, before you ascend, though it be but through the lattice on your nuptial morning. Third, let fall your mantile that I may be means of it be enabled to divide Jordan, yea, the Red Sea, if God calls me to it, and not sink like the Egyptians in the mighty waters, Psalm 32:6. Fourth, if there be any remembrance of things below in heaven, Luke 16:24-28, will you when you are in the blessed haven think of your poor friend, and the rest of your fellow-soldiers left behind and laboring in the storm until Christ shall come to them as He doth to you. Surely the church triumphant doth not forget the church militant, and prayer is no paradox in heaven, till the body of Christ be perfected, Revelation 6:9-10. If justice makes them pray against enemies, why should not charity draw out supplications for their friends? Surely there is a communion of saints between the church militant and triumphant; we may bless God for them, and cannot they pray for us? The martyrs would not pray to dead saints, but some of them desired living saints to pray for them, both on earth and in heaven, and I think therein they were not superstitious.

Sweet sir, I know to whom I speak, and am assured that love will not be puffed up with that which would soon burst a bladder of pride. None higher in God's eye than those that are lowest in their own. I see your time is short and, therefore, though my affections be like Jordan in the time of harvest, I must set bounds and banks to my words lest I divert and trouble you in your passage.

I doubt not but you remember that you must pass through Jordan to the fiery chariot. Jordan was not more effectual to cleanse Namaan's leprosy than the river of repentant tears is to purge the leprosy of sin, Psalm 119:136, next after the immense ocean of the blood of Christ. It is not Abana and Pharpar will wash away the leprosy but Jordan, nor will every tear wash away sin but penitent tears. You have but little time to mourn. Christ stands by with His towel and handkerchief, Psalm 56:8, Revelation 7:17, 21:4, Isaiah 45:8. Spiritual sorrow and joy are inseparable companions in this life, and the dove-like spirit of comfort loves these streams, Song of Solomon 3:12, Matthew 3:16. Every true Christian hath this baptism of the river joined with the baptism of fire; and now God honors you with the baptism of blood super-added. The cup of tears and cup of comfort may well go together, and happy is he who can mingle his drink with weeping, Psalm 102:9. Such need not fear to pledge Christ in His cup of blood, and undoubtedly shall sit at Christ's right hand in His kingdom, Matthew 20:22, 23, though not in the sense of the two ambitious brethren. If we could weep or repent for anything in heaven, sure it would be because we wept and repented no more or no better on earth. The Lord enable you and us all to do much work in a little time.

If I see you no more, I must be forced here to take

my long leave; yet why say I so? It may prove but a short leave since, in likelihood (as things stand) a few weeks, yea, days, may bring me to a sight of your blessed soul in the arms of Christ: and surely the communion of saints in heaven is connected with their essential happiness. The Lord enable me to imitate your graces, and then I shall not doubt to inherit your happiness, which is only God, the highest end and chiefest good. The Lord be nearer to you than your danger and support you in the most needful hour. And when men have done their worst, receive your soul to His mercy. Acts 7:55, 56, 59; Luke 2:29-30; 2 Timothy 4:4, 7, 8. So prays your poor unworthy friend and companion in the kingdom and tribulation of Jesus Christ,

Roger Drake

Thomas Manton
(London Minister who preached
Love's funeral sermon)

18

The Saints' Triumph Over Death

"But thanks be to God who giveth us the victory through our Lord Jesus Christ."
1 Corinthians 15:57

[Thomas Manton had a great respect for Christopher Love. He stood by him on the scaffold the day he was beheaded, and Love, as a token of his respect for Manton, gave him his cloak. When it became known that Manton was to deliver the funeral address, government soldiers threatened to shoot him; but Manton was undaunted and preached the following sermon on August 25, 1651 at St. Lawrence Jewry where Love had ministered.]

These words are a part of Paul's triumphant song. In the song there are two parts, and this is the last.

1. A confident challenge.

2. A solemn thanksgiving.

The one is directed to the enemies, the other to the Giver of victory.

1. A confident challenge, in which he outbraves death and all the powers of the grave: "O death, where is thy sting? O grave, where is thy victory?" The words allude to Hosea 13:14, wherein Christ is brought in speaking, "I will ransom them from the power of death, and redeem them from the grave: O death, I will be thy plagues; O grave, I will be thy destruction." There is Christ's engagement and undertaking for a full conquest of death; Christ threatens death and the

apostle insults over it. The form of the words is altered because the enemy was now fallen and Paul proclaims the victory. Hitherto death and the grave had insulted over the misery and frailty of mankind; all the tombs and charnels of the world were but so many monuments of death's conquests. Golgotha, the place of skulls, seemed to be designed on purpose to upbraid and discourage our Redeemer; so many skulls and rotten relics of human frailty as there were in that place, so many trophies and monuments of triumph did death produce before the eyes of Christ; as if it were said to Him, "Canst Thou, darest Thou, grapple and enter into the lists with such an enemy?"

But our Lord was not discouraged. When He ascended upon the cross, He did, as it were, answer these bravings of death thus: "O death, I will be thy plague; O grave, I will be thy destruction;" and because He was as good as His word, and every way performed His engagement, the Apostle, as one of Christ's followers, comes and insults over this proud adversary that was now fallen. "O death, where is thy sting? O grave, where is thy victory?"

This challenge is illustrated by a prolepsis, or an anticipation of the object. Some might ask, "What is the sting of death? What is the power of the grave?" The Apostle answers, "The sting of death is sin, the strength of sin is the law." Death cometh to have this power by sin, and sin to have this power by the law.

The sting of death (*kentron*) the prick. It implies both the stroke of death and the anguish of it, as in the sting of a serpent, there is the deadly touch and the pain and torment of the wound. And so it notes the power of death over us—the prick or weapon by which it strikes is sin: Romans 5:12, "By one man sin entered into the world, and death by sin"—and the terrors and horrors of it, which also arise from sin. Now, by horrors I mean not only the natural aversion, retirement, or flights of the spirits, but the bondage, torment, and despair that is upon the conscience. As death is a penal evil, inflicted by the justice of God, guilt makes death terrible, so that a sinner is "all his lifetime subject to bondage," Hebrews 2:14-15, and kept under an awe of judgment to come. It is not always felt, but soon awakened, especially in sickness and approaches of death. When we feel the cold hands of it ready to pluck out our hearts, conscience is whipped with a scourge of six strings—fear, horror, distrust, grief, rage, and shame.

"The strength of sin is the law." How is that to be understood? The law gives strength to sin. "By reason of knowledge, obligation, and aggravation." These are the words of Pareus, a German divine, and will yield us a fit method wherein to open this matter.

1.) The law exposes sin and makes it appear in its own colors. The more light and knowledge of the law, the more sense of sin, as in transparent vessels dregs are soon discerned. Romans 7:9, "I was alive without the law, but when the law came, sin revived and I died." When, by a sound conviction, disguises are taken off from the conscience, we find sin to be sin indeed. Paul was alive before, that is, in his own hopes, as many a stupid soul makes full account he shall go to heaven, till conscience is opened and then they find themselves in the mouth of death and hell.

2.) The law gives strength to sin in regard of the obligation of it; it binds over a sinner to the curse and wrath of God. God has made a righteous law which must have satisfaction, and till the law is satisfied we hear no news but of a curse, and that makes death to be full of horrors. Hebrews 10:27, "There remaineth nothing but a fearful expectation of the fiery indignation of the Lord."

3.) It augments and increases sin by forbidding it; lusts are exasperated and rage upon a restraint, as the yoke makes the young bullock more unruly. Now, put all together and you will understand the force of the expression, "The strength of sin is the law." The discovery of the law stops the sinner's mouth, and the curse of the law shuts him up and holds him fast unto the judgment of the great day, by which restraint sin grows the more raging and furious; all which put together make death terrible; not an end of misery but a door to open into hell.

Now, this being the case of every man, what shall we do? And how shall we extricate our souls from such a labyrinth of endless horror? You have an answer to that in the next verse in the Apostle's thanksgiving, where he acquaints you not only with grounds of hope but triumph. "Thanks be to God, who giveth us the victory through our Lord Jesus Christ."

In this thanksgiving you may observe:

The author of the mercy: God, by Jesus Christ.

The manner how we may come to be interested in it: "He giveth us victory." Or rather, you may observe: (1) the act of the Father as to Jesus Christ, in that He appointed Him to get the victory; or (2) the act of the Father as to us, in that He applies this victory to our souls. Christ's victory and the application of it are the two grounds of this thanksgiving.

First, Christ's victory over sin, death, and the law,

for it must be extended to all the things mentioned in the context; they are enemies by combination and knit together in a fast league. The law gives strength to sin and sin gives a sting to death. As long as the law has power, sin will be strong; and as long as sin has strength, death will be terrible. But Christ has overcome death. He foiled it in His own person, as I shall show you anon fully. And for sin, He has taken away the guilt of it by His own merit, and will destroy it more and more by the power of the Holy Ghost. When He stood before the tribunal of God, He stood there as a Surety and Undertaker. Hebrews 7:22, "A surety of a better testament." He was a Surety, mutually God's and ours, to work God's work in us and our work for us. Among other things which He understood there, He undertook the abolition of sin. On God's part, He obliged Himself that it should be performed by His Spirit; on our part, He obliged us to endeavors of mortification. Now, because Christ is an able Surety, the work is as good as done already. Romans 6:6, "Knowing this, that our old man is crucified with Him, that the body of sin might be destroyed, that henceforth we should not serve sin." Mark, it "is crucified with Him," implying His undertaking upon the cross, that the "body of death might be destroyed," noting the work of God's Spirit which was engaged and made sure by Christ's death upon the cross "that we should not serve sin," noting the concurrence of our endeavors to which we are obliged by the same sponsory act of Christ. Thus much Christ has done for the abolition of sin. Now for the law. That was an enemy that could not be overcome but must be satisfied, and so it was by Christ, who both performed the duty and sustained the penalty of it, chiefly that latter. And therefore it is said, "He was made a curse for us," Galatians 3:13. The sting is lost in Christ and the honey is left for us. But this is matter of another respect and cognizance.

Second, the next reason for the Apostle's thanksgiving is the application. He "hath given us the victory," for understanding of which you must note that:

1. Christ's victory is imputed to us as if it were done in our own person. When we are actually united to Him, we are possessed of all His merit. Christ fought our war and joined battle in our stead. We have a mystical victory in Christ and are said to overcome when Christ overcame. This is the reason why the acts of believers are complicated and folded up with Christ's acts in the expression of Scripture, "crucified with Him", "quickened with Him", "raised with Him", and "set down with Him in heavenly places," Ephesians 2. All these terms are proper to the judicial union, which is different both from the moral and mystical, as I could easily show you were it not a matter of another nature. Now, this mystical victory is of great use to a believer in time of discouragements.

If the law challenges, Satan and conscience say, "You are a sinner under a curse."

And you may answer, "I am a sinner, but I am crucified in Christ, in my Surety. His payment and suffering is mine."

If death or the world discourages you may say, "This is a beaten enemy; I foiled it in Christ, I ascended in Christ."

2. The benefit of this victory is imparted and applied to us, by which He makes us conquerors over death and sin. All Christ's work was not done on the

cross; there is much to be accomplished in our hearts. Romans 16:20, "The God of peace shall tread Satan under your feet," not only under Christ's feet but ours; as Joshua called his fellows to come and tread upon the necks of the Canaanitish kings, Joshua 10:24, "Come, put your feet upon the necks of these kings," so Christ will see us conquer. He that got a victory *for* us will get a victory *in* us over sin, death, and hell. Christ has trodden them under foot already when His own heel was bruised, Genesis 3:15; now He will do it under your feet.

Having laid this foundation, the point and head of doctrine which I shall discuss is Christ's victory over death for the comfort and profit of believers.

Death is either the first or second, temporal or eternal. Sinners are under the sentence of both, and both are, in a sort, put into the hands of Satan. He has the power of death, Hebrews 2:14, as God's executioner, and the one makes way for the other. Death to the wicked is but taking them away to torment, as unruly persons are committed to prison that they may molest no more. God's patience expires with their lives and then His vengeance begins. The curse of that first covenant was eternal death, Genesis 2:15, "Thou shalt die," that is, eternally. The curse must carry proportion with the blessing. The blessing was eternal life and the curse was eternal death. I say, the sorrow and pain must have been perpetual, answerable to the life which he should have enjoyed; therefore, Christ is said to have "delivered us from the wrath to come," which certainly was our portion and inheritance by Adam. And without Christ there is no escape. But to come to particulars, I shall show you:

1. How Christ delivered us from death.

2. How far.

1. How He delivered us the Apostle answers that in Hebrews 2:14, "By death He destroyed him that had the power of death." Now, Christ's death comes under a twofold consideration—as a merit, or as a glorious act of war and combat; as the act of a Redeemer or the act of a conqueror, which answers to the double evil in death. It is a natural evil and a penal evil. It is a natural evil as it is the dissolution of soul and body; it is a penal evil as it is a curse of the covenant or the punishment of sin.

1.) There was merit in Christ's voluntary death; it was a ransom for the elect. He died not only for their good and profit, but in their room and stead. As when the ram was taken Isaac was spared, so Christ's death was instead of ours. God will not exact the debt twice, from us and from our Surety. Job 33:24, "Deliver him from going down into the pit, for I have found a ransom." The sinner must die or the Surety. "Now," says the Lord, "I accept the death and passion of Christ for this penitent man." If we go down to the pit, we do not go down by way of vengeance. By Christ's death, the merit of our sin is expiated, justice satisfied, God's wrath appeased, the law fulfilled, sin pardoned, and so the jaws of death are broken. Death in itself is the sentence of the law, the fruit of sin, and the recompense of angry justice, and so it has no more to do with us, for God has found a ransom.

2.) You may look upon it as the act of a conqueror. Christ foiled death in his own person. Ever since he rifled the grave, death has lost its retentive power. Acts 2:24, "loosing the pains," etc. It is an allusion to the throes of a travailing woman. The grave was in travail till this precious burden was egested, for He could not be held by it, and ever since the grave is a womb rather than a dungeon and pit of vengeance. It does not destroy life but renew it. In almost the same metaphor, Christ is called "the first born from the dead," Colossians 1:18; not that He was the first that was raised from the dead, howbeit He was the first that arose. Others were raised by the power of another, but Christ arose by His own. So He is called, 1 Corinthians 15:20, "the first fruits from the dead." As the offering of the first fruits was a blessing to all the store, so Christ dying and rising is a ground of conquest to all the elect. Christ, before His death, had been combating with the powers of darkness and all the subordinate instruments. Death was Satan's beast of prey that was set upon Him; but our Lord foiled it in its own dungeon. The battle between Christ and death was begun upon the cross; He grappled with it there and they went tugging and wrestling to the grave. Christ, like a prudent warrior, carried the war into His enemy's country, and there got loose of the grasp of death, foiled it in its own territory. He arose and left death gasping behind Him, so that the quality of the grave is quite altered. Before it was a prison, Satan's dungeon; now it is a chamber of repose, a bed of ease, ever since Christ slept there. When the prophet speaks of Christ's resurrection, He said, Isaiah 53:8, "He shall be taken from prison and from judgment"—by prison meaning the grave; but speaking of the death of the faithful He said, "Isaiah 57:2, "They shall rest in their beds." It was, for a while, to Christ a prison that to us it might be a bed of ease.

2. The next question is how far he has delivered us from death. We see the godly are obnoxious to the changes and decays of nature, yea, to the strokes of violence, as well as others; and how are we delivered? I answer, it is enough that the second death has no power over us, Revelation 20:6; nothing to do with us, Romans 8:1: "not one condemnation." We may die, but we shall not be damned; and, though we go to the grave, yet we are freed from hell. But this is not all. In the first death, believers have a privilege: they do not die as others do.

1.) The habitude and nature of it is changed. That which is penal in death is now gone. It is not a destruction but a delivery. Believers have wrong thoughts of death. We are delivered from it as it is a punishment and a curse. Now it is a blessing, one of Christ's legacies to the church. 1 Corinthians 3:22, "all things are yours." While death was in the devil's hands, it was an enemy; but it is made a friend and a blessing in Christ, a passage from the vale of tears to the kingdom of glory, the end of a mortal life, and the beginning of that which is immortal. As Haman to Mordecai, it is intended a mischief, but it proves a privilege. To a wicked man it is properly an execution, but to the godly it is a dismissal of their souls into the bosom of Christ. Luke 2:28, "Now lettest thou thy servant depart in peace." They quietly send away their souls, but a wicked man's soul is taken away. It is twice so expressed: Luke 12:20, "this night shall they take away thy soul from thee"; and Job 27:8, "When God taketh away his soul." They would fain keep it longer, but God takes it away whether they will or not. A godly man resigns and sends away his soul in peace. His life cannot be taken away; it is only yielded up upon the call of providence, and he dies not because he must die but because he would die; for when God wills it, he submits.

But to return, the blessing of death lies in three things:

First, the funerals of the godly are but the funerals of their sins, frailties, and weaknesses. Sin dies, misery dies, but the man does not die. All other means and dispensations but weaken sin, but death destroys it. When God justifies, the damning power is gone; when God sanctifies, the reigning power is gone; but when by death we come to be glorified, then the very being of it is gone. When the house was infected with leprosy so that scraping would not serve the turn, then it was to be torn down. We are so infected with sin that all other remedies are too weak; nothing but death will serve the turn. When ivy has gotten into a wall, it cannot be wholly destroyed till the wall is demolished; cut off the stump, the body, the boughs, the branches, there are still some strings that are ready to sprout again. So it is here: original sin cannot be destroyed. The constant groans of the faithful are, "Who shall deliver us from this body and mass of sin?" Romans 7:24. But now, death is a sudden cure. Sin brought in death and, as if a revenge, death destroys sin.

Second, there is a way made for a present and complete union of the soul with Christ. Philippians 1:23, "I desire to be dissolved and be with Christ." We are loosed from the body and joined to Christ. It is better that a soul is separated from the body than absent from Christ. We have a union here, but not a presence.

Now you judge which is better—to be present with the body or to be present with the Lord? To have the company of the body or the company of Christ? Here the soul is enclosed and imprisoned, as it were; but there you have the free enjoyment of Christ without the clog of an earthly estate. When Potiphar's wife laid hold on Joseph's coat, he escaped; so you can leave your upper garment in death's hand, but the soul flies to God. The body came from Adam and runs in a fleshly channel, and what we had from Adam must, for a while, be moldered to dust to purge it from the impurity of the conveyance; but the soul, by a natural right, returns to God who gave it, and by a special interest to Christ who redeemed and sanctified it by His own Spirit.

Third, the body, which seems most to suffer, has much advantage; a shed is taken down to raise up a better structure. "It is sown a natural body, it is raised a spiritual body," 1 Corinthians 15:44. Here it is not capable of high enjoyments; it is humbled with diseases and unfit for duties. Again, "it is sown a corruptible body, it is raised an incorruptible body." Here it is liable to changes; there it may live forever without change and decay. If we love long life, there is eternal life. It is carnal self-love that makes us willing to abide in the flesh; if we did love ourselves, we would be afraid to die; for to die is to be perfected, to have the body and soul free from sin and corruption.

2.) The hurt of it is prevented. As you are chosen and sanctified in Christ Jesus, it cannot hurt you. I say again, death may kill you, but it cannot hurt you; it has no power over the better part. Like a serpent, it feeds only upon your dust; nay, and for your bodies, that which dies as a creature is sure to live as a member of Christ. The Lord Jesus is our head in the grave; your bodies have a principle of life within them; believers are raised by the Spirit of holiness; the same Spirit that quickens them now to the offices of grace shall raise their mortal bodies. So says Romans 8:11, "He shall quicken your mortal bodies by His Spirit that dwelleth in you." The Holy Ghost can never leave His old mansion and dwelling place. How many grounds of comfort have we against the mortality of the body! Christ is united to body and soul, and He will not let His mystical body lack one sinew or joint. In the account that He is to make to the Father, He says that He is to lose nothing, John 6:39. Mark, He does not say none, but "nothing." Christ will not lose a leg or a piece of an ear.

Again, God is in covenant with body and soul. When you go down to the chambers of death, you may challenge Him upon the charter of His own grace. God is the God of Abraham's dust, of a believer's dust; though it is mingled with the remains of wicked men, yet Christ will sever it, Matthew 22:32. Christ proves the resurrection of the body by that argument that "God is the God of Abraham, the God of Isaac, and the God of Jacob." The ground of the argument is that God made His covenant not only with the souls of the patriarchs, but with their whole persons.

Again, Christ has purchased body and soul, so much is intimated in 1 Corinthians 6:20, "Ye are bought with a price, therefore glorify God with your bodies." Christ has paid price enough to get a title to body and soul and, therefore, He will not lose one bit of His purchase. The Lord will call the grave to an account: "Where is the body of My Abraham, My Isaac, My Jacob?" It is said, Revelation 20:13, "The sea gave up her dead, and the grave gave up her dead, and hell gave up her dead." Let me note that "hell" is there taken for the state of the departed, or else what is the meaning of that passage that follows afterward, "and death and hell were cast into the lake that burneth"? Well, then, all the dead shall be cast up. As the whale cast up Jonah, so the grave shall cast up her dead

The grave is but a chest wherein our bodies are kept safe till the day of Christ, and the key of this chest is not in the devil's hands but Christ's. See Revelation 1:18, "I have the keys of death and hell." When the body is laid up in the cold pit, it is laid up for another day. God has a special care of our dust and remains; when our friends and neighbors have left it, Christ leaves it not, but keeps it till the great and glorious day.

3.) We are eased from the terrors and horrors of death. Death is terrible as it is a penal and natural evil, as I distinguished before.

As it is a natural evil. Death in itself is the greatest of all evils. Job called it "the king of terrors," Job 18:14. We gush to see a serpent, much more the grim visage of death. Moral philosophy could never find out a remedy against it. Heathens were either desperate, rash, stupid, or else they dissembled their gripes and fears; but Christ has provided a remedy. He has delivered us not only from the hurt of death but from the fear of death. Hebrews 2:14, "To deliver them from the fear of death, that all their lifetime were subject to bondage." By His Spirit, He fills the soul with the hopes of a better life. Nature may shrink when we see the pale horse of death approaching, but we may rejoice when we consider its errand: it is to carry us home. When old Jacob saw the chariots come from Egypt, how his heart leaped within him because he would see his son Joseph. Death, however we figure it with the pencil of fancy, is sent to carry us to heaven, to transport us to Jesus Christ. Now, who would be afraid to be happy? To be in the arms of our beloved Jesus? Let them fear death who do not know a better life! A Christian knows that when he dies he shall "not perish but have everlasting life," John 3:16. The world may thrust you out, but you may see heaven alluring, ready to receive you, as Stephen saw heaven opened, Acts 7:56.

There is an intellectual vision or persuasion of faith which is common to all the saints, though every one does not have such ecstasy and sensible representation as Stephen had. Yet usually, in the hours of their departure, faith is mightily strengthened and acted so that they are exempted from all fear and sorrow.

As it is a penal evil. It is sad when death is sent in justice, and clothed with wrath, and comes in the quality of a curse. You know what was said before: "The sting of death is sin." They die indeed who die in their sins. Death is a black and gloomy day to them; they drop down like rotten fruit into the lake of fire. Now Christ has taken away the sting, the dolors and horrors of it; He has taken away death as He has taken away sin. He has not cast it out, but cast it down; He has taken away the guilt and power of it, though not the being of sin. So the hurt, the sting is gone, though not death itself. It is like a serpent disarmed and unstinged; we may put it into our bosoms without danger. There are many accusations by which Satan is apt to perplex a dying soul.

These make death terrible and full of horrors, but "they overcome by the blood of the Lamb," Revelation 12:11, and get the victory of these doubts and fears. When sins are pardoned, fears vanish. Luther said, "Strike, Lord, strike; my sins are pardoned."

4.) It will be utterly abolished at the last day. We scarcely know now what Christ's purchase means till the day of judgment. It is said, 1 Corinthians 15:26, "The last enemy that shall be destroyed is death." It is weakened now, but then it shall be abolished as to the elect. Revelation 20:14, "And death and hell shall be cast into the lake of fire, this is the second death." The dominion of death is reserved for hell; it must keep company with the damned while you rejoice with God. For the present, it is continued out of dispensation; it does service to promote God's glory, but then the wicked must share death and hell among them and be kept under a dying life or a living death; but all tears shall be wiped from your eyes, Revelation 7:17. Death shall be no more, and you shall take the harps of God in your hands, and in a holy triumph say, "O death, where is thy sting? O grave, where is thy victory?" It is true, we may say it, yea, and sing it now in hope, as some birds sing in winter, but then we are properly said to triumph.

To apply it now.

USE 1. Here is terror for wicked men. You may think it strange that I should draw terror out of such a comfortable doctrine, but consider that Jesus Christ has conquered death for none but those who have an interest in Him. Others, alas, are under the full power of it! For the present, the case of wicked men is sad; in death it will be worse; in hell it will be worst of all.

1. It is sad for the present. There is a bondage upon your souls, not always felt but soon awakened. You cannot think of death and hell without torment. The thought of it, like Belshazzar's handwriting against the wall, smites you with trembling in the midst of all your cups and bravery. A small thing will awaken a wicked man's conscience, the fingers of a man's hand upon the wall. Belshazzar seemed a jolly fellow, a brave spirit; he set light by the Persian forces that were even at his door. But God soon took the edge off his bravery and then his joints trembled, his knuckles smote one against another for fear. If the Lord will but whist to conscience, the bravest spirits are soon daunted; He needs arm nothing against you but your own thoughts. Certainly none but a child of God can have a true and solid courage against death; you cannot suppose it without consternation. David said in Psalm 23:4, "Though I walk through the valley of the shadow of death, yet I will fear no evil." That is a grisly, sad, dark place to walk in, the very borders of death, side by side with terrors and destruction; yet there David would be confident. It is otherwise with wicked men; hereafter they would not live, and here they would not die.

2. In death it will be worse; the nearer you draw to the everlasting state, the more will conscience be opened and scourge you with horror and remorse. I confess, every wicked man does not lie sensible. Some are stupid and foolhardy; they may sacrifice a stout body to a stubborn mind, but at last they die uncertain, doubtful if not anxious, and full of horror. As Adrian said to his soul, "O poor soul! Whither dost thou go now? Thou shalt never sport it more, jest it more." Or,

as he said, "I have lived doubtfully and die uncertainly; alas! whither do I go?"

A man that leaps in the dark near a deep gulf knows not where his feet shall land, and this is the case of wicked men. But this is not all. Usually their death is full of terror. When things written with the juice of a lemon are brought to the fire, they are plain and legible. So, when wicked men are within the stench and smell of hell, they howl upon their beds. Few or none are able to look death in the face with confidence. Oh! Consider, when you come to die, sin stares in the face of conscience, and conscience remits you to the law, and the law binds you over to hell, and hell enlarges her mouth to receive you. What will you do in such a case? Satan insults; your old tempter has become your new accuser. Nay, you are at odds with yourself; the body curses the soul for an ill guide, and the soul curses the body for a wicked instrument. It is a sad parting when they can never expect to meet again but in flames and torments and, therefore, curse the memory of that day whenever they were joined together. A godly man can take fair leave of his body. Farewell, flesh! Go, rest in hope. You shall one day awake out of the dust, and then I shall be satisfied with God's likeness. I have a longing desire of your reunion. We have lived together and glorified God together this long, God will not suffer you to see corruption."

3. In hell it will be worst of all. Envy will be a part of your torment as well as despair. In Luke 16:23, it is said of the rich man, "In hell he lifted up his eyes, and seeth Lazarus in Abraham's bosom, and saith, I am tormented in this flame." It will be an additional torment to compare the believers' eternal happiness with

your own misery. They are in the presence of God and His holy angels. You have no company but the devil, death, hell, and the damned, and are held under the power of everlasting torments. You would not live and you cannot die. When you have run through many thousands of years, you cannot look for one minute of rest. Conscience gnaws more and more; you burn but are not consumed. Oh! "It is a dreadful thing to fall into the hands of the living God," Hebrews 10:31. Mark that attribute, *living* God. We do not speak in the name of an idol who cannot avenge his quarrel upon you, or of a God who shall die and suffer decay, but in the name of a *living* God who lives forever to see vengeance executed upon His adversaries. There is no hope of release; as long as God is God, hell is hell.

USE 2. It serves to exhort us all to get an interest in this conquest of Christ. Every one is not fit to make use of Christ's victory over death. There are many things necessary to enjoy the full comfort of it. I shall name them.

1. A care to get sin pardoned. All the power of the devil and death hangs on sin; therefore, see sin buried before you are buried or it will not be well with you. There are two deep pits wherein you may bury your sins, and you shall never hear of them any more: the ocean of divine mercy and the grave of Christ.

See them buried in the ocean of mercy. Micah 7:19, "Thou wilt cast all their sins into the depths of the sea." There is depth enough to bury and drown them so that they may no more come into remembrance.

Then there is the grave of Christ. The merit of Christ is a deep grave, deep enough wherein to bury all the sins of the world. We are "buried with Him in baptism," Romans 6:4. Otherwise, if this is not done, you will desire to be buried eternally and never to rise more. Let me use one metaphor more in this matter, and it shall take its rise from that expression of the Apostle in 2 Corinthians 5:3. He says, "We shall be clothed upon if so be that we shall not be found altogether naked." It is the great fault of Christians, when they come to die, that they are to seek for a shroud and are found altogether naked. It is uncomely to see a man in his nakedness; you should be wrapped in the winding-sheet of Christ's righteousness. There is no shroud like that. Come thus to the grave and the grave shall have no power over you. But to leave the metaphor: this must be your great work and care, Christians, to reflect upon these things in the serious applications and discourses of faith, the infinite mercy of God, the abundant merit of Christ, and the sufficiency of His righteousness for your acceptance with God.

2. Do not only act faith, but strive after assurance of God's love to your souls. Old Simeon said, Luke 2:29-30, "Mine eyes have seen Thy salvation; now let me depart in peace." He held the Messiah not only in his arms but in his heart, and then he could comfortably dismiss his soul. "Now let me die," said Jacob when he had seen Joseph. As for his own comfort and profit, he can never die too soon who has seen Jesus. His death is not untimely and immature by whatever stroke he is cut off. Whereas otherwise, if you live a hundred years, you die too soon if you die before you have gotten an interest in Christ. "The sinner of an hundred years shall be accursed." Old sinners who are left to be eaten out by their own ruse are chimneys long foul, and

come at last to be fired.

3. Mortify corruptions. Sin must die before we die; he dies well whose sins are dead before him. Either sin must die or the sinner. As the prophet said in another case I say in this, "Thy life must go for its life." You will find those sins mortal that are not mortified. What should an unmortified man do with heaven? There are no sports nor carnal pleasures there; those blessed mansions seem to him but dark shades and melancholy retirements. The Apostle has an expression in Colossians 1:12, "He hath made us meet to be partakers of the inheritance of the saints in light." We are first made meet for heaven before we enter into it; we are weaned from the world before we leave it. When men hang upon the world as long as they can, and, when they can hang no longer, think then to make use of God, the Lord will refuse them with disdain. "Go to the gods which you have chosen," Judges 10:14. Let the world now help and save you. In short, a mortified man is prepared and ready. He merely waits for wind and tide, and falls like a shock of corn in season.

4. A holy life and conversation. Men live as if they never thought to die, and then die as if they never thought to live. The best way to die well is to live well; they who are not ashamed to live are not afraid to die. Balaam desired to "die the death of the righteous," but would not take pains to live a godly life. Every man cannot say, "Thanks be to God that giveth us the victory by Jesus Christ." You cannot die in Christ unless you live in Him and, in the power of His life, advance towards heaven. Oh, labor to exercise yourselves in these things that you may be in a constant preparation. You never enter into the combat with death but once.

It is impossible to mend oversights; either we are slain or saved eternally. Now, if you do what I have here exhorted you to, you may wait until your change comes, and, when it comes, your last hour will prove your best.

USE 3. It serves to press God's children to improve the comforts of Christ's victory; do not let it go out of your hands.

1. Improve it for your friends who are departed in the Lord. Our weeping puts some disparagement upon Christ's conquest. Why should we weep in the day of their preferment, in the day of their solemn espousals to Jesus Christ? In the primitive times, at funerals, they were wont to sing psalms of thanksgiving. We should bring them as champions to the grave as those who have passed the pikes, finished their course, kept the faith, and have conquered the world, sin, death, and danger. Chrysostom, in one of his homilies on the Hebrews, spoke of the ancient rites at funerals, of their hymns, psalms, and praises: "All of these signify joy; and will you weep and sing a psalm of praise and triumph at the same time?"

I confess it is said, Acts 8:2, that "devout men carried Stephen to his burial and made great lamentation over him." It is our loss when the church is bereaved of such excellent persons; there is cause of sorrow, but there should be a mixture. We should not mourn as those without hope, 1 Thessalonians 4:13. As Christians must not rejoice without sorrow, so they must not be sorry without some mixture of joy. Let us declare that we hope for a resurrection, that we expect to meet our friends again in heaven, and when we weep let it be like rain when the sun shines. There should be something of joy in our countenances as well as tears in our eyes.

2. Improve it for yourselves, and that:

1.) In lifetime, that in your resolutions you may be willing to die. Many times we are like Lot in Sodom, or like the Israelites in Egypt: we could wish for Canaan but are loathe to go out of Egypt. This argues little faith. Can we believe there is a heaven so excellent and glorious and yet shun it? Can we hope for such an "incorruptible inheritance," 1 Peter 1:4, and yet be afraid that we shall enter upon it to soon? What prince would live uncrowned? What heir would whine when he is called to come and take the inheritance? What thoughts do we have of eternal life? Do we count it a privilege or a misery and burden?

And again, it argues little love. Can we pretend to love Christ and be shy of His company? He should be unwilling to die who is unwilling to go to Christ.

Again, it argues little judgment and consideration. Wherein is this life valuable? The world is nothing else but a place of banishment. Here is nothing but groaning; all the creatures join in comfort with the heirs of promise, Romans 8:23. What do you see in the world, or in the present life, to make you be in love with it? Are you not weary of misery and sin? The longer you live, you sin the more. Certainly you have provoked God long enough already; it is high time to breathe after a better estate, and you have had taste enough of the world's misery and deceit, and of the frailties and weaknesses of the body. A longer life would be but a longer sickness. What is the matter if we are so loathe to let go our hold of present things? If it is not for lack of faith or lack of love to Christ, or too much love of the world, certainly it must be fear of death. And what a baseness and lowness of spirit is this, to fear an enemy so often vanquished by Christ and His saints? If you are at this pass, I have preached all this while in vain, and the victory of Christ of which I have discoursed is to little purpose.

Oh, consider, generous heathens may shame you! You make all the provision of Christ in the gospel to be of less effect than mere moral principles.

2.) Especially improve this in the very season and hour of death. The great Goliath is now fallen, and you may come forth and look upon the carcass, Isaiah 66:4. Death itself, which startles the creatures and seems to be the great check and prejudice of Christian hopes, is vanquished by Christ. Therefore, in the very season when it seems to prevail over you, apply the victory and say, "Thanks be to God." When the pangs come upon you, remember this is death's last pull and assault. You may bear with it; it shall molest you no more, as Moses said, Exodus 14:13, "The Egyptians which ye have seen today, ye shall see them no more again for ever." So you shall feel these things no more. In heaven there are no groans, nor tears, nor sorrows; have but a little patience and, as soon as the last gasp is over, the soul shall be carried by angels to Christ, and by Christ to God. Believers have the same entertainment that Christ had; He was carried into heaven by angels. Daniel 7:13, "They brought him to the Ancient of days." And so we are carried by angels into Abraham's bosom, Luke 16:22. They have a train to accompany them into heaven, as their friends accompany their bodies to the grave. And as Christ was welcomed into heaven with acclamations, and God said, "Sit down at My right hand," Psalm 110:1, and "Ask of Me, and I will give it thee," Psalm 2, so are believers welcomed: "Well done, good and faithful servant, enter into thy master's joy."

What remains, then, but that we die by faith as well as live by faith; but that we welcome death with confidence and breathe out our soul in triumph? When Moses took up the serpent in his hand, it was but a rod; death thus welcomed and entertained by faith will prove at most but a correction, yea, rather a blessing of the covenant, a means of passage into glory.

One thing I almost forgot, to press you to thankfulness to Christ. Oh! Bless your Redeemer who has delivered you from the fear of death; admire His love and condescension, that He should come down from heaven and substitute Himself in our room and place, and take the horrors of death into His own soul. It is said, Matthew 20:28, "The Son of man came not to be ministered unto, but to minister, and to give His life a ransom for many." Christ was a prince by birth, heir of all things, yet He came not in the pomp and equipage of a prince. If He had come in state to visit us, and to deliver comfort to us by word of mouth, it would have been much; but Christ did not come in this way, not in the pomp of a prince, but in the form of a servant, to minister to our necessities, and that in the highest way of self-denial: He gave His life as a ransom for many. Other princes are lavish of their subjects' blood, and do not care how many lay down their lives for them. Many give their lives as a ransom for the prince, but here it is quite otherwise. This prince lays down His life to redeem the subjects, and He suffered death that it might not be terrible and destructive to us. Oh, blessed be the Lord Jesus Christ for this love forevermore!

Some may expect that I should speak something concerning the servant of God, our dear brother now departed, but I need not say anything other than what I have spoken already all along the discourse. I have indeed spoken of him, and that in the judgment of your consciences. The duties which I pressed upon you he performed; the comforts which I have propounded to you he enjoyed. I shall not make any particular rehearsal of the passages of his exemplary life. I do not judge it convenient. Only to you of this place I may take liberty to commend his doctrine and entreat you to be careful of those precious truths which he sowed among you while the Lord used him here as a skillful seedsman. God looks for some increase, and takes special notice of the time that you have enjoyed his labors. There is an exact account kept in heaven, as in that parable in Luke 13:7, "These three years came I seeking fruit." Probably the three years of Christ's ministry are intended, for then He was entering upon His last half year. God reckons how many years, how many months, your minister has been with you, and accordingly expects fruit. Your pastor, a little before his suffering, professed high and worthy thoughts of you; let him not be deceived. It will be sad for you in that great day of separation that, when he expects to find you among the sheep, and to be his crown and rejoicing, he should see you among the goats. He will know you there; memory in heaven is not abolished but perfected. I say he will know you, though without any lessening of his own happiness, or repining at God's righteous judgments.

Thomas Cawton
(Minister of St. Bartholomew's behind the Royal Exchange, London, who was arrested in Love's Plot)

19

My Dear Friend, and Beloved in the Lord

[John Jacquel testified against Christopher Love before the High Court of Justice. In this letter, he refers to his testimony against Love and repents of that deed.]

My bowels are troubled within me. I am pained, I am pained, even at the very heart. The Lord knows, I want words to express the thoughts of my heart to you. I say, right Christian friend, and true soldier of Jesus Christ, I was thinking to have been silent, being even ashamed to send you a line written by that hand which is very much slackened and taken off from the plow, which I thought not many weeks ago had been very fast settled. Give me leave to breathe forth my heart to you in such rude words and language as I can utter, and I pray you receive them and spell out my heart towards you which at this time is so full that I know not how to empty it but in tears before the Lord for you night and day. And oh that the remembrance of the seventh and one and twentieth of June might often come into my thoughts to keep my heart humble for my folly in taking my own and carnal friend's counsel, and not the counsel of those that are right godly; which (as I now perceive) did help to bring forth that sad and never to be forgotten day, and sentence on the fifth of July against my dear friend.

Truly, I could not appeal to God who knoweth all things what the intention of my heart was, thinking I might rather do you good than hurt, knowing one had gone before me, and fearing he had much wronged you, made me willing to testify what I did, being told and informed it would do you good and not hurt, being but misprisoned at the most. I say, were it not for the testification in mine own conscience, I were not able to bear up my spirit, but should (I fear) even sink under the burden. But when I consider to whom I now write, who, I know, is full of charity and doth believe what I say, and will forgive what wrong I have done him, and, I hope, will pray for me to your God and my God, to your Father and my Father, that He will not lay this to my charge; for you may charge me to be as one of those Paul chargeth in 2 Timothy 4:16. And, dear sir, if the Lord will be pleased to let me see your face one more time, that I may open myself to you, I hope I shall stand right in your affections. Some promises I have met withal in the word that do (me thinks) add wings to my faith that God will not suffer you to fall by the hands of violence, as in Psalm 79, Psalm 91, Psalm 94, Psalm 3, Isaiah 41:10, Isaiah 66:5, and many others that I know you are better acquainted with them than I am, and can beat them out and lay them by you as a glass of cordial water for fainting times.

But, dear sir, let me earnestly beg you that you will use what means you can for your own preservation, and go as far as you can in your petition to them in whose power your life is, for many reasons. As first, because if you should fall, O! how would the enemies rejoice! Malignants and others would make songs at your death and say, "Where is all his fastings and prayers? His God will not help him." Oh, sir, it would be a day of reproach and blasphemy.

Second, consider how it would sadden the hearts of God's people and make them wring their hands if they should miss the fruit of their prayers in your deliverance; which (I am confident) have been poured out in an extraordinary way for you?

Third, consider the service you may yet do in the Church of Christ. How many souls may God make you instrumental to bring home to Christ? And what service may yet this poor, bleeding nation have by your life?

Fourth, I need not remember you of your dear and precious consort who, I am confident, is dear in the heart of God, and also to you; and her life even bound up in yours, and her condition being as it is.

And then I humbly beg you will consider my condition. For surely, in that day, I should hear of your life being violently taken away, mine would be but little comfort to me, being instrumental in taking yours away, although (the Lord knows) not intentionally, but accidentally. Therefore, for these reasons, I humbly beg of you again and again that you will do what you dare, and go as far as you can for your preservation; and the Lord will make you instrumental for His glory; if not here, yet in some other place. And me thinks wherever the Lord casts you, I could willingly make that promise and perform it that Ruth made to Naomi; and so I am confident, could my dear wife, whose addresses remember me to God that I may learn to lean upon Him more firmly and rely upon the Rock of Ages and not upon broken reeds. And I hope through the strength of Christ and the supply of your prayers, I shall be better fortified for the time to come as Peter was after his fall.

I would fain be remembered to my good friend, Doctor Drake. I hope I have got better armor of proof than I had before, but I hope there will be no need of showing it about him. For poor Po. [I have been unable to identify this person.—Ed.] hath wronged himself more than any man can, for I hear he hath sent more papers of his confession since he was there.

Good sir, I have many more things to say, but will not presume to be more burdensome to you at this time. Will the lord let me see your face once more here? I hope He will. However, it will not be long before we shall enjoy one another in that place where violent hands shall not touch us; and then eternity shall be little enough to praise and magnify the Lord for His riches of mercy he shows to us.

The Lord stand by you. The Lord preserve you, and put His everlasting arms under you and deliver you. Which shall be the earnest groans and sighs of him who is (he hopes) a dear, yet most unworthy friend, not worthy to be looked upon by you.

John Jacquel

Christian Reader

Grudge not now to receive this unexpected Birth from a Woman, the Conception was long since (I may say) formed tho' I cannot say perfected. Thine Eyes may be witnesses that it comes forth otherwise. It is the only one of its Mother, yet far from being doted on nor hath it any Brothers from whome to beare the honour, like Jabez, tho' it also like him was borne with (more than ordinary) Sorrow, Call it Soriah, or Ichabod or Benoni &c.

I know not how far it may worke upon thy bowells and affections (if thou pleasest to looke upon it while it weeps) Surely all mine were moved in the working of it; yet the Debt I owed unto the truth, the testimonie I owed unto the Grace of God, and the memorie of his Servant suffred me not to decline, either the Sorrowes which by such a rehearsall were renewed in mee or the Censure which for it and its imperfections, may possibly light upon mee.

No, tho' noe consecrated hand appeare at its delivery tho' some constellations seeme to threaten at the instant of its Nativitye, yett it must goe, and crye (when it comes abroad & is once understood) that none know better how to love their King even to the death than they who best

best know how to love their God and a good conscience, and this much I hope it will speake in time be believed:

Reader if this relation (which Conscience hath clothed with truth, and greife left plaine, and without ornament) be any way blessed by God, to excite his Grace in thy Soule and to provoke thee to love, Loyaltye, and good workes; Thou then enjoyest what is sincerely aimed at by

Thy Freind in the best of Freindships M: L.

The first page of Mary Love's memoirs

Epilogue

Christopher Love was indeed "a burning and shining light," one "of whom the world was not worthy." The Church today could certainly use a few more like him in their ranks. As his wife said of him, "He lived too much in heaven to live long on earth."

This historical narrative shows that devout Christians can be on both sides of a political issue, both absolutely convinced they are guided by Scripture. Christopher Love paid for his convictions with his life. He was a man of honor, a hero, not just because he was a faithful covenanter, but because he was a faithful minister of the gospel in an age of compromise. All the other men who were arrested with him spent a short amount of time in jail and were then released because they promised submission. Love would not compromise and was put to death.

The death of Christopher Love reminds us today that faithfulness to the truth can be (and usually is) costly. It was only eleven years following Love's execution that over 2,000 of England's finest ministers, including men such as Manton, Watson, Calamy, and Owen were ejected for non-conformity to the Church of England. Love's words still ring true, "And you think this an evil time? No, no; this is the very time when grace and true godliness can be distinguished from hypocrisy."

Today we face similar circumstances. There is an intense push for unity; but unity must be based upon truth. Often what passes for unity is really compromise. For it is never the low standard that rises; it is always the high standard that is asked to come down. But the standard must always be kept high, even at the cost of so-called "unity." While love is always important, Scripture says that love rejoices in the truth. Christopher Love rejoiced in the truth to the end; he would not compromise. That, too, makes him a hero.

As I researched the material for this book, I felt great sadness for his wife and children, yet I also know that "the Judge of all the earth must do what is right." God always gives extra grace to those whom He calls to extra duty. I am content with the knowledge that He took good care of His precious little lambs.

Soli Deo Gloria has reprinted three of Love's most famous works as Volume 1 of *The Works of Christopher Love.* It contained "The Combat between the Flesh and the Spirit (twenty-seven sermons on Galatians 5:17)," his treatise on eternal felicity, "Heaven's Glory," and his treatise on eternal punishment, "Hell's Terror." Since then, we have also published *Grace: The Truth, Growth, and Different Degrees; A Treatise of Effectual Calling and Election;* and *The Mortified Christian.* Many more are in process at this time (1998).

It is my prayer that the writings of this godly man will urge more men and women to speak the truth boldly, to better discern grace and true godliness from hypocrisy, and, should God call us, as He did Love, may we stand firm and be willing to be made "a spectacle unto God, to men, and to angels."

Soli Deo Gloria!
Don Kistler

King Charles II
(His father, Charles I, was ousted by Oliver Cromwell)

Appendix A

The Tragedy of Christopher Love at Tower Hill, August 22, 1651

(A Poem by Robert Wilde)

[Robert Wilde was a bystander at the execution of Christopher Love. He wrote this poem which was published afterwards. In it, he makes reference to several of the men involved with Love's Plot: Jenkyn, Drake, and others.]

Prologue

Now from a murdered monarch's urne I come,
A mourner to a martyred prophet's tomb:
Pardon, Great Charles his ghost, my muse had stood
Yet three years longer, till she had wept a flood;
Too mean a sacrifice for royal blood.
But she must go, heaven doth by thunder call
For her attendance as Love's funeral.
Forgive Great Sir, this sacriledge in me,
The tenth tear he must have, it is his fee;
'Tis due to him, and yet 'tis stolen from thee.

Argument

'Twas when the raging dog did rule the skies,
And with his scorching face did tyrannize,
When cruel Cromwell, whelp of that mad star,
But sure more fiery than his syre by far;
Had dried the northern fife, and with his heat
Put frozen Scotland in a bloody sweat:
When he had conquered, and his furious train
Had chas'd the north-bear, and pursue'd Charles' wain
Into the English orb; then 'twas thy fate
(Sweet Love) to be a present from our state.
A greater sacrifice there could not come,
Than a Divine to bleed his welcome home:
For he, and Herod, think no dish to good,
As a John the Baptist's head serv'd up in blood.

Act I

The Philistines are set in their High Court
And Love, like Sampson's fetched to make them sport:
Unto the stake the silent prisoner's brought,
Not to be tried, but baited, most men thought;
Monsters, like men, must worry him, and thus
He fights with beasts, like Paul at Ephesus.
Adams, Far, and Huntington, with all the pack
Of foisting hounds are set upon his back.
Prideaux and Keeble stand and cry A'loo;
It was a full city, yet it would not do.
Oh, how he foiled them, standers-by did swear,
That he the judge, and they the traitorts were:

For there he prov'd, although he seem'd a lamb,
Stout, like the lions, from whose den he came.

Act II

It is decreed; nor shall thy worth, dear Love,
Resist their vows, nor their revenge remove.
Though prayers be joined to prayers, and tears to tears,
No softness in their rocky heart appears;
Nor heaven nor earth abate their fury can
But they will have thy head, thy head, good man.
Sure some the sectary longed, and in haste
Must try how Presbyterian blood doth taste.
'Tis fit she have the best, and therefore thine,
Thine must be broach'd, blest soul, 'tis drink Divine.
No sooner was the dreadful sentence read,
The prisoner straight bow'd his condemned head.
And by that humble posture told them all,
It was a Head that did not fear a fall.

Act III

And now I wish the fatal stroke were given
I'm sure our martyr longs to be in heaven,
And heaven to have him there; one moment's blow
Makes him triumphant, but here comes his woe.
His enemies will grant a month's suspense
If't be but for the nonce to keep him thence:
And that he may tread in his Saviour's ways,
He shall be tempted too his forty days:

And with such baits too, cast thy self but down,
Fall, and but worship, and your life's your own.
Thus cried his enemies, Oh 'twas their pride
To wound his body, and his soul beside.
One plot they have more, when all the rest do fail,
If devils cannot, disciples may prevail.
Let's tempt him by his friends, make Peter cry
Good Master, spare thy self and do not die.
One friend entreats, a second weeps, a third
Cries your petition wants the other word:
I'll write it for you, saith a fourth; your life,
Your life, Sir, cries a fifth; pity your wife,
And the babe in her: Thus this diamond's cut
By diamonds only, and to terror put.
Methinks I hear him still, you wound my heart;
Good friends forbear, for every word's a dart:
'Tis foolish pit, this I do profess:
You'd love me more if you did love me less:
Friends, children, wife, life, all are dear I know,
But all's too dear, if I should buy them so.
Thus like a rock that routs the waves he stands,
And snaps asunder, Sampson-like, these bands.

Act IV

The day is come, the prisoner long to go,
And chides the lingering sun for tarrying so.
Which blushing seems to answer from the sky,
That it is loath to see a martyr die.
Methinks I hear beheaded saints above
Call to each other, Sirs, to make room for Love.
Who, when he came to tread the fatal stage,

Which prov'd his glory, but he enemies' rage,
His blood ne're run to his heart, Christ's blood was
There reviving it, his own was all to spare;
Which rising in his cheeks did seem to say,
Is this the blood you thirst for; take it I pray.
Spectators in his looks such life did see,
That they appear'd more like to die than he,
But oh his speech, methinks I hear it still;
It ravish'd friends, but did his enemies kill,
His keener words did their sharp axe exceed,
That made his head, but it their hearts to bleed:
Which he concludes with gracious prayers, and so
The lamb lay down, and took the butcher's blow:
His soul makes heaven shine brighter by a star,
And now we're sure there's one Saint Christopher.

Act V

Love lies a bleeding, and the world shall see
Heaven act a part in this black tragedy.
The sun no sooner spied the head on the floor,
But he pull'd in his own and look'd no more:
The clouds which scattered, and in colors were,
Meet all together, and in black appear:
Lightning, which filled the air with blazing light,
Did serve for torches all that dismal night:
In which, and all next day for many hours,
Heaven groaned in thunder, and did weep in showers.
Nor do I wonder that God thundered so
When His Boanerges murdered lay below.
Witnesses trembled, Prideaux, Bradshaw, Keeble,
And all the guilty court looked pale and feeble.

Timorous Jenkyn and cold-hearted Drake
Hold out, when called no base petitions make;
Your enemies thus thunder struck no doubt,
Will be beholding to you to come out.
But if you shall recant, now thundering heaven
Such approbation to Love's cause hath given,
I'll add but this, your consciences, perhaps,
Ere long may feel far greater thunder claps.

Epilogue

But stay, my muse grows fearful too, and must
Beg that these lines be buried with thy dust:
Shelter, blest Love, this verse within thy shroud,
For none but heaven dare take thy part aloud.
The author begs this, lest if it be known,
That he bewails thy head, he lose his own.

Finis

Matthew Poole
(London Minister who helped Simeon Ashe
get many of Love's works reprinted)

Appendix B

[Christopher Love was a Covenanter. As a Presbyterian, he swore to uphold this document; and, since Charles II took the same oath, Love was a staunch supporter of the King's position, if not his person. This is a decidedly Presbyterian document, as will be evident from the reading thereof.]

The Solemn League and Covenant

for Reformation and Defence of Religion, the Honor and Happiness of the King, and the Peace and Safety of the three Kingdoms of Scotland, England, and Ireland. Taken and Subscribed several times by King Charles II, and by all ranks in the said three Kingdoms. With an Act of the General Assembly, 1643, and an Act of Parliament 1644, ratifying and approving the said League and Covenant.

Jeremiah 1:5, "Come and let us join ourselves to the Lord in a perpetual Covenant that shall not be forgotten."

Proverbs 25:5, "Take away the wicked from before the king, and his throne shall be established in righteousness."

2 Chronicles 15:15, "And all Judah rejoiced at the oath, for they had sworn with all their heart."

Galatians 3:15, "Though it be but a man's covenant, yet if it be confirmed by an oath, no man disannulleth or addeth thereto."

The Solemn League and Covenant

for

Reformation and Defence of Religion, the Honor and Happiness of the King, and the Peace and Safety of the three Kingdoms of Scotland, England, and Ireland; agreed upon by Commissioners from the Parliament and Assembly of Divines in England, with Commissioners of the Convention of Estates, and General Assembly in Scotland; approved by the General Assembly of the Church of Scotland, and by both Houses of Parliament and Assembly of Divines in England, and taken and subscribed by them, Anno 1643; and thereafter, by the said Authority, taken and subscribed by all Ranks in Scotland, Anno 1644; And again renewed in Scotland, with an acknowledgment of Sins, and Engagement to Duties, by all Ranks, Anno 1648, and by Parliament 1649; and taken and subscribed by King Charles II at Spey, June 23, 1650; and at Scoon, January 1, 1651.

We Noblemen, Barons, Knights, Gentlemen, Citizens, Burgesses, Ministers of the Gospel, and Commons of all sorts, in the kingdoms of Scotland, England, and Ireland, by the providence of GOD, living under one King, and being of one reformed religion, having before our eyes the glory of GOD, and the advancement of our Lord and Saviour Jesus Christ, the honour and happiness of the King's Majesty, and his posterity, and the true public liberty, safety, and peace of the kingdoms, wherein every one's private condition is included: And calling to mind the treacherous and bloody plots, conspiracies, attempts, and practices of the enemies of God, against the true religion and professors thereof in all places, especially in these three kingdoms, ever since the reformation of religion; and how much their rage, power, and presumption are of late, and at this time, increased and exercised, whereof the deplorable state of the church and kingdom of Ireland, the distressed estate of the church and kingdom of England, and the dangerous estate of the church and kingdom of Scotland, are present and public testimonies; we have now at last (after other means of supplication and remonstrace, protestation, and sufferings), for the preservation of ourselves and our religion from utter ruin and destruction, according to the commendable practice of these kingdoms in former times, and the example of GOD's people in other nations, after mature deliberation, resolved and determined to enter into a mutual and solemn League and Covenant, wherein we all subscribe, and each one of us for himself, with our hands lifted up to the most High GOD, do swear:

I. That we shall sincerely, really, and constantly, through the grace of GOD, endeavour, in our several places and callings, the preservation of the reformed religion in the church of Scotland, in doctrine, worship, discipline, and government, against our common enemies; the reformation of religion in the kingdoms of England and Ireland, in doctrine, worship, discipline, and government, according to the word of GOD, and the example of the best reformed Churches; and shall endeavour to bring the Churches of GOD in the three kingdoms to the nearest conjunction and uniformity in religion, confession of faith, form of church government, directory for worship and catechising that we and our posterity after us, may, as brethren, live in faith and love may delight to dwell in the midst of us.

II. That we shall, in like manner, without respect of persons, endeavour the extirpation of Popery, Prelacy (that is, church-government by Archbishops, Bishops, their Chancellors, and Commissaries, Deans, Deans and Chapters, Archdeacons, and all other ecclesiastical Officers depending on that hierarchy), superstition, heresy, schism, profaneness, and whatsoever shall be found to be contrary to sound doctrine and the power of godliness, lest we partake in other men's sins, and thereby be in danger to receive of their plagues; and that the Lord may be one, and His name one, in the three kingdoms.

III. We shall, with the same sincerity, reality, and constancy, in our several vocations, endeavour, with our estates and lives, mutually to preserve the rights and privileges of the Parliaments, and the liberties of the kingdoms; and to preserve and defend the King's Majesty's person and authority, in the preservation and defence of the true religion, and liberties of the kingdoms; that the world may bear witness with our consciences of our loyalty, and that we have no thoughts or intentions to diminish his Majesty's just power and greatness.

IV. We shall also, with all faithfulness, endeavour the discovery of all such as have been or shall be incendiaries, malignants, or evil instruments, by hindering the reformation of religion, dividing the king from his people, contrary to this League and Covenant; that they may be brought to public trial, and receive condign punishment, as the degree of their offences shall require or deserve, or the supreme judicatories of both kingdoms respectively, or others having power from them for that effect, shall judge convenient.

V. And whereas the happiness of a blessed peace between these kingdoms denied in former times to our progenitors is, by the good providence of GOD, granted unto us, and hath been lately concluded and settled by both Parliaments; we shall each one of us, according to our place and interest, endeavour that they may remain conjoined in a firm peace and union to all posterity; and that justice may be done upon the willful opposers thereof, in manner expressed in the precedent article.

VI. We shall also, according to our places and callings, in this common cause of religious liberty, and peace of the kingdoms, assist and defend all those that enter into this League and Covenant, in the maintaining and pursuing thereof; and shall not suffer ourselves, directly or indirectly, by whatsoever combination, persuasion, or terror, to be divided and withdrawn from this blessed union and conjunction, whether to make defection to the contrary part, or to give ourselves to a detestible indifferency or neutrality, in this cause, which so much concerneth the glory of GOD, the good of the kingdom, and honour of the King; but shall, all the days of our lives, zealously and constantly continue therein against all opposition, and promote the same, according to our power, against all lets and impediments whatsoever; and, what we are not able ourselves to suppress or overcome, we shall reveal and make known, that it may be timely prevented or removed: All which we shall do as in the sight of God.

And because these kingdoms are guilty of so many sins and provocations against GOD, and His Son, JESUS CHRIST, as is too manifest by our present distresses and dangers, the fruits thereof; we profess and declare, before God and the world, our unfeigned desire to be humbled for our own sins, and for the sins of these kingdoms: especially that we have not as we ought valued the inestimable benefit of the gospel; that we have not laboured for the purity and power thereof; and that we have not endeavoured to receive CHRIST in our hearts, nor to walk worthy of Him in our lives; which are the causes of other sins and transgressions so much abounding amongst us: and our true and unfeigned purpose, desire, and endeavour for ourselves, and all others under our power and charge, both in public, and in private, in all duties we owe to GOD and man, to amend our lives, and each one to go before another in the example of a real reformation; that the Lord may turn away His wrath and heavy indignation, and establish those churches and kingdoms in truth and peace. And this Covenant we make in the presence of ALMIGHTY GOD, the Searcher of all hearts, with a true intention to perform the same, as we shall answer at that great day, when the secrets of all hearts shall be disclosed; most humbly beseeching the LORD to strengthen us by His HOLY SPIRIT for this end, and to bless our desires and proceedings with such success, as may be deliverance and safety to His people, and encouragement to other Christian churches, groaning under, or in danger of, the yoke of antichristian tyranny, to join the same or like association and covenant, to the glory of GOD, the enlargement of the kingdom of JESUS CHRIST, and the peace and tranquility of Christian kingdoms and commonwealths.